MURDER
at the
COUNTRY CLUB

BOOKS BY HELENA DIXON

HELENA DIXON

MURDER
at the
COUNTRY CLUB

Bookouture

Published by Bookouture in 2022

An imprint of Storyfire Ltd.
Carmelite House
50 Victoria Embankment
London EC4Y 0DZ

www.bookouture.com

ISBN: 978-1-80314-305-7
eBook ISBN: 978-1-80314-304-0

Murder at the Country Club is dedicated to all of the incredible volunteers of the Friends of Oldway tea room and the Oldway gardens volunteer group. Between them and the trustees of the Oldway Trust, this very special house is being brought back to life and the gardens give pleasure to so many people. Thank you to all of them.

PROLOGUE

Torbay Herald August 1934

Advertisement

Torbay Country Club and Golf Club is delightfully situated in the extensive private grounds of Oldway Mansion, Paignton. The club, once home to the Singer family, goes from strength to strength. Positioned on a major bus route, facilities include seventeen tennis courts (eleven of which are grass and six are hardcourts), two squash courts, two bowls courts, three badminton courts, three billiards tables, bridge, croquet, swimming bath and shower bath and a superb ballroom.

The eighteen-hole golf course, designed by Mr James Braid, which opened just over a year ago, provides excellent views and easy walking along cinder paths to take advantage of the undulating and attractive grounds. Refreshments are available at the windmill at the halfway point of the course where golfers may enjoy extensive views over the bay.

Day visitors are welcome on payment of the green fees payable to the club secretary.

For those less inclined to the sporting way of life, the mansion itself, modelled on the Palace of Versailles in France, offers many other pleasurable recreations and boasts a marvellous tea room and terrace overlooking the landscaped gardens and wooded walks. This month there are several special events taking place to charm and intrigue club members. Why not apply today for membership?

ONE

Kitty's eyelids drooped and she settled her head back against the chenille-covered armchair in her grandmother's salon at the Dolphin Hotel. Even with all of the leaded pane windows of the large bay window open, the late afternoon heat still felt oppressive. A wasp buzzed angrily and her grandmother swatted it away from the jam dish as she replaced the cover. Outside the walls of the ancient hotel, the hum and clatter of people and traffic on the river and the embankment below floated up to her.

She blinked and tried to stay awake to join in the conversation between her fiancé, Matt, and her grandmother. They had almost finished enjoying a delicious high tea with crab sandwiches and fruit scones with clotted cream and strawberry jam. The combination of a full stomach, a hot summer's day and exhaustion from the sheer volume of work she had been doing lately were combining to overcome her.

'Are we keeping you awake, Kitty dear?' her grandmother asked as Kitty pressed the back of her hand to her mouth to try and stifle a yawn.

There was a twinkle in her grandmother's eyes as she asked her question, although Kitty detected a note of concern too.

'I'm sorry, Grams. It's so warm today.' Kitty forced herself to sit up straighter in her chair and to open her eyes wider. Bertie, Matt's blue roan cocker spaniel who had been snoring softly at her feet, lifted his head and made a mild grumble of protest at her movement.

'And you have been working so hard too,' Matt observed before popping the last bit of his scone in his mouth.

'It's always very busy at this point in the season. I'm so glad that we have young Dolly now to help us,' her grandmother remarked as she set her cup and saucer back on the tea trolley.

Dolly was one of the younger sisters of Kitty's maid and particular friend, Alice. Alice was the eldest of eight children and also worked at the hotel. Usually she was employed as a chambermaid but often accompanied Kitty as her personal maid whenever she went travelling or needed to attend a formal event.

Kitty murmured her agreement with her grandmother's sentiment. Dolly was proving to be a great asset to the Dolphin. While her grandmother had been away for a few weeks visiting Kitty's Great-Aunt Livvy, Dolly had given Kitty a good deal of support.

'Now that I am back from Scotland, you must take a couple of days off, Kitty darling. You should too, Matthew. Your business has also been quite busy or so I've heard.' Her grandmother looked at Matt.

Kitty realised that he did look quite tired. There were dark smudges beneath his bright blue eyes and the faint lines at the corners of his mouth were deeper. He worked as a private investigator, and like Kitty, his busiest period was during the main holiday season. An influx of holidaymakers unfortunately also meant a rise in crime.

'Well, if you can spare Kitty on Sunday, Mrs Treadwell, I

have been invited to Torbay Country Club for the afternoon.' Matt grinned at Kitty.

'Oh?' Kitty asked. She had heard a great deal about the country club and had often wondered if the interior of the mansion there was as grand as rumours made out.

'Sir William Winspear has invited me as his particular guest. I undertook a small job for him a while ago and he is taking a party there on Sunday. There is to be an archery demonstration amongst other things, and I must admit I'd quite like to take a look at the golf course,' Matt said.

'There has been a lot in the newspaper lately about the country club. I've heard the tea dances there are very good.' Kitty looked at her grandmother. She wasn't overly fond of sports but a nice tea on the terraces and a stroll around the gardens with Matt sounded a lovely way to spend a sunny Sunday afternoon.

'Of course you can be spared, darling. Sundays are often quieter, as you know, and a day out would do you good. It sounds delightful. I must admit I haven't been there myself since I was a young girl and Mr Singer's father had the place, but it is supposed to be quite something, and the gardens are wonderful,' her grandmother said.

'I take it Bertie will be welcome too?' Kitty asked. Matt's dog, a recent acquisition from their last murder case, was quite an anxious beast and tended to create havoc if left alone for any period of time. Bertie lifted his nose at the mention of his name.

'Yes, I believe so, at least in the grounds.' Matt stretched out a hand to rub the top of the dog's head.

'I rather think Millicent knows Sir William. Is he the one with the much younger wife? She used to be on the stage, I think?' Kitty's grandmother asked.

Millicent Craven, former mayoress of Dartmouth and her grandmother's friend, knew everyone who was anyone, so Kitty was unsurprised by this statement. It would have been more shocking if Mrs Craven had not known them.

'Yes, Lettice is Sir William's second wife. There is quite some disparity in their ages. Sir William is not an easy man, and I must admit I was a little surprised by his invitation.' Matt frowned.

'He must have been pleased with your work,' Kitty suggested. Her suspicions were suddenly aroused. She hoped that the outing would be just for pleasure and that Sir William did not have some ulterior motive in mind for his invitation.

'Perhaps. Either way it should prove an interesting afternoon out and who knows, we may even become tempted to join as members.' Matt smiled at Kitty.

'You mean you might like the golf course as much as the one next to your house.' Kitty smiled back at him. Matt's modern white square villa was sited very near to the club at Churston, and he played there at least a couple of times a week.

The dimple flashed in his cheek as he responded, 'And you, old thing, will probably enjoy the afternoon teas and dancing.'

Kitty couldn't deny the truth of his response. The odd game of tennis or croquet might be pleasant, and the sprung parquet floor of the mansion's ballroom was reputed to be excellent.

'Then it's settled. Kitty darling, you take Sunday and Monday as your days off and then you can accompany Matt to the country club.' Her grandmother smiled genially at them.

Kitty was not about to argue. A lovely day out with Matt sounded just the ticket.

———

Sunday morning turned out to be another clear and sunny day. Kitty drove her small, bright red Morris car through the town and onto the ferry to cross the Dart. The roof was down, and a very light breeze ruffled the curls beneath the brim of her hat.

She had arranged with Matt to collect him from his house at Churston and from there to drive the short distance into Paignton and then on to the country club. Matt's standard mode of transport was his Sunbeam motorcycle, so it usually fell to Kitty to act as his chauffeur.

The sun sparkled on the river as she made the crossing before motoring up through the small village of Kingswear. The fields were yellow with ripe cereal crops and the farmers were busy with the harvest. A faint haze had already started to shimmer over the fields and the air smelled of dust and heat.

She pulled to a halt outside Matt's house and tooted the horn to let him know she had arrived. He quickly appeared looking very dapper in a smart, dark blue blazer and paler blue silk cravat, with Bertie at his side.

Matt stowed the black-and-grey cocker spaniel safely on the back seat of her car before taking his place in the passenger seat.

'You look very lovely today, old girl.' He placed a kiss on Kitty's cheek, making her face heat up. She was secretly quite pleased that she had spent extra time taming her short blonde curls and that the band on her new straw hat matched the colour of his cravat.

'Are we to meet Sir William's party at the club?' Kitty asked as she pulled away and set off along the coast road towards Paignton.

'Yes, he mentioned that there would be a small group of us. He said he would leave our names at the gate, and we could find him on the small side lawn for the archery display. I believe it is a private event just for his party.' Matt glanced at Kitty.

'It's very generous of him to have invited us.' Kitty concentrated on overtaking a small horse and cart.

'I was surprised at the invitation, but he is quite a capricious man. He either likes you or he doesn't, and he does have the influence to be able to put quite a lot of work my way. I rather fear there may be more to this invitation though, as he mentioned consulting me on a small matter. But with Sir William, who knows what that may be.'

Kitty raised her brows but refrained from commenting as she took the turn slightly inland towards the Oldway estate. It sounded as if Sir William was indeed quite an interesting character.

She parked her car in one of the side streets and they walked the short distance to the entrance. A large archway constructed of cream-coloured stone spanned the driveway with two iron-gated entrances. One was much wider for vehicles and the other one narrower for pedestrians. A uniformed attendant at the gate took their name and checked them off his list before permitting them to continue into the grounds.

'I must admit I'm looking forward to seeing the club. The house was remodelled a few years ago to look like Versailles, and it is supposed to be simply marvellous inside.' Kitty slipped her hand into the crook of Matt's arm as they strolled along the broad pathway towards the house. Mature trees initially hid the mansion from view until they had walked further up the incline to where the vista opened out.

The house was a huge creamy-white building with a broad flagstone terrace on one side and ornate Italian-style gardens. Statues with the bodies of what appeared to be lions with the heads of women guarded the entrance to the terrace. The tennis courts and bowling greens were to the one side and paths ran down into the cooler-looking, green, wooded glades.

On the larger lawn a cricket match appeared to be in progress, and they paused for a moment to watch.

'The Paignton team are hoping to try out for new recruits today, I think,' Matt said. 'I don't believe cricket to be a regular feature here.'

Walking along the paths, Kitty could see smartly attired young men and women, some of them in groups seated on the terrace taking tea. The cricket match and the advertisements of a tennis exhibition match probably accounted for the number of visitors present in the grounds. Several of the tennis courts were already in use and the thwack of balls hitting racquets could be heard above the birdsong.

'Sir William said the archery display was taking place on the far side lawn. It's his latest hobby apparently,' Matt said.

'This is all most impressive.' Kitty enjoyed looking about her as they continued to stroll towards the other side of the mansion. As they rounded a neatly clipped hedge, they came upon what Kitty assumed was Sir William's party.

A group of rattan lounge chairs were grouped around a table with a uniformed maid serving tea and cakes. Several elegantly dressed ladies and gentlemen were enjoying the hospitality. Set out on the grass at the far end of the field were several hay bales with targets attached.

A couple of older men stood near to the group carrying bows and two quivers full of arrows.

'Ah, Captain Bryant! And this must be your fiancée. Enchanted to meet you my dear, enchanted.' Kitty found her hand firmly grasped and kissed by a tall, elderly man with an impressive silver moustache. Shrewd but watery pale blue eyes assessed her from top to toe.

'Sir William, may I present Miss Kitty Underhay,' Matt said.

'Most delightful.' Sir William continued to gaze at Kitty for slightly too long, making her feel a touch uncomfortable.

A very beautiful and expensively dressed blonde-haired woman of around Kitty's age came over to greet them.

'May I introduce my wife, Lettice. Letty dear, this is Miss Underhay and Captain Bryant. The private investigator fellow I told you about.' Sir William finally relinquished Kitty's hand and she breathed a subtle sigh of relief.

'Delighted, I'm sure.' Lettice smiled at Matt and ignored Kitty.

'Come and meet the rest of the party. Captain Bryant, you've met my sister, Elspeth. She's also my secretary, Miss Underhay. Bit of a battleaxe. Keeps me in order, eh.' Sir William nudged the elbow of a tall, well-built woman of about fifty. She didn't appear terribly pleased by her brother's introduction.

'My brother, Henry, and his wife, Padma. They've just come back from India. Oh, and this is Natasha and Ivan Bolsova. Russian, don't you know. You may have heard of them. Very famous dancers. They are going to give an exhibition dance in the ballroom here this evening. Lettice is quite a patron of the arts.' He looked at his wife as he spoke, and Kitty thought she detected a faint note of derision in his tone.

Henry Winspear was a younger, shorter and plumper version of Sir William. He was more tanned and lined but minus the moustache. His wife was dressed simply in a pale pink silk dress with her long black hair secured in a bun at the nape of her neck. Gold bangles glittered along her arms, and she too appeared younger than her husband.

The Russian dancers were both quite striking in appearance. Ivan was tall with dark hair and dressed fashionably in a lightweight linen suit while his sister sported a dark green chiffon dress and sleek bobbed hair.

The other members of the group murmured their greetings and Kitty took a seat beside Natasha Bolsova as Sir William walked across the lawn to address the archers. It looked as if they were in for an interesting afternoon.

TWO

Lady Lettice Winspear attached herself to Matt's arm as he stood next to Kitty's chair.

'My husband tells me you have worked on several cases now with the local police?' Lettice turned her artfully made-up gaze on him. Her question drew the attention of the rest of the party.

'Um, yes, Lady Lettice, both Kitty and I have been involved in quite a few incidents now.' Matt glanced at Kitty.

'What sort of crimes? Divorce cases? Missing cats?' Henry Winspear looked up from where he was tucking into a slice of sponge cake to join in the conversation. There was a jeering tone to his remark that didn't impress Kitty.

'Murders, actually.' She smiled sweetly at Henry Winspear.

Padma Winspear gave an audible gasp and Elspeth rolled her eyes.

'Oh really, how absolutely thrilling. Do tell us more?' Lettice continued to cling to Matt's arm, her crimson-painted nails digging into the sleeve of his blazer.

'Really, Letty, the man is here to enjoy an afternoon out with his fiancée,' Elspeth chided, and Matt guessed there was not much love lost between Elspeth Winspear and her much younger sister-in-law.

'Quite, and you know that Padma is sensitive.' Henry Winspear joined forces with his sister to rebuke an unrepentant-looking Letty.

Sir William strode back across the lawn to join them, rubbing his hands together with glee. 'Right then, we're all set up and ready to go. These fellows are going to talk us through the demonstration and then we can all have a go.' He came to join his wife. 'I can show you what I've learned, eh, Lettice.'

———

Matt took the opportunity to extricate himself from Lettice Winspear's clutches and subsided gratefully onto an empty seat beside the tea table. He could see Kitty trying somewhat unsuccessfully not to smile at his relief. Bertie however seized the opportunity to wriggle under the table in a quest to discover any dropped crumbs of cake.

The archers took up their positions and demonstrated the correct way to hold the bows before firing several arrows into the distant targets. The smattering of applause had scarcely died down before Sir William had bounded to his feet to give his own demonstration of his archery prowess.

Matt surmised that the entire display had been orchestrated so that Sir William could show off his newest hobby. Certainly, Elspeth had a resigned expression as she was cajoled into attempting a passable shot at the target. She was followed by Lady Winspear. Lettice made a great deal of fuss, giggling and protesting before her attempt, which sailed wide of its mark.

Henry Winspear merely looked bored as he hit the centre of the target with his first arrow. Matt assumed that he must have used a bow and arrow before. Padma, his wife, refused to make an attempt, and the Russian dancers both acquitted themselves well.

'Miss Underhay, Kitty, my dear, do come and have a go.' Sir William pounced, leering over Kitty until she was forced to stand and take a turn with the bow.

Sir William fussed about her, giving instructions on how to position her hands until she had taken her shot. Her arrow landed near the centre of the target.

'Bravo, splendid attempt, my dear.' Sir William beamed approvingly.

'Thank you, Sir William. That was most interesting.' She handed the bow back to him and removed herself back to her seat. Matt held back a smirk at the expression on her face as she passed him.

'Captain Bryant, care for a turn?' Sir William asked.

Matt handed Bertie's lead across to Kitty and dutifully walked over to his host. He had used a bow before some years ago so was familiar with how to place the arrow. Sir William seemed quite pleased with his shot, praising his attempt.

'Jolly good show.' Sir William accepted the bow once Matt had fired, then fired a few more arrows to demonstrate his own prowess. He crowed aloud with delight when one of his arrows neatly split one of those already in the target.

'Very good, sir,' Matt said politely as Sir William looked around at his party in search of praise.

'Thank you. I've been practising daily on the lawn at home. Archery is good for the health, you know. Lots of life in this old dog yet, eh, Letty?' Sir William beamed at his wife. The men looking after the equipment retrieved the arrows from the targets, replacing them in the quivers. They placed the feathered end of the broken one down on the tea table for everyone to see.

Sir William waited for a moment until he could ensure everyone's attention was focused on the broken tail of the arrow with its bright orange and yellow feathers. Matt realised the man was visibly preening himself as everyone passed the arrow around, commenting on his prowess as an archer.

'By the by, if you are free a little later this afternoon, I wouldn't mind a quick word. Could use a spot of advice.' Sir William dropped his voice very slightly and glanced about him theatrically.

'Of course, sir.' Matt wondered if this was really what his and Kitty's invitation had been about. He noticed that the rest of the party were busy pretending they hadn't heard the conversation.

'Meet me back here after the tennis match, say at about four. They've got that fellow who played at Wimbledon here today. Elspeth is very keen that we go and watch.' Sir William glanced at his wristwatch and raised his voice. 'Starts in a minute, exhibition match on the third court.'

Ivan and Natasha both stood up from their seats. 'I hope you will excuse us, Sir William. We are very keen to see the views from the golf course. We have been told there is a windmill at the top, which offers a panorama of the bay,' Ivan said.

'We have heard a great deal about the beauty of the countryside here, and of course we have never visited this area before,' Natasha agreed. Both she and her brother had a faint accent.

'Of course, of course. Everyone is free to do their own thing. What say we all meet up on the terraces at the mansion at around four thirty? Elspeth can organise a table for us all. I dare say we shall all be ready for some refreshments by then.' Sir William smiled convivially at his group.

Elspeth looked a little sour at having this task thrust upon her by her brother. 'Very good. Now, if anyone wishes to see the exhibition tennis match, we need to make our way there.'

'Padma and I may take a turn around the Italian gardens.

The heat is rather oppressive today.' Henry offered his hand to his wife to assist her from her seat.

'Yes, I do have something of a headache starting,' Padma murmured.

'Captain Bryant, are you and Miss Underhay keen on tennis?' Elspeth asked.

'I rather think Bertie might be a nuisance. Bertie always wants to play with the balls,' Kitty said apologetically.

'Very well.' Elspeth gave a rather tight smile. 'We shall all meet again on the terrace at the mansion later, then.' She gathered her cardigan from the back of her chair and walked off at a brisk pace in the direction of the tennis courts.

'Come along, Lettice, time and tennis and all that.' Sir William took his wife's arm and the party dispersed.

———

'Is it me, or was that whole thing rather awkward?' Kitty asked once she and Matt were safely out of earshot of any of the Winspear party.

'It was very odd. You probably heard that Sir William has asked to meet me after the tennis match away from the others. I'm rather afraid this was why he invited us along today. He clearly has something that is troubling him.' Matt paused to allow Bertie time to sniff at the trunk of a large tree.

'Hmm, and I think it must be something to do with one of the people we just met,' Kitty said.

Matt looked at her. 'What makes you think that?'

'Well, why else would he have asked you here today? If it was to do with anything else, then surely, he would have asked invited you to his office or his home. Why bring you here unless it was to meet everyone?' Kitty thought the atmosphere at the archery demonstration had been most peculiar. 'It seemed to me

that he wanted everyone to know he was meeting you too. He
made a bit of a performance of the request, didn't he?'

'Yes, you're right, it was all a bit odd,' Matt agreed.

Lettice Winspear was at least thirty or more years younger
than Sir William, and, from her behaviour towards Matt she
was quite a flirt. Henry Winspear was a boor and Kitty thought
Padma, his wife, had looked very much as if she were attending
the afternoon under sufferance. Elspeth Winspear was clearly
Sir William's dogsbody and the Russian brother and sister had
been largely silent.

The sun was high in the sky now and Kitty was glad of the
shade from the trees as they wandered along the pathways
admiring the grounds. In the distance they could hear applause
and cheering from the direction of the tennis courts. The cricket
match was still in progress too, with small groups of spectators
sitting on blankets at the edges of the pitch in the shade of some
of the mature trees.

Eventually they found a vacant, wrought-iron bench in the
shade of a large pine tree and took a seat. Bertie spragged out on
the neatly manicured grass, panting.

'It's so warm again today. I think we may well get a storm
when this weather breaks.' Kitty unpinned her straw hat and
fanned her face with it.

'I think you're right,' Matt agreed.

A faint breeze ruffled the leaves above their heads, bringing
some welcome relief from the heat.

'I wonder what Sir William wishes to discuss with you,'
Kitty mused.

'I have no idea. The job I did for him before was a simple
one. A case of theft within his household.' A frown creased
Matt's forehead. 'This new issue must be either very personal or
delicate in nature.'

'I agree.' Kitty glanced at her watch. 'The exhibition match will be finished shortly so I expect you'll soon learn what this is all about.'

'I had better head back to the archery lawn,' Matt said.

'While you are meeting Sir William, I'll take Bertie down to the grotto. I saw a signpost earlier and I've heard it's very pretty. Bertie can cool his paws in the stream before we walk back to the mansion for tea.' Kitty rose, replaced her hat and smoothed the creases from her skirt before taking Bertie's leash from Matt.

'I'll meet you back at the terrace after the meeting.' Matt kissed her cheek, knocking her hat slightly askew.

'If you get there before me, I'd love a cool drink and an ice cream.' Kitty grinned at him as she straightened her hat once more.

She heard him chuckle as he hurried off for his meeting. Kitty followed the narrow gravel path deeper into the shade. The small stream running alongside the path gurgled and burbled over the stones and a small blue butterfly danced along in the air before them. Bertie paused for a drink and Kitty marvelled at the quiet seclusion of the place.

As she rounded the corner to enter the glade, she spotted something colourful peeking out from the shrubs on the far side near the edge of the pool. The sound of the waterfall filled the air as the stream tumbled over the rocky ledge into the waters below. She hesitated for a moment, wondering if she had inadvertently disturbed a courting couple.

Bertie however had no such qualms and tugged forward on his lead, his nose down snuffling at the grass.

'Bertie!' Kitty hissed as she tried to get him back.

In her quest to pull Bertie back, she had taken a few steps nearer to whoever was lying in the bushes. She suddenly realised that the well-tailored trouser legs and highly polished brown brogues were vaguely familiar. The owner of them was also strangely still.

Kitty swallowed hard and walked closer. To her dismay she

realised the colour she had seen from the far side of the glade was the bright yellow and red of the broken arrow from earlier, and it was sticking straight out of Sir William Winspear's back.

She looked around the clearing but there was no one in sight and no one had passed her and Bertie as they had walked along the path. She looked around the grass and spotted a tiny fragment of pale blue chiffon snagged on a branch nearby.

Sir William was lying face down with his head turned to one side, a surprised expression on his face. She reached out a hand and cautiously touched his cheek. The host of their party was now most definitely dead. His skin was still slightly warm so he must have been killed recently. She hadn't heard any noise when they had been walking to the grotto, so he hadn't cried out.

Kitty straightened back up and tugged at the dog's leash. 'Come on, Bertie, we have to go and get help.'

She hurried from the grotto back towards the mansion, all thoughts of her ice cream and cold drink gone from her mind. She had to find Matt and alert the police.

THREE

Her heart hammered in her chest as Bertie loped along beside her. Her rapid pace drew curious stares from some bystanders on the pathways, but Kitty was intent only on finding Matt.

She was hot and breathless by the time she reached the wider paved path leading to the side lawn. Matt was standing under the shade of a large tree as she approached.

'Kitty? What's wrong?' He hurried towards her a surprised expression on his face at her haste to reach him.

'Sir William is dead. Murdered in the grotto. We need to get the police.' Kitty gasped out the words.

Matt stared at her. 'Dead? How?'

'Stabbed in the back with that broken arrow.' Kitty pressed her free hand deep into her side to try and ward off the cramps that she could feel were imminent.

Matt grasped the tops of her arms and peered at her, concern for her welfare clearly showing in his gaze. 'Are you all right, Kitty darling?'

She nodded. 'Yes, I'm perfectly fine, just a little winded from hurrying. Go and telephone the police before someone else happens on the scene.'

He hurried away towards the house and Kitty sank down onto a nearby bench to recover her breath. She hoped no one else would stumble upon Sir William before the police could arrive.

Her mind worked overtime as she recovered from her exertions. Had someone realised why Sir William wished to consult Matt? Was that why he had been murdered? The use of the broken arrow suggested that it was likely to be someone in Sir William's own party who was the culprit. It would be too much of a coincidence surely for a random stranger to have seized the arrow from earlier and used it to murder the man.

Matt returned to her side within a few minutes.

'Inspector Greville is on his way. He has requested that we say nothing to the family until he arrives. The club are sending some staff to the grotto to ensure that the body is not disturbed. Are you all right to walk down there with me now to wait for the police?' Matt asked as he peered anxiously at her. 'I have asked the staff to tell Sir William's party that there has been an accident.'

Kitty frowned. 'Has no one missed him?'

Matt shrugged. 'I'm not sure. I don't think that everyone in the party has returned yet for tea. The staff have set aside one of the salons inside the mansion and are keeping the family in there until the police come.'

Bertie stood and shook himself as Matt took his leash from Kitty.

'Very well. Let's return to the grotto.' Kitty quickened her pace to match Matt's longer stride as they made their way back towards the scene of the murder. By the time they had reached the turn in the path however, a small crowd had already begun to gather.

The entrance to the glade was blocked by a large man dressed in old tweed gardening clothes with a cloth cap on his head. In his one hand he held a lawn rake, which he appeared to be using as a barrier to prevent anyone from entering.

'It looks as if the police have not arrived yet,' Kitty murmured to Matt.

'I expect they will attend quite quickly.' Matt placed his arm around her waist and steered her out of the crush of onlookers threatening to envelop them. 'There is nothing more we can do here for the moment. The grounds staff seem to be doing a good job at keeping everyone at bay.'

'Then shall we return to the mansion? We can wait for the inspector there,' Kitty suggested.

Matt hesitated and she could see that he really would have liked to enter the grotto to see Sir William's body for himself. Bertie gave a small whine as if to remind them that he was still there.

'Very well.' Reluctantly, Matt agreed and they turned around and extricated themselves from the crowd.

The calves of Kitty's legs ached by the time they arrived at the mansion once more. En route to the tea terrace, she briefed Matt on everything she had noticed when she had discovered Sir William's body, including the chiffon fragment.

Matt found the manager of the tea room who quickly and discreetly led them inside, across the vast marble floor of mansion's entrance hall, to a side room.

'I have arranged refreshments in here, sir, as you requested and have directed the other members of the party to wait here for news.' The man opened the large dark oak door for them to enter and promptly returned to his duties.

The room was sunny and pleasant, with tall windows framed by dark green velvet curtains and elaborate pelmets. Ornate plasterwork cornicing decorated the ceiling and a large marble fireplace stood at the one end, the grate filled with a display of summer roses in shades of pink and white. The room was furnished with velour-covered sofas and cushion-backed chairs grouped around small, heavily carved oak occasional tables.

Elspeth Winspear hurried over to greet them, her round face creased with worry. 'Captain Bryant, Miss Underhay, have you heard? The staff have indicated that something untoward has happened to my brother?'

Kitty could see Henry and Padma Winspear sitting together on one couch and Lettice Winspear apparently being comforted by Ivan Bolsova on another. Natasha Bolsova was standing beside the open windows smoking a small, black cigarette in a long jade holder.

'Yes, we heard. I think the police have been called,' Matt replied cautiously.

'The police? What have the police to do with anything? Is William hurt? Is a doctor on the way? Where is he? What's happened?' Lettice jumped up from the couch, wrenching her hands free from Ivan's hold. Her pretty, pale blue chiffon dress was floating around her as she moved.

'I'm sure we'll find out more in good time, Lettice. It's probably something quite trivial.' Henry Winspear leaned back and stretched out his legs. 'You know what William's like. He adores some drama, being the centre of attention. He's probably fainted or got himself hit on the head by a cricket ball.'

Elspeth Winspear took a seat on the edge of one of the armchairs. 'I know William loves fuss, but this seems extraordinary even by his standards.'

Lettice took out a lace-edged handkerchief and dabbed at the corners of her large blue eyes. 'Poor William. What if something bad has happened to him?'

Kitty noticed that there seemed little sign of any actual tears. It seemed that Sir William was not the only family member that enjoyed being the centre of attention. She tried to discreetly look for any sign of damage to Lettice's dress.

'There, there, Lady Winspear, you are overwrought. Come

sit, I will fetch you a drink, it is very warm today. I am certain all will be clear very soon.' Ivan rose from the couch in one graceful move and steered Lettice back to her previous seat.

Kitty walked over to the table to pour herself and Matt a glass each of cold fruit squash. Bertie flopped down on Matt's feet and immediately started to snore. She handed a glass to Matt before making her way over to the open windows, hoping she might feel a breeze.

'It's frightfully close today. There is so little air,' Kitty remarked to Natasha in an attempt to draw the girl into conversation. She hoped the police would arrive soon as it was uncomfortable knowing Sir William was dead and keeping that information from his family.

The other girl shrugged eloquently. 'You English are always so obsessed with the weather.' She flicked ash from the end of her cigarette into a marble ashtray. 'In Russia we do not concern ourselves in such a way. It is either cold or not so cold.'

'It must seem very strange to you,' Kitty agreed. 'I understand that Lady Winspear is your patron?'

Natasha flicked a glance towards Lettice who was still being consoled by Ivan. 'We are most fortunate. We demonstrate various dances at her soirees, and also she has secured for us some prestigious venues. We are very grateful for her generosity.'

'That is very kind of her.' Kitty took another sip of her drink. 'Is Sir William keen on the arts too?'

Natasha's dark ruby lips curled up in a half smile. 'He is supportive of whatever Lady Winspear enjoys. I wonder what has happened to him, this seems to be most strange.'

Kitty shifted uncomfortably. She was aware that when Inspector Greville arrived, her role in the discovery of Sir William's body would no doubt be made public.

'Have you and your brother been in England for long?'

Natasha stubbed out her cigarette. 'Only for a few weeks.

We were working in Paris when Lady Winspear saw our show there.'

'This is ridiculous. Where on earth is William?' Elspeth was on her feet once more.

'I agree.' Padma looked at her husband. 'Henry, you really should do something.'

Henry didn't look as if he agreed with his wife, but before he could respond, the door to the room opened. To Kitty's relief the familiar, slightly rumpled figure of Inspector Greville, flanked by a uniformed constable, entered the room.

He removed his hat as soon as Elspeth approached him. 'Lady Winspear?'

'No, I'm Elspeth, Sir William's sister.'

Lettice was on her feet once more, supported by Ivan. 'I am Lady Winspear. Where is William? The staff said there has been an accident? Is he all right?'

The inspector twiddled with the brim of his hat. 'I'm very sorry, Lady Winspear.'

Lettice's face paled and she swayed on her black patent heels. 'William?'

'I'm afraid that your husband was found dead a short while ago in the grounds of the club.'

A collective gasp met the inspector's statement and Lettice swooned into Ivan's arms. He carried her onto a nearby couch and began to pat her hands in an attempt to revive her.

'William dead? What, a heart attack or something? I always said high living would do for him one day.' Elspeth's lips pursed and Kitty couldn't tell if she was about to cry or if she was angry.

Padma stooped over Lettice, offering her a sniff of the smelling salts she had produced from her capacious cream leather handbag.

'Well? Is my sister correct?' Henry was on his feet, glowering at Inspector Greville.

Lettice appeared to be recovering now with colour creeping back onto her cheeks. Ivan placed a silk-covered pillow under her head.

'I regret to say that your brother was murdered.' Inspector Greville's expression was impassive, and Kitty noticed that he was scrutinising each member of the Winspear party to study their reaction.

'Murdered.' Natasha sat down on the armchair next to Kitty.

'Murdered? How?' Henry Winspear asked.

'I understand from the club staff that Sir William had recently taken up archery and had arranged a private demonstration here today?' The inspector had taken out his notebook.

'Well, yes, but what has that to do with anything?' Elspeth demanded.

'Sir William was killed by an arrow that we believe was used in the demonstration.' The inspector's reply again caused an outburst from the group.

'Poppycock! How could that be the case? The members of the archery club packed everything up and took all the equipment away with them.' Elspeth's cheeks flushed with indignation.

Henry stepped closer to the inspector in a threatening manner and the constable also moved forward. 'My sister is right. Besides, William was perfectly well and went off to watch the tennis match when the demonstration finished. What has the archery to do with anything? How could he have been killed by an arrow?'

Lettice was sobbing noisily now. 'Poor William. He loved showing off with his bow and arrows.'

'The weapon used was a broken arrow.' Inspector Greville met Henry's gaze.

'The one William split? But how?' Elspeth was trembling, her shoulders quivering.

Kitty stayed quiet. She could see that Matt too was observing the Winspear party. She wondered which of the group would be the first to realise the implications of the arrow being used to kill Sir William.

'This is not possible.' Ivan looked to his sister.

'And you are, sir?' the inspector asked.

'Ivan Bolsova, and this is my sister, Natasha. We are guests of Sir William and Lady Lettice.'

Kitty noticed a defensive note in Ivan's reply.

'Perhaps someone could tell me what happened at the archery demonstration?' The inspector glanced around before allowing his gaze to rest on Matt. 'Captain Bryant, were you and Miss Underhay present?'

'Yes sir,' Matt answered, and Kitty detected a change in the atmosphere in the room. Where before everyone had appeared shocked by the news of Sir William's murder, she now felt as if mistrust and suspicion were appearing.

Matt gave a succinct description of the events of the demonstration and of Sir William splitting the arrow. The others all agreed with his version of events.

'What happened to the broken arrow?' the inspector asked.

'The one part was buried in the target. I presumed that the men looking after the equipment collected it up with the rest of the arrows,' Elspeth said.

'And the other part?' the inspector asked. Kitty realised that Inspector Greville had very cleverly not let on which part of the arrow had been used to murder Sir William. She supposed that most people would assume it to be the half with the tip.

'William collected it and placed it on the tea table so we could all marvel at his prowess with the bow.' Henry strode about the room.

'Thank you, sir. Do you know what happened to that half of the arrow?' Inspector Greville asked mildly.

'I presume it was collected up by the archer chappies, the

same as the rest.' Henry paused in his striding about. 'Inspector, what is this all about?'

'Did anyone see the arrow on the table being collected?' Inspector Greville disregarded Henry's question to continue with his own line of enquiry.

'I did not notice anything. My brother and I were keen to walk up on to the golf course to see the views. I think it was on the table when we left.' Natasha shrugged dismissively.

'I didn't take any notice as my brother wanted me to make arrangements for tea and I didn't wish to miss the start of the exhibition tennis match.' Elspeth looked puzzled.

'My wife and I were hot and wished to visit the gardens for more shade. I think it was still on the table when we left.' Henry looked at Padma for confirmation.

Attention fell on Lettice.

'I have no idea. I accompanied William up to the tennis match and then sat with Elspeth when William said he had to go and see someone.'

Kitty glanced at Matt. Of all the people in the room, Lettice was the only one who seemed keen to establish an alibi.

'Did Sir William say who he intended to meet?' The inspector was scribbling in his notebook.

Lettice looked blank and turned her gaze to Elspeth who appeared flustered.

Kitty felt certain that no one would own up to having over-heard Sir William's plans and yet she was sure they were all aware of the intended meeting.

'I rather think the meeting was with me.' Matt spoke out when it became apparent that no one was going to answer the inspector's question.

'Have you any idea what Sir William wished to speak to you about?' Inspector Greville asked.

Matt shook his head and Kitty thought she detected a sense of relief in the room.

FOUR

'You said, Lady Winspear, that your husband accompanied you and Miss Winspear to the tennis match. At what time did he leave the match for this meeting with Captain Bryant?' Inspector Greville had his pen poised once more over his notebook. The questioning had been going on for a while now and it seemed to Kitty that the inspector was digging deeper.

'The match was coming towards the end, and we were discussing going onto the court to meet the players, so it must have been around three forty-five, perhaps a little earlier.' Elspeth looked at Lettice for confirmation.

'Oh yes, absolutely,' Lettice agreed.

'I am puzzled about something, Inspector,' Kitty said.

'Yes, Miss Underhay?' Inspector Greville turned his attention to Kitty.

'Sir William arranged to meet Matt back where the archery demonstration had been held and yet he was killed in the grotto.' Her words caused a ripple to run around the room.

The inspector's moustache twitched. 'You are suggesting there may have been another meeting arranged by Sir William?'

'It seems likely, sir,' Kitty said.

'And you found Sir William at what time, Miss Underhay?' the inspector asked.

Another ripple ran around the room and Kitty felt the weight of accusatory stares from members of the Winspear family.

'It would be about twenty past four. I glanced at my watch just before I went into the grotto as I didn't wish to be late meeting up with Matt at the tea room.'

'You found William and didn't say anything to us? You knew he had been killed?' Elspeth's face contorted in fury.

'It was not Miss Underhay's place to say anything until she was instructed to do so. She has previous experience with these kinds of unfortunate events,' Inspector Greville replied in his most official tone.

'It was very distressing.' Kitty couldn't help feeling guilty that she had stayed silent. She did her best to look shocked and upset.

Natasha gave her a suspicious look.

'Oh, it must have been. I can imagine you would not know what to do,' Padma said, and Kitty was grateful for the older woman's apparent empathy.

Inspector Greville consulted his notebook. 'So it seems that we have a period of time between Sir William leaving the tennis match at three forty-five and Miss Underhay discovering his body at four twenty. Did any of you see Sir William during that time?'

There was a collective shaking of heads.

'And no one has any idea what may have led to Sir William being in the grotto? Or who else he may have been intending to meet?' The inspector looked around the room.

Once more there was a shaking of heads.

'I see, thank you.' The inspector closed his notebook and quietly consulted with the constable.

The constable nodded and left the room.

'I will need to speak to each of you individually, after which point you will be free to return to your home.' Inspector Greville focused his attention on Lettice. 'I understand, Lady Winspear, that everyone is currently residing with you at Palm Lodge?'

Lettice sniffed and dabbed at her nose with her handkerchief as she nodded at the inspector. 'Yes. Elspeth lives with us, and Henry and Padma have been staying since they returned to England. Natasha and Ivan are our guests.'

'Thank you.'

The constable returned to the room and spoke quietly to the inspector.

'The staff have arranged for me to use one of the housekeeping offices for the interviews. Lady Winspear, I'm sure this has been a most distressing day for you. Perhaps you would care to accompany me. Miss Underhay, would you and Captain Bryant also please attend? No doubt Lady Winspear would be grateful for your support.' Inspector Greville's brows raised as his gaze met Kitty's and she stood up, ready to follow Lettice to the small side room.

The staff area was slightly less grand than the public rooms but still boasted the beautiful marble floor that ran throughout the ground floor of the mansion. Lettice seated herself on a small, red, velvet-upholstered seat as the inspector took his place behind a mahogany desk. Kitty, Matt and Bertie installed themselves discreetly behind Lettice's seat on a couple of plain wooden chairs.

Inspector Greville placed a glass of water on the desk for Lettice and leaned forward in a fatherly manner. Kitty wondered if he had seen the fragment of chiffon next to Sir William's body in the grotto. The colours and fabric would match Lettice's dress.

'I realise this must be very distressing for you, Lady

Winspear, but anything at all that you can recall may be helpful in catching your husband's murderer.'

'I don't understand why anyone would want to kill William.' Lettice twisted her handkerchief in her fingers.

'It was your husband that organised today's party?' the inspector asked.

Lettice sniffed. 'Well, Elspeth did all of the organisation, but it was William's idea. He was keen to demonstrate his skills. He thought it would be nice to make an outing of it here to the club as Ivan and Natasha were keen to see the area and Elspeth wanted to see the tennis exhibition. Natasha and Ivan are dancing here tonight.' She paused to blow her nose. 'William loved to show off and he was terribly proud of his archery prowess. He was like a small boy when he had a new hobby.'

'I see. Did he say why Captain Bryant had been invited to attend today?'

Kitty and Matt both leaned forward slightly at this question.

'No, I had no idea anyone else was to join us until Elspeth mentioned it when the men arrived to set up the demonstration. There were extra chairs on the lawn. She told everyone that Captain Bryant and his fiancée would be attending. Elspeth always took care of everything, she might know why William had invited them.' Lettice flicked a glance in Kitty and Matt's direction.

'Do you know of anyone who might have wished to harm your husband? Any discord within your household?' Inspector Greville waited while Lettice took a sip of water.

'No, well, not really. No one who would wish to kill him. I mean, there were a few disagreements.' Her lips trembled.

'That is normal in most families,' the inspector soothed. 'What kind of disagreements, Lady Winspear?'

Lettice sighed. 'Well, Henry and Padma were cross that William wouldn't give them any money for a business idea of

Henry's. Henry is terrible with money. William disapproved of what he called Henry's wild ideas and well, Padma, well, she's from India.' Lettice shrugged as if this explained everything. Kitty decided she really did not care much for Lady Winspear.

'What about Sir William's relationship with Elspeth? You said Miss Winspear did everything for your husband?' Inspector Greville asked.

'Oh yes. She has been his secretary for years. She organises everything for his business and in the house. Takes his letters, sets up meetings, organises the staff. She has always lived at home, you see.' Lettice smiled brightly.

'Forgive me, Lady Winspear, but is Elspeth paid for her work for Sir William?' Kitty asked.

Lettice looked affronted by the question. 'Of course not. She lives with us, and William gives her an allowance. But she is his sister after all, what else would she do with her time?'

Inspector Greville coughed. 'And I understand that Ivan and Natasha Bolsova are staying with you at Palm Lodge at your invitation? Your husband was happy with this?'

'Of course. William encouraged my support of the arts. It reflected well on him, made him appear cultured. He was a self-made man, you see. Ivan and Natasha are superb dancers. We discovered them in Paris.' Kitty noticed that Lettice dropped her gaze as she said this, and she wondered if Sir William had been happy about the arrangement. Ivan Bolsova had certainly been very attentive to Lettice earlier.

'I see. Thank you, Lady Winspear. One last question, do you have any idea if your husband had made a will?'

Lettice had started to stand when the inspector's question made her sink back down onto her seat. 'Yes, William had a will. The house belongs to the family, held in trust, so I suppose it goes to Henry now – although there is provision of course for Elspeth to continue living there.' She frowned. 'I think I inherit his money and the London townhouse.'

Inspector Greville scribbled some notes. 'Do you know the name of your husband's solicitor?'

Lettice shook her head. 'Elspeth will know. He's an elderly man who practises locally. I'm afraid I don't recall his name.'

The inspector reached across the desk. 'I think you may have damaged your dress, Lady Winspear?'

Kitty noticed a small tear on the edge of the sleeve and realised her suspicions had been correct; it must match the scrap she had seen in the grotto.

Lettice turned her arm to examine the damage to the material just above her elbow. 'Yes, it's most annoying. I caught it on a nail earlier this afternoon.'

'I must inform you that a piece of material matching your dress was found near your late husband's body.' Inspector Greville had fixed his full attention on Lady Lettice's face.

The woman looked bewildered. 'I don't understand. I tore my dress before the archery started. How could it have ended up in the grotto?'

The inspector made no reply as he scribbled a final note then escorted Lettice from the room before returning to Kitty and Matt.

'She has an alibi,' Matt observed when the inspector rejoined them. 'And so does Elspeth if they remained together during the match and afterwards.'

'Hmm, and yet there was a scrap of material in the grotto that clearly came from her dress, and she cannot account for how it arrived there. Let us have Elspeth Winspear in next and hear what she has to say.' The inspector looked at the notes he had made in his book.

Elspeth Winspear still looked quite cross when she was shown in by the constable. She glanced at Kitty and Matt as if unsure why they would be present during the interview.

'Miss Winspear, do take a seat.' The inspector indicated the chair that Lettice had recently vacated.

Elspeth took her place, a belligerent set to her lips.

'Lady Winspear said that you were the person who organised the archers for today's event?' The inspector had picked up his pen again.

'Yes. I organised everything for William, and for Lettice. William couldn't organise himself out of a broom closet left to his own devices.' Elspeth gave a disdainful sniff.

'Why at the country club?' Inspector Greville asked.

Elspeth sighed. 'William loved to show off. There was no point in having the demonstration at home because he wanted people to know about his new hobby and that he was wealthy enough to stage it here at the club. My brother always had to be at the centre of attention, like a child.' Her lip curled.

'Did your brother tell you why he was inviting Captain Bryant? I understand that his invitation to attend today was issued by Sir William personally'

A tinge of colour crept into Elspeth's cheeks. 'He didn't tell me anything, no. He told me when we arrived at the club that I needed to make provision for two more guests and to expect Captain Bryant and Miss Underhay.'

'Do you have any guesses about why I was asked to attend?' Matt asked.

'Well...' Elspeth looked most uncomfortable. 'I did accidentally hear William on the telephone to his solicitor, Mr Morley. He mentioned his will and that he wanted to consult a private investigator before he acted. He had an appointment with Mr Morley for this coming Wednesday.' Elspeth's cheeks were now a rosy hue.

'And you have no idea about what the changes to the will may have been?' Inspector Greville pressed the point.

'No, not at all.' Elspeth's lips compressed together into a straight line.

Kitty was certain that Elspeth was not telling the truth. She suspected that Sir William's sister had a very good idea of what the changes may have been.

The inspector questioned Elspeth on when she had last seen Sir William and where she had been during the window of time when her brother had been murdered. In turn she supported Lettice's earlier statement that they had been at the tennis and had then gone to the terrace for tea.

The inspector returned to the question of the arrow.

'Do you recall, Miss Winspear, when you last noticed the broken arrow shaft on the tea table?'

'We were all looking at it and we took turns picking it up. I remember someone, I think it may have been William, advising us to be careful as it was quite sharp where it had been broken.' Elspeth frowned.

'Was it still there when you left to organise tea for the party for after the tennis exhibition?' the inspector asked.

'I don't know. I suppose so,' Elspeth said.

Kitty had been racking her own brain to try to recall when she had last noticed the arrow. It had been on the table while Sir William had been directing Elspeth to organise tea but then she had turned away. Had it been there when Elspeth had collected her cardigan and walked off?

It would have been possible to conceal the arrow inside a gentleman's jacket or indeed under a shawl or cardigan. Padma and Lettice had both been carrying handbags, something the inspector confirmed with Elspeth.

'Do you know if your brother had any enemies? Someone who may have wished to harm him?' Inspector Greville asked.

Elspeth sighed. 'My brother was not an easy man, Inspector. He was a walking ego. He loved to be the centre of attention. He could be very kind and generous but at the same time terribly vindictive if he was crossed or thwarted. If he believed someone had wronged him in some way, then it did not bode well for that person. I'm sure Captain Bryant will recall the man who was dismissed for stealing a brooch. Above everything though, he liked to control people.'

Matt nodded.

'He controlled you?' Kitty asked in a gentle tone. She was beginning to build a picture of Sir William's character in her mind.

A bitter expression crossed the older woman's face. 'Oh yes, especially me. He refused to pay me a salary. He said that he put a roof over my head and paid for my keep and gave me a generous allowance for my clothes so what need had I for a wage? When I was younger, any man that showed any kind of interest in me, he scared off. Either by bribery or threats of some kind.'

'Forgive me, Miss Winspear, but do you know if your brother has provided for you in his will?' the inspector asked.

Elspeth wriggled a little on her seat. 'I have a home for life at Palm Lodge, as indeed does Henry. The house will pass to Henry now. I think William may have left me an annuity. Certainly, he always promised that he would do so.' She fidgeted with the edge of her cardigan and Kitty wondered if the reality of the changes her brother's death would bring might be starting to dawn on Elspeth.

'And what of Sir William's relationships with the other members of the household? Did he control them in the same way?' Matt asked the question this time.

'Lettice certainly knew which side her bread was buttered. She was just a jobbing actress working in third-rate theatres when William found her, and she made sure she always played to his ego. Henry was livid when William refused to support him setting up in business when he returned from India. William disapproved of the marriage and of Henry generally. Said he was a wastrel.' Elspeth sounded resigned.

'And what of the Russian couple? They are proteges of Lady Winspear's, I understand?' Inspector Greville asked.

Elspeth's lips twisted in amusement. 'Lettice is certainly very interested in Ivan Bolsova. I think William was starting to catch on but of course Natasha, being young and pretty, was a good distraction. My brother liked young, attractive women.'

Kitty recalled the way Sir William had fawned over her hand and decided Elspeth was telling the truth there.

'One more thing, Miss Winspear, did you observe Lady Winspear damaging her dress at any point this afternoon?'

Elspeth's brows raised. 'Yes, she snagged it on a nail on the garden furniture, she made the most frightful fuss.'

The inspector thanked Elspeth for her time and escorted her from the room before returning.

'A cup of tea is needed, I think, before we see Henry and Padma Winspear. It seems we have a lot to think about.' The inspector signalled to the constable.

FIVE

A few minutes later there was a knock at the door, and a gilt and marble tea trolley was wheeled inside the room. Kitty smiled when she saw the inspector's gaze alight on the accompanying plate of cakes and biscuits.

She had to admit that a cup of tea and a biscuit was very welcome after all the events of the afternoon.

'I take it that you believe whoever killed Sir William was most probably one of the Winspear party, sir?' Kitty asked.

Inspector Greville helped himself to several of the biscuits, balancing them on his saucer. 'Yes. Sir William was obviously lured to the grotto to meet someone. This had to be someone he knew who had heard that he intended to meet Captain Bryant after the tennis match. The use of the arrow to stab him confirms this, otherwise they could have just bashed him over the head with a rock or something. This whole murder feels very personal, especially with the scrap of material from Lady Winspear's dress being found within the grotto.'

'Yes, *especially* as it doesn't sound as if she were the one to have left it there. There certainly seems to be a lot going on under the surface, between the various household members,'

Matt observed as he fed Bertie one of the biscuits that had escaped the inspector's attention.

'Hmm, and it sounds as if Sir William intended to make some changes to his will in the next few days. They all seemed to be financially dependent on him in some way so until we know what the changes were, we have to assume that it's something that could have affected any or all of them.' The inspector chewed thoughtfully on a biscuit. 'I don't suppose you picked up anything before when you worked for Sir William?' He looked at Matt.

'I'm afraid not, sir. Elspeth contacted me a few months ago and I met Sir William in the study of his house. There were concerns about some missing money and a small item of jewellery. It was quickly established that a new member of staff was responsible for the thefts – the man Elspeth mentioned. Henry Winspear was in India and I think that Lady Winspear was in London at the time. I only met Elspeth briefly and Sir William a couple of times.' Matt rubbed the top of Bertie's head as the dog retrieved a crumb from the knee of Matt's trousers.

'You told me you were a little surprised when he contacted you again and invited you to the club?' Kitty asked.

'I was surprised that he telephoned me himself, rather than Elspeth contacting me to make the arrangements. He said it would be a nice day out, and to bring my fiancée. He said there was a small matter he wanted advice about, and we could talk about it on the day. I thought it would be a nice way to see the club and have a pleasant day out. Sorry, old thing, I hadn't anticipated you would find our host pushing up the daisies in the grotto.' He smiled apologetically at Kitty.

Inspector Greville brushed biscuit crumbs from his tie and looked regretfully at the empty plate. 'Hmm, I see, well, we'd better get on. Let's have Mrs Padma Winspear next.'

Suitably refreshed, Kitty resumed her seat beside Matt and waited for the constable to show Padma Winspear into the room. From Elspeth and Lettice's tone, it seemed that Padma's arrival at Palm Lodge had not been especially welcomed by Sir William, or indeed, his family.

Padma took her seat on the red velvet chair and Kitty realised that Padma was even younger than she had first thought. She was dressed in a slightly old-fashioned style and her dark hair had a small grey streak at the front.

She was probably in her mid-to-late thirties, which must make her at least twenty years younger than her husband. Although the age gap was nothing compared to the one that had been between William and Lettice.

'Mrs Padma Winspear? You arrived in the country about three weeks ago with your husband, Henry?' The inspector had taken out his notebook once more.

Padma nodded. 'Yes, that's correct, we stayed in London for a few days and then came to Devon to stay with my brother-in-law.' She had a soft, clear voice with a pronounced accent.

'You had not met Sir William before this visit?' the inspector asked.

'I had met him once before, many, many years ago. I was employed as a housekeeper by Henry at that time. It was obviously before we were married, and Sir William came to stay at the house in India for a few days. He had business interests in my country. It was shortly after his first wife had passed away and many years before he married Lettice.'

Padma's information took Kitty by surprise. She hadn't considered that Sir William might have known Padma before her marriage to Henry.

'I see. When did you and Henry marry, Mrs Winspear?' Inspector Greville asked.

'We married shortly before we came to England. Henry telegraphed William with news of our wedding. I have to say that he did not approve of our marriage.' Padma lifted her chin defiantly to meet the inspector's gaze squarely.

'He expressed his displeasure to you personally?' Inspector Greville scribbled furiously in his book.

Padma nodded. 'Of course. My brother-in-law was the kind of man that had no scruples about rudeness. I am Indian and I was Henry's servant before our marriage. William disapproved of both of these facts and had no hesitation in voicing them both to me and to my husband. My husband and his brother did not have a close relationship, Inspector. William disapproved of everything Henry did so I tried not to take it personally. It would not matter who he married, William would have found fault.'

'And yet you came to stay at Palm Lodge?' Matt asked.

'The house belongs to the family, so we were entitled to come and stay. Henry has no money and William had lots of it. Henry hoped his brother would back him in a business idea; he felt that if he could appeal to William's ego then he would change his mind. I rather think Henry felt we would simply stay until William got tired of us and might pay us to go away.' Padma gave a small shrug. She sounded both pragmatic and resigned to her situation.

'Did you notice the arrow on the table after the demonstration, Mrs Winspear?'

Padma nodded. 'We all had to pick it up and admire William's skill with a bow. It was quite beautifully made. William said the feathers had been dyed in the colours on his standard.'

'And do you recall if it was it still on the table when you and your husband left...' The inspector paused and flicked back a couple of pages. 'To go to the Italian garden?'

Padma's brow creased in a frown. 'I think so, but I'm not really sure. I wanted to avoid having to sit in the heat watching tennis, so I was eager to get away.'

'Thank you, and are you aware of anyone in the house or outside it that might have wished harm to Sir William?'

Padma gave a mirthless smile. 'I detested him, but I didn't kill him and neither did Henry. Elspeth, I think, was very resentful of the way he treated her.' She laughed. 'I may have been Henry's servant before our wedding, but I was paid and treated well. Poor Elspeth, for all she looks down on me, is in a much worse position.'

'And Lettice?' Kitty asked.

'We were very surprised when William remarried. I do not think it was a love match, not on Lettice's side. As Henry said, "there's no fool like an old fool", especially when it comes to love. I think Sir William had noticed the attentions of that dancer towards Letty.'

'And, one last thing: Lady Winspear damaged her dress earlier in the afternoon, I believe?' the inspector asked.

Padma's lip curled. 'Oh yes, she caught it on the lounger and made such a pantomime. It's the kind of material that catches on everything, most impractical.'

Padma left the room and Kitty looked at Matt. 'Well, that was interesting, wasn't it?'

'Yes, no love lost there at all for the Winspear family. It'll be interesting to hear what her husband has to say for himself.' The inspector nodded to the constable who promptly left to collect Henry Winspear.

An air of belligerence surrounded Henry Winspear like a thunder cloud as he entered the room. Before he was even seated, he started on the inspector.

'I hope this isn't going to take long? My wife will have found all of this most distressing.' He settled on his seat and crossed his legs before glaring at the inspector once more.

'Thank you, sir. I shall endeavour to take as little of your time as possible.' The inspector's tone was smooth.

'I should think so too. I hope you have your men out combing the grounds for whoever did this.' He glared at the policeman.

Inspector Greville appeared untroubled by Henry's ire. 'I assure you, Mr Winspear, that all appropriate steps are being taken to capture whoever killed your brother.'

'Humph, wouldn't be surprised if that wife of his wasn't behind it. Her and that Russian dancer chappie. You must have noticed his attention towards her?' Henry uncrossed his legs and leered.

'I can assure you sir, that I shall consider everyone. You believe then that Lady Winspear is involved romantically with Ivan Bolsova?' Inspector Greville asked.

'Dash it all, it's as plain as the nose on your face that they are carrying on together. Even my brother had begun to notice.'

Kitty glanced at Matt. She wondered how much Sir William had observed about his wife's friendship with the Russian dancer.

'What led you to this conclusion, Mr Winspear? Had your brother spoken to you about any concerns?' Inspector Greville asked, lifting his gaze to meet Henry's.

Henry shuffled on his seat. 'Well, no, not as such,' he mumbled, dropping his gaze.

Inspector Greville waited silently, his pen poised over his notebook for the man to continue.

'Um, well, I might have accidentally overheard a bit of an argument between William and the Russian fella, about Lettice' Henry muttered.

'I see. And when was this exactly, sir?' The inspector asked.

'About a week or so ago. Not long after Padma and I had arrived at Palm Lodge. William was in the library, and I was outside on the terrace having a smoke. The windows were open.'

'Of course, I understand. What exactly did you hear, sir?' The inspector made a brief note in his book.

'I heard William mention Lettice's name and the other chap say something about her in reply, but he was quieter. Then I heard William say, "Stay away from her if you know what's good for you."'

'Did Mr Bolsova respond?' Inspector Greville lifted his head.

'No, the next thing I knew, I heard the library door bang and then Bolsova came storming out onto the terrace. He looked furious.' Henry moved his shoulders in a slight shrug. 'I didn't let on that I had heard anything. I thought it better to keep out of it.'

Inspector Greville nodded. 'Very wise, sir. Do you know of anyone else who may have had a grudge against your brother? Or who may have wished to harm him?'

'I've wanted to murder him myself a few times and I'm sure Elspeth feels the same.' Henry chuckled then caught the inspector's eye and subsided. 'Not that either of us would ever have done anything to William. He was our brother after all,' he added hastily.

'Of course, sir. Did you notice if the arrow was still on the table when you and your wife left the group to go to the Italian gardens?' The inspector directed the conversation back to the events of the afternoon.

Henry gave another shrug. 'No, I'm afraid I can't say as I did. The girl, Natasha, she was very interested in it. Kept stroking the feathers.'

'May I ask, sir, if you noticed any of the other members of your party while you were seated in the gardens?' Matt asked.

Kitty knew the Italian gardens – which consisted of fine paths and miniature box borders with roses – offered a view over the grounds. It occurred to her that if anyone were seated there, they might have seen someone walking on the top path in the direction of the grotto.

Henry appeared to consider Matt's question. 'Not that I can say for certain. I thought I saw the Russian girl or someone wearing a dress like hers. A distinctive shade of green, you know, but she and her brother had gone to the golf course to see the windmill.' He blinked owlishly and Kitty could see him working it out in his mind.

'And you and your wife remained together in the gardens until shortly before four thirty when you returned to the mansion for tea?' Inspector Greville asked.

'Yes, of course, yes.'

Kitty thought Henry's reply sounded a touch over-vehement to her ears.

'One last thing, sir, may I ask if you are aware of the terms of your brother's will?' Inspector Greville's gaze rested innocently on Henry's face.

Kitty watched as Henry's cheeks grew florid. 'Of course, yes. The house is held in trust, so naturally Padma and I will continue to live there. Elspeth too, and Lettice if she wishes to remain. I believe he will have made provision financially for my sister and Lettice will no doubt be a very wealthy widow. He always implied that I would have control over some of his companies. There is also a substantial sum of money that came from our mother's will, which by rights should come to me.'

'And you had no idea that he intended to make some changes to his will this coming week?' Inspector Greville's tone remained mild.

Henry's face was scarlet now and Kitty noticed he had clenched his hands into fists where they rested on the arms of the chair. 'No, not at all.'

'Thank you, sir.' The inspector nodded to the constable and Henry Winspear was shown out of the room.

'I don't think Mr Winspear was being very truthful,' Kitty remarked once Henry was out of earshot.

Inspector Greville's moustache twitched in amusement. 'I am inclined to agree with you there, Miss Underhay.'

'He was very keen to throw suspicion on Lettice and the Bolsovas,' Matt observed.

'He was, rather,' Kitty agreed. 'There are some very compli-
cated threads to unpick here. Either Henry or Padma or both of
them could have killed Sir William.'

'It seems to me that someone wanted to place Lettice in the
frame by planting that scrap of fabric.' Matt frowned as he stood
to stretch his legs, eliciting a grumble of complaint from Bertie
who was still snoozing peacefully.

'Well, if Lettice and Elspeth are telling the truth and they
were both in each other's company the whole time after the
archery then they are in the clear. It can't have been Lettice
who left that bit of chiffon,' Kitty said.

'If she tore her dress earlier in the day, why would she leave
evidence to implicate herself in her husband's death?' Inspector
Greville scowled at the notes he had made in his notebook.

'I agree. It looks more as if someone else wished to try and
implicate her in the murder or possibly to try and divert attention.' Kitty sighed. 'This surely must be to do with the will, or
Matt's invitation to the archery demonstration, or even both of
those things.'

'Henry Winspear was not very subtle about trying to high-
light Natasha Bolsova's name as a suspect.' Inspector Greville
tapped the end of his pen thoughtfully on the table. 'I think we
should talk to Miss Bolsova next. Let's find out if Henry did see
her on the path when she was supposed to be accompanying her
brother on a walk to the windmill.'

He spoke to the constable who promptly left the room in
search of Natasha while Kitty and Matt settled back in their
seats.

SIX

Natasha Bolsova entered the room quietly, her head held high as she walked with lithe grace to take her seat in front of the inspector. Her expression was inscrutable although Kitty thought she caught a flash of something in Natasha's eyes. Fear? Anger? It was gone in an instant and the Russian girl met the inspector's gaze with apparent equanimity.

'Miss Bolsova, thank you for seeing me. You and your brother are staying at Palm Lodge as the guests of Sir William and Lady Lettice Winspear?' Inspector Greville's tone was mild.

Natasha inclined her head, the edges of her sleek, dark bob swaying gracefully forward to frame her face with the movement. 'Yes, that is correct. Lady Winspear is very supportive of all of the arts. She is our sponsor for this visit to England.'

'Lady Winspear mentioned that she first met you and your brother in Paris?' Inspector Greville continued.

'She and Sir William attended a demonstration dance at the apartment of the Comtesse de La Remarques. Lady Lettice was gracious enough to take an interest in our dancing. She has been involved in the theatre herself.' Natasha's heavily kohl-lined eyelids helped to veil her gaze and Kitty wondered what the girl was thinking.

'Her husband, Sir William, was he also a patron of the arts?' the inspector asked.

Natasha stirred in her seat. 'I believe he was supportive of Lady Lettice. He liked to be considered a cultured man. Lady Lettice has sponsored other artistes before, a sculptor and a prominent painter.' She mentioned a couple of names and the inspector made notes in his book.

'And you came to London when?' Inspector Greville lifted his pen and looked at Natasha.

'We arrived in London just over two weeks ago and stayed with Sir William and Lady Lettice at their invitation to perform for some clients of Sir William and some other interested society people. Then after a few days we came here, to Palm Lodge.'

'I see. You are due to dance here at the club this evening?'

Natasha nodded once more as the inspector continued with his notes. 'Yes, I do not know if Lady Lettice will wish that to go on now this terrible thing has happened to Sir William. No doubt she will let us know what is to happen.'

Kitty wasn't sure if the dance exhibition would be affected or not. She supposed that a good many of the club members would be looking forward to seeing Ivan and Natasha perform.

'I expect the club and Lady Lettice will make the decision about the performance this evening. Were you aware of any conflicts or ill feeling amongst Sir William's household that might lead someone to wish to harm him?'

Natasha opened her eyes wide. 'I do not think that it is my place to speculate on such things. Lady Lettice and her husband have been most kind and generous to us.'

'Sir William is dead, Miss Bolsova. As an outsider looking in, your impressions are important and may lead to Sir William's murderer being caught.' Inspector Greville sounded stern, and Natasha's eyelids fluttered downwards to shield her gaze once more.

The girl sighed. 'Very well, then. I shall give you my impressions. I think that Miss Elspeth is most unhappy and was resentful of Sir William. He ordered her about like a servant. I think too that she had recently made a new acquaintance, a gentleman of the clergy, and Sir William did not approve of this. Mr Henry Winspear and his wife also disliked Sir William. I heard many arguments about money and also about Sir William's treatment of Mrs Winspear. He was very rude to her and would make what you call snide remarks within her hearing.'

'Thank you for being so frank, Miss Bolsova. May I also ask your impression of the relationship between Sir William and Lady Lettice?' The inspector caught and held Natasha's gaze and a delicate flush mounted on the girl's high cheekbones.

'My impression? Sir William was an old man and Lady Lettice is young, beautiful and full of life. He regarded her as his property, something he owned and liked to show off about. Sir William was inclined to be jealous of any friendships that Lady Lettice formed that did not include him or reflect well on him in his opinion.'

The inspector raised his eyebrows at this and waited for Natasha to fill the silence.

'I think he also often accused her of improprieties if she was friendly towards other men,' Natasha finally supplied, her mouth prim with disapproval.

'Was there anyone in particular that he suspected of engaging in this behaviour with Lady Winspear?' Inspector Greville asked. 'Your brother, for instance?'

The flush deepened in colour on the Russian girl's cheeks. 'Ivan is teaching Lady Lettice to tango. It is a very intimate dance.'

Inspector Greville nodded and made more notes in his

book. 'Did you notice the shaft of the damaged arrow that was on the tea table earlier today, shortly before the party dispersed?

Natasha's shoulders dropped and Kitty sensed the girl was relieved at the change in the line of the policeman's questions.

'Of course. We all examined it and praised Sir William's skill with the bow. It was a very beautiful thing, so much work to make an arrow balance. I had not realised.' Natasha sounded unconcerned.

'Did you notice it on the table when you and your brother left to walk up the golf course to the windmill?'

The dancer appeared to consider the inspector's question carefully. 'No, I do not remember. I think Mrs Winspear was looking at it, but I could be mistaken.'

The inspector asked her a few more questions about the time she and Ivan had left the group and the route they had taken to walk along the paths leading into the hills above the mansion.

'And did you reach the windmill?'

Again, the colour crept into the girl's cheeks. 'No, it was very hot, and we were tired, so we stopped and rested on a bench halfway there before turning back. We had not realised how steep the climb was or how far we needed to go in order to reach the windmill.'

'And you and your brother were together the whole time?' Inspector Greville asked.

Natasha nodded. 'Yes, we came back to the terrace together in time for tea and the staff said something had occurred, so we were shown inside to meet the rest of the group.'

Inspector Greville glanced over in Kitty and Matt's direction. Kitty presumed this was to check if they had any questions for Natasha before he allowed her to rejoin the group.

Matt gave a faint shake of his head.

'Did you see Lady Winspear catch her dress on the cane chair before the archery demonstration?' Kitty asked.

Natasha's lip curled. 'No, I do not think so.'

'Thank you,' Kitty replied.

The inspector nodded to the constable who duly escorted the dancer from the room.

'One more to go.' Inspector Greville scratched the bridge of his nose absentmindedly with the end of his pen.

'Indeed, sir,' Matt agreed.

Kitty was finding it all very illuminating as the relationships within the house were revealed. She had so many questions and theories buzzing around in her mind. It would be very interesting to hear what Ivan had to say.

The constable returned and ushered in Ivan Bolsova. He was tall and dark like his sister, with an almost leonine cast to his dark features. He was strikingly handsome, and Kitty could well imagine Sir William thinking the worst if he found Lady Lettice in the dancer's arms.

Inspector Greville waited until the Russian was seated. 'Mr Bolsova, my apologies for the wait.'

Ivan waved a lean languid hand in a dismissive gesture. 'You have a job to do, Inspector.'

He confirmed his sister's story of how they had come to secure Lady Winspear as their patron.

'And Sir William? He was also a supporter of the arts?' Inspector Greville asked.

Ivan shrugged. 'This I cannot say for sure, it would seem so. He attended performances with Lady Lettice and invited his business contacts.'

'I've been led to believe that Sir William was a very jealous man?' The inspector looked directly at Ivan.

A small tic appeared in the corner of the dancer's jaw. 'Indeed. He often made baseless accusations to his wife who was perfectly blameless.'

'You were involved personally, I understand, in some of these accusations?' Inspector Greville asked calmly.

'I am teaching Lady Winspear to tango. Sir William was not happy about this.' Ivan scowled.

The inspector made a note in his book. 'Did you have the impression that there were other people in the household who Sir William may have also upset in some way? Or who may have disliked him?'

Ivan reached inside his jacket pocket and took out a silver cigarette case. He opened it and took out a small, dark-coloured cigarette for himself before offering the case to the inspector. The policeman shook his head, and the dancer closed the case with a snap, returning it to his pocket before lighting his cigarette.

'Henry Winspear and his wife disliked Sir William. I hear them many times arguing over money, and Sir William, he did not like Mrs Winspear. All the time he made little jibes about her country or her waiting on her husband. Elspeth too, she argued with him also. I heard them only a couple of days ago.'

'Do you know what Elspeth's argument with Sir William was about?' the inspector asked.

Ivan inhaled and the blew out a thin stream of smoke before replying. 'Elspeth had been calling on the new vicar. I think she had made a present for him. Sir William told her she was an old fool, and a man prefers a younger, more tender chicken, not an old boiler. Miss Elspeth was crying afterwards in the garden.'

The inspector's brows rose into his hairline at this statement and Kitty had to stifle a gasp at this example of Sir William's cruelty.

'You and your sister said that you planned to walk to the windmill at the top of the golf course, is that correct?'

'That is so. The others were going to watch the tennis. Miss Winspear is very fond of the game. It holds no interest for myself and Natasha, and we were keen to see more of the views. Henry Winspear said he was going to the Italian gardens with his wife.' Ivan tapped the ash from the end of his cigarette into a large marble ashtray on the corner of the desk.

Inspector Greville scribbled more notes. 'Did you and your sister reach the windmill?'

Ivan shook his head. 'No, it was hotter than we had realised so we stopped at a seat in the shade of a tree partway up the course.'

'And did you see any other members of the party while you were there?' Matt asked.

Ivan frowned. 'No one came near us but as we walked back towards the terrace, I thought I saw Miss Winspear approaching from the direction of the woods, but I must have been mistaken.'

'I see. Thank you, sir. Now, can I ask if you recall if the shaft of the arrow that Sir William broke earlier was still on the table when you left the group to go for your walk?'

'I don't know. I thought it was but after we had all looked at it and put it down again, I confess that I rather lost interest.' The dancer shrugged.

'One final question for now, sir. Do you recall Lady Winspear tearing her dress on a nail earlier in the afternoon?' The inspector flashed a quick look in Kitty's direction.

'I'm not sure. If she did then I did not notice.'

Kitty found the dancer's response unconvincing, yet she couldn't see why Ivan and Natasha should lie over such a small thing. No one had mentioned to them the scrap of fabric found at the scene of the murder so they couldn't know anything about that.

Ivan stubbed his cigarette out in the ashtray. 'Oh, one thing – one of the arguments I heard was between Miss Elspeth and Henry Winspear. Elspeth had discovered that Sir William had telephoned his solicitor about changing his will. They were arguing about this very loudly until they saw me enter the room and then they went quiet.'

Inspector Greville's pen scurried over the page in his notebook. 'Hmm, very interesting, sir, thank you. Can you recall any particular phrases?'

Ivan's brow puckered in thought. 'Henry said something about Lettice getting everything and then Elspeth said something about not if he finds out.'

Kitty looked at Matt.

The constable stepped forward once more and escorted Ivan from the room with instructions from the inspector that the party were now free to return to Palm Lodge.

'Well!' Kitty turned to face Matt and Inspector Greville. 'What do you make of all of that?'

The inspector sighed, his moustache drooping. 'I'm afraid to say, Miss Underhay, that I don't believe a single blessed one of them. All of them are lying over something or other, or holding something back. The trouble is I can't for the life of me work out why.'

Matt inclined his head in agreement. 'I know what you mean, sir.'

'I've asked that they all resume their residence at Palm Lodge while my enquiries continue. My men and the staff here at the club are speaking to the other guests as they leave today to see if anyone saw or heard anything that might prove pertinent.' The inspector closed his notebook and returned it to his jacket pocket.

'Yes, it would be useful to know if anyone saw Henry and Padma together in the gardens or Natasha and Ivan on the edge of the golf course,' Kitty said. From the way both pairs had responded during the interviews she had her doubts that they had been together for the whole of the time period between leaving the archery demonstration and reuniting for tea.

Both couples had implied that they had seen other members of the party in places where they were not supposed to be. Was this deliberate, or a simple error? Or spite, perhaps?

'Do you think that Lettice and Elspeth's alibi is true? That they were together during the match and afterwards?' she asked thoughtfully. It was true that there seemed little love lost between the sisters-in-law, but Kitty was sure that even there she had detected a note of evasion.

Inspector Greville sighed. 'There was something there that did not ring true. I'm hopeful that we can gain more information from the staff here at the club. It's possible that someone may have noticed their movements.'

There was a knock at the door of the room. Bertie scrambled to attention as the door opened a crack and Dr Carter's cheery face appeared.

'What ho! We meet again, Miss Underhay, Captain Bryant.' He stepped inside the room and Bertie trotted across to greet him, sniffing at the doctor's tweed-clad trouser legs with interest.

Kitty and Matt had met Dr Carter many times before on previous cases. A round, eternally cheerful man with a love of fast cars, even the most gruesome of deaths failed to dent his naturally happy disposition.

He shook hands with Matt and the inspector and tipped his Panama hat to Kitty. 'All finished in the grotto, Inspector.'

'Thank you, Dr Carter, is there anything to report?' Inspector Greville asked.

'Nothing at present beyond the obvious. Death was caused by someone skewering the poor fellow through his back with that broken arrow. It looks as if it went straight through his ribs and into his heart. Death would be pretty instant, no time to cry out or anything,' the doctor reported cheerfully.

'Would it take a great deal of strength to do that?' Matt asked.

The doctor smiled. 'If you are asking if a woman could have killed him, Captain Bryant, then I would have to say that it could have been done by either sex. Our victim was taken by surprise, his back was to his killer and he was dressed in a very light linen jacket and thin cotton shirt. The wooden shaft of the arrow is strong and where it was broken is very sharp. It would have gone in like a knife through butter.'

A cold shiver danced along Kitty's spine at the doctor's description. She recalled Sir William's surprised expression and the pool of dark red blood that had surrounded the protruding tip of the arrow.

'That is so horrid.' She shuddered and Bertie nudged her leg as if in sympathy.

Matt placed his arm around her waist. 'Are you all right, old thing?'

'Oh, Miss Underhay, I am so dreadfully sorry. I quite forgot, you were the one who found him, weren't you?' Dr Carter immediately rushed to apologise, his expression contrite.

'I'm perfectly all right, really,' Kitty assured them. 'It just struck me how cold-blooded and cruel the manner of Sir William's death was. He was so proud of his archery accomplishments and so eager to prove his skills. I think the inspector was right when he said that this was a very personal murder.'

SEVEN

The intense heat from earlier in the day had settled into a slightly gentler warmth by the time they made their way out of the mansion and back into the sunlit grounds. Matt held on to Bertie's leash with one hand as the dog sniffed and snuffled his way along the path leading towards the exit. Matt's other hand was firmly around Kitty's narrow waist.

Her complexion still looked a little too pale beneath the brim of her hat for his liking. The doctor's words had clearly hit a nerve. He felt guilty that he had not realised that discovering Sir William's body had affected her so much. Perhaps Kitty's involvement with their recent cases was taking a toll upon her.

'It seems that Lady Winspear is insisting that the dance demonstration is to go ahead here tonight,' he said. 'She has told the manager that it is what Sir William would want and that it is honouring his memory. She herself will not be attending, of course.'

'Of course. I wonder how Ivan and Natasha feel about performing,' Kitty mused. 'They are professional dancers, but even so it cannot be easy in such extraordinary circumstances.'

All around them the day guests were making their way out

of the grounds in the same direction. The cricket match had ended, and the lawn was now empty. A few guests were passing by in the opposite direction, their day clothes changed for evening attire ready for a night of supper and dancing in the ballroom.

Matt gave her a gentle squeeze. 'I'm sorry that today has not been the relaxing, carefree outing that I promised.'

Kitty smiled and looked up at him. 'You could hardly have anticipated that our host would end up being murdered.'

'True, but I should have been more thoughtful. Finding Sir William so unexpectedly in the grotto must have been a huge shock.' Kitty had been exposed to more murder victims than almost anyone else that he knew, and he wondered if he had become a little blasé about her ability to cope with such scenes.

'I think it was just the realisation that overwhelmed me when Dr Carter described how the poor man was killed. It struck me as almost vindictive that he had been murdered by his broken arrow. From what the other members of his party have said, he was not a particularly nice man but even so, to die in such a manner.' A faint shudder ran through her small frame as she spoke.

They paused momentarily while Bertie investigated a particularly interesting tree trunk. Kitty looked around at the people walking in and out of the grounds.

'This is such a lovely place. I can quite see why Mr Singer decided to build his mansion here. Poor Matt, we never did get to look at the golf course.' She smiled impishly at him.

'And you didn't have the opportunity to test out the dance floor or sample a cream tea.' He smiled back at her.

They resumed their stroll towards the large stone archway that spanned the drive. Matt fell back into step beside her, relieved to see her usual bubbly good spirits had returned.

'I would quite like to see Ivan and Natasha dance,' she remarked thoughtfully as they reached the wrought-iron gate.

'I suppose I do owe you a nice supper and a spot of dancing might be rather fun after the events of today,' Matt agreed.

Kitty glanced back towards the mansion, just visible through the trees lining the avenue at that point in the driveway. 'It's a shame we are not members.'

'I'm sure that for one evening it could be arranged, if I have a word with Inspector Greville. If you feel you are up to it, of course?'

Her smile widened. 'Oh, I think I could manage it.'

———

Kitty drove back to Dartmouth after leaving Matt and Bertie back at his house. Matt had assured her he would arrange their entry to the mansion and the ballroom this evening with the inspector. In the meantime, she needed to bathe, change into her evening gown and arrange for Mr Potter, her regular taxi driver, to take her and Matt to Oldway for the evening.

Matt had been insistent that she didn't drive, saying she had done enough for one day and she deserved a night of drinking cocktails and dancing. Kitty hadn't put up much of an argument since it sounded like a fine idea to her too.

She secured her car inside the shed that she rented from one of the fishermen and walked the short distance along the riverside embankment to the Dolphin. The ancient, black-and-white, half-timbered building was a landmark in the small town and the path was still bustling with holidaymakers and walkers as she approached the entrance.

A prickly sensation tickled at the back of her neck accompanied by a faint sense of unease. She paused and looked about her, certain that she was being watched. The crowds around her ebbed and flowed and she saw nothing unusual, yet the sensation remained.

Unnerved, Kitty quickened her pace until she was safely

inside the familiar wood-panelled surroundings of the hotel lobby. A few months ago she would have chalked such a notion up to her sometimes fanciful imagination. Events since then had taught her to take notice of her instincts.

Only a few weeks earlier the man who had been responsible for the murder of her mother many years before had drowned in the river at Exeter while attempting to flee from prison.

He had taken Kitty as his hostage, and she had barely escaped with her own life. She had thought that nightmare to be at an end but the man's sister, Esther Hammett, had vowed to take revenge. Kitty knew enough of the woman to know how cold-blooded and evil she truly was. It seemed Esther blamed Kitty for her brother's death and had sent a bloodcurdling bouquet along with a threat.

Ever since then, she was always careful to check any odd feelings or sightings just to be on the safe side. It probably was simply that she was overwrought from discovering Sir William's body, but it was better to be safe.

'Oh, Miss Kitty, you'm back. Mrs Treadwell asked that you go straight to see her in her salon when you come in.' Mary the receptionist's cheeks were pink with excitement when she saw Kitty enter the lobby.

Kitty's heart sank. Not that she normally had any worries about answering her beloved Grams' commands, but coming after the murder of Sir William this sounded ominous. She wondered if the news of his death had already reached Dartmouth. And, if it had, how had it got there?

'Thank you, Mary, I'll go straight up. By the way, could you telephone Mr Potter and ask him if he could collect me at around seven thirty?' Kitty said.

'Yes, miss, right away.'

Kitty left the girl reaching for the telephone as she made her way up the broad flight of oak stairs to the first floor and her grandmother's salon. As she tapped on the door to let her grandmother know she was there, she heard the faint murmur of voices from inside the room.

'Come.'

Kitty automatically smoothed the skirt of her dress and took a deep breath before fixing a smile to her face as she opened the door to the salon.

'Hello, Grams, Mary said you were asking for me.'

Her grandmother was seated on a fireside chair while opposite her, placidly sipping tea, sat Mrs Craven, her grandmother's friend and Kitty's particular bête noire.

'Oh, my dear, I'm so glad you've returned. Millicent has just been telling me the most alarming story.' Her grandmother turned an anxious face to Kitty, her hand resting on the fine pearl necklace that encircled her throat.

'Oh?' Kitty could tell from the slightly haughty expression on Mrs Craven's face that the news of Sir William's demise had indeed already reached the Dolphin Hotel.

She unpinned her hat and hung it on one of the hooks beside the door.

'Do come and sit down, Kitty darling. Tell me, is it true? Millicent says that Sir William Winspear has been murdered this afternoon at the country club.' There was a faint tremor in her grandmother's voice and Kitty almost wished someone would murder Millicent Craven.

Kitty took a seat on the sofa and helped herself to one of the fingers of fruitcake from the china plate on the side table. 'Yes, I'm afraid so, this afternoon, just after the archery demonstration,' she confirmed in between dainty bites of cake.

'There, I knew it,' Mrs Craven said smugly. 'As soon as my friend, Joan Ponsonby-Bell telephoned me and said poor Sir Winspear had been killed at Oldway, well, I had to come and let you know. Especially as you'd said Kitty and Captain Bryant were supposed to be meeting him there today.' She looked at Kitty's grandmother who had grown quite pale.

Kitty blinked and wondered who Joan Ponsonby-Bell might be, and how she had discovered that Sir William had been killed.

'What on earth happened? You and Matthew were supposed to be having a relaxing day out, not tripping over corpses at the country club. I mean, at Oldway Mansion of all places.' Colour was gradually returning to Kitty's grandmother's cheeks.

'Quite. It is such a lovely place,' Kitty agreed.

'I agree, but of course, my dear, the membership is not as exclusive as one would wish. They really should be more particular about who is permitted to join. No doubt some miscreant took the opportunity to attack and rob Sir William.' Mrs Craven helped herself to a shortbread biscuit.

'How did your friend discover that Sir William had been murdered?' Kitty asked.

Mrs Craven waved her hand dismissively. 'Her maid is walking out with Lady Winspear's chauffeur. He called round to see her as soon as he had taken poor Lady Winspear and her family back to Palm Lodge. Naturally, as I am friendly with Sir William, Joan telephoned me. She assumed that I would wish to know, and I came straight here to be with your grandmother.'

Kitty sighed. The speed with which news could travel via various networks never failed to amaze her.

'Well, I think it's perfectly horrid. Is Millicent right, Kitty? Does the inspector – I presume it will be Inspector Greville – think it is some rogue member of the club? Or some villain who has crept into the grounds and attacked Sir William?' her grandmother asked.

Kitty picked the crumbs from her skirt and placed them neatly on a spare saucer. 'I don't know what happened, Grams.' She knew she had to be careful or anything she said would be halfway to Totnes before supper was served.

'I do hope that you are not going to become embroiled in

this investigation, Kitty. You have a wedding to plan for December and we are very busy here at the hotel.' Her grandmother fixed her with a stern look.

'Exactly. Once you are a married woman, Kitty, you will not have time for such shenanigans. It's far better to make this plain to Matthew now,' Mrs Craven advised, nodding her head sagely.

Kitty gritted her teeth and took a calming breath. 'Thank you for your concern, Mrs Craven but I don't think my fiancé expects me to sit at home knitting once we are married. Indeed, if he did, I rather doubt that I would agree to say "I do".' She softened her words with a smile and a quick apologetic glance at her grandmother. 'I'm afraid you must excuse me, Grams darling. I need to change as I'm meeting Matt again shortly for supper and dancing.'

She made a swift exit from the sofa, only pausing to place a kiss on her grandmother's cheek. As she closed the salon door behind her she heard Mrs Craven huff.

'Well, really. She gets more like her mother every day.'

Kitty had bathed and changed into a pale green evening gown with a low back and chiffon-capped sleeves when there was a tap at her bedroom door. She paused in her struggle to fasten her silver chain around her neck.

'Oh, let me do that for you, Miss Kitty.' Alice, her maid and trusted friend, hurried into the room to take the necklace from her.

She was wearing a thin, pale blue knitted cardigan over the top of her black maid's dress, and she had removed her starched white apron and cap.

'I was just about to get off home when Mary said as you'd come back. She said as how there had been a murder at that country club in Paignton. She said as Mrs Craven arrived all of a bustle just before teatime to see your grandmother to tell her.' Alice's deft fingers made short work of fastening the chain.

Kitty met her friend's gaze in the reflection of the dressing table mirror. 'I dare not let on to Grams, but I was the one who found Sir William's body. Well, Bertie and I, to be precise.'

Alice's eyes widened. 'Oh, miss, how awful.'

'He was in the grotto by the side of the pool. Someone had speared him in the back with one of his own arrows.' Kitty bit her lip as her friend took a seat on the end of Kitty's bed.

'Heavens above, what a thing to happen, miss. Do the police know who's done it?' Alice asked.

Kitty shook her head as she picked up her comb. 'No, not yet. Sir William doesn't seem to have been a very nice man so I think a few people might be in the frame.'

Alice jumped up and whipped the comb from Kitty's hand. 'Here, let me do your hair for you, miss.'

Kitty acquiesced to Alice's expert ministrations and her blonde curls were soon looking neat and smooth against her head. 'I'm going back to Oldway this evening with Matt. There is a dance demonstration being given by a Russian brother and sister who are staying with the Winspears.'

'I take it as you and Captain Bryant are on the case, then, miss?' Alice asked as she fixed a jewelled side comb in Kitty's hair.

'We are, but my grandmother doesn't approve, and truthfully, Alice, we are so busy here I'm not certain how much help I can be to Matt.' Kitty was aware that her tone was more than a little regretful. She would much rather be out hunting for a murderer than adding up accounts sheets or dealing with complaints from guests.

'Well, you know as you can count on me and Dolly if you wants some extra help.' Alice stood back and gave Kitty's hair a critical look.

Kitty grinned at her friend. 'You're an absolute brick, Alice. I don't know what I would do without you.'

The girl's narrow face flushed the same shade of crimson as her hair. 'Get on with you, Miss Kitty. Just promise me as you won't go putting yourself in any danger this time. I don't like the sounds of someone wandering about shooting innocent folks with arrows.'

'Well, tonight is mostly about dining and dancing, I promise. I am very eager to try out the dance floor there. It was built for Isadora Duncan, you know, so it's reported to be the best of the best.' Kitty picked up her pale pink lipstick.

'Dancing in a ballroom sounds safe enough. It's the poking about for clues that might get you in hot water,' Alice rejoined tartly.

'I'll be careful. Thank you for dressing my hair, you have such a good touch.'

The black Bakelite candlestick telephone on the side table rang out and Alice picked it up and answered.

''Tis Mary, she says as Mr Potter's taxi is here for you, miss.' Alice replaced the receiver and looked around for Kitty's delicate evening shawl.

Kitty stood and picked up her matching silver evening purse before taking her shawl from her friend. 'Thank you, Alice.'

Her friend accompanied her down the stairs and out to the taxi. Alice had been walking out with Mr Potter's son, Robert, for a few months now and the taxi driver greeted her cheerfully.

Alice stood aside as Mr Potter opened the door for Kitty. 'Have a good evening, miss.'

'I will, and I'll tell you all about it tomorrow,' Kitty promised as the girl assisted her inside the car.

EIGHT

Matt had managed to persuade his housekeeper's son to stay at the house with Bertie while he and Kitty went out for the evening. Left alone, the dog would howl constantly and destroy anything he could get his paws or teeth on. Although his behaviour was slowly improving, he was still quite a handful.

He stood in front of the fantail-shaped, silver hall mirror and adjusted his bow tie. It would be interesting to see Ivan and Natasha dance this evening, to witness the dynamic between brother and sister. A car horn sounded from the driveway, and he guessed the taxi had arrived.

Kitty was seated in the back seat, a fine silver knit shawl loose around her shoulders and a diamante clip gleaming in her blonde curls. The evening air was still warm, and the light was only just starting to fade, streaks of pink and gold creeping into the pale blue of the evening sky.

'You look rather lovely.' He kissed her cheek as he slid onto the seat beside her. His compliment sent colour into her cheeks.

'Thank you. You look quite spiffing yourself. Did the inspector mind when you telephoned and said we wished to attend the dance demonstration?'

Matt cracked open the window in the back of the taxi to allow a stream of air to enter as they drove along. His time in the trenches during the Great War had left him with a dislike of enclosed spaces.

'No, not at all. I think he is hoping we might learn more about our Russian friends this evening.' He leaned back and looked out at the view over the sea before the car took the turn to drive in land towards the mansion.

'What time are Ivan and Natasha due to perform?' Kitty asked.

'Ten o'clock, so we have time for supper first. I have managed to reserve a table for us, with Inspector Greville's assistance. I think he used the Chief Constable's name to secure us a seat.' He smiled when his fiancée's expression brightened at the mention of supper.

She told him of Mrs Craven's visit and her grandmother's disapproval of her becoming involved in the investigation.

'Trust dear Mrs C to be first with the news. Oh dear, though, I can see your grandmother's point about the hotel being busy.' He looked at Kitty, knowing full well that she would have no intention of being side-lined no matter how busy the hotel might be.

'Then I shall just have to find a way,' Kitty said in a prim, butter-wouldn't-melt-in-her-mouth tone.

Matt couldn't help feeling sorry for Mrs Treadwell. Kitty's poor grandmother might well find her granddaughter slacking off just a little from her duties until Sir William's murderer was captured.

Mr Potter drove the taxi slowly up the driveway to the stone arched gate where they had entered earlier in the day. The gate keeper allowed the taxi to proceed through and up to the parking area outside the mansion. Matt clambered out and held the door for Kitty, helping her down. They arranged for Mr Potter to return for them at eleven thirty and then strolled towards the front door of the mansion.

Lights spilled out under the stone-colonnaded entrance and a uniformed doorman stood at the open door, greeting the club members and directing people. Kitty took Matt's arm as they walked inside the vast marbled hallway with the huge painted mural and ornate ceiling. His housekeeper had told him that the mansion had been used as a hospital for wounded American servicemen during the Great War. He wondered what they had thought when they had arrived at such grandeur.

He had met his own wife, Edith, in a similar setting when she had nursed him after he had been injured on the battlefield. He recalled his own feelings of confusion mixed with gratitude at finding himself recuperating in a grand country house not unlike Enderley Hall, the home of Kitty's aunt and uncle.

The restaurant area was busy, and they had to wait for a few minutes before being shown to their table. All around them the air buzzed with the hum of chatter and the clinking of silverware on fine china. Elaborate crystal chandeliers set a glittering light over the pristine white tablecloths and sparkling glassware.

The waiter pulled out a chair for Kitty and she took her place opposite Matt, her blue-grey eyes shining as she smoothed the linen napkin across her knees.

'I know we are really here to investigate Sir William's death, but this is rather splendid, isn't it?' she murmured as the waiter left to bring the wine list and menu.

Matt smiled at her. 'This evening is as much about pleasure as gathering background information.'

'I saw the poster in the entrance way about the dance demonstration this evening.' Kitty changed the subject when the waiter reappeared.

Matt accepted one of the burgundy leather-covered menus. He too had seen the brightly coloured poster with an artistic sketch of Ivan and Natasha in a dance embrace advertising the event. A black ribbon had been discreetly placed on one corner with a note to say that the event was celebrating the life of the late Sir William Winspear, patron.

'Yes, They're an interesting pair. I'm looking forward to seeing them perform.' Matt waited while Kitty made her choices from the menu before placing his own order.

Wine and food orders placed, Kitty leaned back in her chair, busy surveying their fellow diners.

'I can see why one would wish to become a member here even if the sporting activities were not to one's tastes.' She smiled impishly at Matt as an elderly lady glittering with diamonds swept past them on her way to her table.

'Sir William would have enjoyed this immensely. He was a man who enjoyed feeling that he was someone important.' Matt had been giving a great deal of thought to Sir William's character.

The waiter returned to place white china dishes containing mock turtle soup before them. 'He certainly liked to be noticed and thought important. I wish we knew what he wanted to speak to you about,' Kitty mused as she started her soup.

'I think it might have been connected in some way to the changes he was considering making to his will.' Matt frowned as he took a sip of his wine.

Kitty looked at him. 'I suppose that's a possibility from what Elspeth said. He told you he wanted some advice, didn't he? That doesn't sound as if he wanted you to investigate anything, otherwise surely he would have said he had a job for you.'

'Very true, and it was interesting that he telephoned me himself to invite us. Normally he got Elspeth to do everything. He even said to me when I worked for him before that he didn't see the point of keeping a dog in order to bark himself.' Matt shook his head slightly in disapproval.

'He was a rather horrid man.' Kitty set her spoon down in the empty bowl with a satisfied sigh. 'That was quite delicious.'

Matt bit back a smile. His fiancée had a healthy appreciation for food.

Their empty soup dishes were whipped away and replaced with plates of fillet of dover sole with Dauphinoise potatoes and summer vegetables. Kitty sniffed appreciatively.

'Inspector Greville is speaking to Sir William's solicitor tomorrow.' Matt speared a morsel of fish with his fork.

'That will be interesting. I wonder if a new will had been drafted or if he had merely spoken to him about any changes he intended to make.' Kitty's eyes brightened.

'It would be good to know too if any of the inspector's men learned anything from their questioning of the country club members and staff from this afternoon.' All of the Winspear party's alibis had sounded rather too pat. Henry and Padma had vouched for each other, as had Ivan and Natasha. He was not even convinced by Lettice and Elspeth's assertion that they had remained together.

They finished their main course and opted for a dessert of lemon and raspberry tart with Chantilly cream before ending their dinner with a selection of petit fours and coffee served in exquisitely tiny white china cups in the modern style.

'That was very good.' Kitty set her empty cup down carefully on her saucer and sighed with satisfaction.

'Do you think you will be able to dance?' Matt teased her gently. 'Or are you too full?'

'I think perhaps a stroll outside on the terrace first might be in order.' Kitty smiled back at him.

Matt settled the bill and escorted Kitty back outside the mansion through one of the open French windows. Light spilled through the tall open windows onto the terrace, and they could hear the faint strains of music emanating from the ballroom.

The night air was still pleasant and all around them on the terrace and in the Italian gardens other couples were walking together, enjoying the moonlight. He moved his arm to place it around Kitty's slim waist as they paused to look out over the grounds towards the grotto.

'This afternoon all feels like a bad dream now. It's so lovely and peaceful here,' Kitty said.

'And yet it seems that one of the people we met this afternoon killed our host in cold blood.' Matt kept his voice low so they would not be overheard.

Kitty shivered. 'I know, and the manner of his death was so bizarre. Whoever killed him left nothing to chance. They must have lured him to the grotto and even took a weapon with them.'

'Yes, it was premeditated and cold. To spear him in the back...' Matt broke off and shook his head. The whole affair was deeply troubling. 'Let's go back inside. There should be enough time for us to take to the floor for a few spins before Natasha and Ivan give their performance.'

———

Kitty accompanied Matt back inside the mansion. They opted to walk back up the grand marble staircase to the ballroom rather than entering via the French doors from the far terrace. The brass insets of the balustrading glittered like gold against the brown and cream.

They followed the stream of guests in their evening finery into the grand ballroom. The music was provided by the small orchestra positioned on a minstrels' gallery at the far end of the room above the dance floor.

The walls were lined with huge mirrors set in carved and gilded frames and Kitty guessed that this room especially must be modelled on the famous hall of mirrors at Versailles. The mirrors reflected the couples dancing on the polished parquet floor with the light twinkling from the smart, modern, geometrically shaped lights in the ceiling.

Matt took her in his arms and Kitty gave herself up to the music, happily moving around the floor amongst the other couples.

'Does the floor live up to your expectations?' Matt's breath tickled her ear as he deftly steered her around an elderly couple who were in their path.

'Yes, it is wonderful.' Kitty always enjoyed dancing with Matt and the sprung floor was living up to its reputation. There was time for a few more dances and then the announcement was given to clear the floor for the evening's demonstration of dance.

Kitty squeezed her way to the front of the crowd around the edge of the floor so she could have a clearer view of the proceedings. One of the downsides of being petite was that invariably someone tall would stand in front of her if she was further back.

'My lords, ladies and gentlemen. It gives Oldway Country Club great pleasure to introduce the famous international dancer Mr Ivan Bolsova and his sister, Miss Natasha Bolsova. They appear tonight by the generous patronage of the late Sir William Winspear and his wife, Lady Lettice Winspear. This demonstration and performance is a tribute to the late Sir William.'

A ripple of enthusiastic applause greeted the announcement by the dapper, tail-suited compere.

'Ladies and gentlemen, we will commence the evening with a demonstration of the Viennese waltz.'

The conductor in the gallery raised his baton and the music commenced. Natasha appeared wearing a very pale, blue, floor-length gown with a full chiffon-feathered skirt, followed by Ivan in a white tail suit. They bowed to the crowd and commenced their dance.

Kitty had to admit, to her untrained eye they seemed spec-tacularly good. Almost like a scene from one of Alice's favourite films. Natasha appeared to float around the floor, her movements effortless, and Kitty heard some of the crowd gasp in admiration as they sailed past.

They followed their first dance with more waltzing and demonstrations, narrated by the compere of how to hold one's head and arms and where to place your feet in the various dances.

Natasha and Ivan then left the floor briefly and the compere announced that they would now demonstrate the tango. Some of the lighting in the room changed and the Russians made a dramatic entrance. Ivan was now dressed in a crimson bolero-style jacket and black trousers and Natasha in scarlet satin with a slashed skirt.

The dance was passionate and exotic and several ladies standing near to Kitty fanned themselves with their hands when Ivan came closer. The applause was loud and long when the dance ended, and it took a moment before the commentator could make himself heard to say that the next demonstration would be of modern dance.

The couple changed costumes once more with Natasha in a beaded and sequinned above-knee silver dress as they demonstrated the Charleston and other expressive dance moves.

The exhibition ended with Ivan performing a spectacular Cossack dance to rapturous applause. Everyone around Kitty surged forward to talk to Ivan and Natasha and to obtain their autographs. The sudden movement almost knocked Kitty off her heels and she was glad of Matt's strong arm steadying her.

'Well, that was quite something, wasn't it?' She looked up at Matt.

'They are certainly excellent dancers,' he agreed. She noticed his gaze was still fixed on the brother and sister as they talked to the audience members.

After a short intermission allowing everyone who wished to meet Ivan and Natasha to see them and obtain autographs, the music recommenced. The dance floor soon filled up once more with members of the country club eager to show off their own dancing skills.

Matt went to the bar to obtain some cocktails while Kitty stepped out onto the terrace again, in search of some cooler air. The night was still warm, and the stars twinkled overhead like diamonds in the navy velvet sky. The heavy scent of roses mingled with a faint tinge of tobacco as others also took advantage of the summer evening.

Now that she had seen Ivan and Natasha dance, she could understand why Lettice had felt moved to offer them patronage. They were extremely talented. Ivan had certainly caused quite a sensation in the tango.

A mixed group of men and women spilled out onto the terrace, laughing and talking loudly, and Kitty retreated further along the path towards the deeper shadows at the rear of the mansion where the windows, although open, were covered with drapes and only a dim light escaped around the edges to light the paving.

'That went well.'

Kitty froze. She edged carefully and quietly closer to the window. She had recognised the voice as Ivan's.

'It was something to be on the same floor where Isadora Duncan also danced.' Natasha's voice was clearer, and Kitty assumed that she must be closer to the window than her brother.

'Letty says that the will is to be read tomorrow morning. That policeman will be coming to the house.' Ivan's voice was muffled for a moment and Kitty guessed the couple must be changing from their stage clothes.

'No doubt she will be a very rich woman.' There was a hint of scorn in Natasha's tone.

Ivan laughed. 'No doubt.'

'I do not like that the police will be there,' Natasha said. Her voice now sounded very close to where Kitty was standing.

Kitty pressed her back against the wall of the house hoping the girl would not decide to step out onto the terrace. The stone wall was cold against the bare skin of her back.

Ivan laughed again. 'It is only to be expected with Sir William's murder. I am more interested in what he may have said to that private investigator.'

Kitty's heart thumped in her chest as she realised that Ivan was referring to Matt.

'Da, it was very strange that he should turn up this afternoon. The blonde girl who was with him too. They were both present when the policeman was asking questions,' Natasha mused.

'They were in the ballroom just now, watching us dance.' Ivan had seen them. The realisation sent Kitty's pulse racing.

'You think they are here with the police?' Natasha asked.

'I don't know, but we had better be certain that we are saying the same things if they question us once again.' Ivan too now sounded closer to the window. His words to Kitty seemed to hold a warning note to his sister.

'You think that the police will talk to us again?' Natasha sounded worried.

A shuffling sound came from within the room, like someone walking on the parquet flooring. 'Of course. We are foreigners. It would be more convenient if one of us were to be arrested. We must stick together and be certain we are saying the same things. I was with you, and you were with me. Do not forget.' His voice sounded very close now to Kitty's ear and the warning was clear.

NINE

Kitty held her breath and hoped that Ivan wouldn't decide to step through the nearby French door out onto the terrace. If she were caught snooping, she had no idea how the Russian would react. She moved her foot and started to edge silently and cautiously away from the open window.

Ivan must have pulled the curtain open as more light suddenly flooded out onto the terrace beside her. Kitty turned and took a few quick steps along the flagstones, eager not to be seen. With luck, she could reach the group further along and conceal herself in their midst. A courting couple engrossed in each other and clearly intent on finding a more private spot passed her, heading towards the spot Kitty had just vacated.

She hurried on into the small crowd on the area immediately outside the ballroom windows and walked straight into Matt.

'Steady on, old thing, I've been looking everywhere for you.' He handed her one of the two cocktail glasses he was carrying and eyed her curiously.

She accepted a drink and took a reviving sip while peering back along the terrace. 'I was further towards the end.' To her relief, she saw no sign of either Ivan or Natasha on the terrace. That had been a narrow squeak.

He walked with her as they headed for a quieter spot in the opposite direction to where Kitty had been eavesdropping on Natasha and Ivan. Matt reached out a hand and lifted something from her shoulder.

'Wherever you were, darling, it seems to have been a little cobwebby,' he observed.

She told him about the snippet of conversation she had just overheard. 'I rather think that confirms that they weren't together for the whole time, so their alibi looks shaky. Ivan definitely seemed to be warning his sister that they needed to keep their story straight. Not something you would need to do if one were telling the truth,' Kitty said thoughtfully.

'True, but I wonder what the motive for murdering their patron would be. Unless, of course, Ivan and Lettice are conducting a serious liaison and he is hoping to marry a wealthy widow.' Matt's mouth set in a grim line.

'And what of Natasha? She could be the killer. Dr Carter did say a woman could have struck the fatal blow.' Kitty frowned. She couldn't see a motive for Natasha unless she was assisting Ivan. If their motive was so that Ivan could marry Lettice, presumably for her money, would Lettice then become their next victim?

She choked a little on her cocktail at the thought.

'Steady on, darling, these are quite strong.' Matt looked at her as she moved the twist of orange peel adorning the top of the glass.

'It's very nice.' Kitty eyed her drink appreciatively.

'A Hanky Panky.' Matt's eyes twinkled mischievously in the moonlight. 'The bartender said they are all the rage at the club at the moment.'

Kitty gave a faint shake of her head in silent reproof, causing Matt to chuckle.

'Let's forget the Bolsovas for now and go back inside and enjoy the dancing. Mr Potter will be here to collect us soon and it would be a shame not to make the most of our evening.' Matt smiled at her.

'Yes, you're right. I think I may have done enough sleuthing for the moment,' Kitty agreed and accompanied him back inside towards the dance floor.

———

Kitty awoke the following morning with a remarkably clear head, considering she had consumed several more cocktails before Mr Potter had arrived to drive her and Matt home. She glanced at her bedside clock, annoyed with herself that she had woken so early on what was a precious day off.

She was acutely aware that she really needed to see her grandmother before the working day was fully underway. At the very least she should apologise to her for her outburst at Mrs Craven yesterday afternoon. It really was too vexing that she always seemed to allow the wretched woman to get under her skin.

While she didn't really regret the content of what she had said, she didn't wish to be thought rude or to have embarrassed her grandmother. Kitty sighed and slipped out of bed. She could see an apology to Mrs Craven herself being on the cards too.

She had just finished dressing for the day when there was a familiar tap at her door and Alice appeared carrying a tea tray.

'Good morning, Miss Kitty. I thought as you'd be awake now. Have you time for a cup of tea?' the maid asked hopefully, her eyes bright with curiosity.

Kitty guessed that she had given Mrs Homer, the hotel housekeeper, the slip for a few minutes so that she could find out from Kitty what had happened at the mansion.

'Absolutely. I could do with a spot of fortification before I go and see Grams.' Kitty patted the bedcover to encourage Alice to set down the tray and take a seat beside her.

She hid her private amusement when, having poured Kitty's tea, Alice produced an extra cup and settled down for a moment to catch up on the gossip.

'So how was your evening, miss? Was the dancing good?' Alice asked.

'Oh yes, the dinner was wonderful, and the Russian dancers put on a superb exhibition. I do hope they might do some more public performances while they are here in Devon. You would really enjoy seeing them. It was just like that musical we saw a few weeks ago.' Kitty savoured the tea. Perhaps she was a little more affected by last night's cocktails than she had realised. Hanky Pankys indeed.

'And did you find out anything more about the murder, miss?' Alice asked between sips of tea.

Kitty told her friend what she had managed to overhear while she had been standing on the terrace.

'That sounds to me like they were up to no good. It's a good thing as they didn't catch you listening in. I suppose as you or Captain Bryant will tell the inspector what you heard?' the girl said, her expression thoughtful.

'Of course. I rather think it proves that they were not telling the truth about being together all the time on the golf course,' Kitty agreed.

Alice nodded in agreement, causing a few auburn curls to escape from under her cap. 'It sounds like that other film I saw with our Dolly about the old husband being murdered by the glamorous young wife with her lover.'

Kitty laughed. Alice loved going to the picture house and frequently compared events in their small town to the plots of the movies she saw on the silver screen.

'Hmm, there are others though with motives for murdering

Sir William and who equally seem to have been less than truthful. At least, that is what the inspector thinks, and I must admit I am inclined to agree with him. The family solicitor is reading Sir William's will today so Inspector Greville may have new information when that has occurred.' Kitty finished her drink and set her cup back on its saucer.

Alice also returned her cup to the tray and jumped to her feet. 'In the films, the wife will have inherited everything. That would give her ladyship a motive.' She sighed as she headed for the door. 'I'd best get back afore I'm missed.'

Kitty thanked her friend for the drink and promised to let her know of any developments in the case. She checked her appearance in her dressing table mirror and set off down the stairs to her grandmother's salon. She hoped to find her grandmother taking breakfast so that she could make her apologies and start her day off on the right note.

Mrs Treadwell was seated at the dining table in the bay window of her salon, nibbling on a slice of toast when Kitty entered.

'Good morning.' Her grandmother watched as Kitty took her place on the empty seat opposite her own.

'Morning, Grams.' Kitty helped herself to a piece of toast from the silver toast rack and started to spread it with rich yellow butter. 'I hoped I'd see you before you went downstairs to the office. I'm sorry about yesterday afternoon, but you know that Mrs Craven always seems to have an unfortunate effect on me.'

Her grandmother raised immaculate arched eyebrows. 'I had noticed, darling. I realise Millicent can be trying but she does have a good heart really. You will of course apologise to her.'

This was a statement and not a request. Kitty sighed. 'Of course, Grams. By the by, you are still certain that I can take today off?'

Her grandmother added more boiling water from the jug to the teapot and gave the pot a stir before replacing the lid. 'Of course. Although I trust you do not intend to spend all of it on police business? I expect Inspector Greville can manage without your assistance for at least one case.' There was a hint of a smile about her lips as she spoke, softening the dry tone of her words.

Kitty paused from her investigation of the marmalade pot. 'Mr Morley, Sir William's solicitor, is going to Palm Lodge today to read the will. I doubt that either Matt or I would be welcome for such an event. I think our intention was to take a picnic to Goodrington for a spot of sea bathing.'

'Well, that sounds a much pleasanter occupation and far more suitable.' Her grandmother smiled her approbation of Kitty's plan. 'You and Matthew work so terribly hard and with the wedding to organise too, you are going to have your hands full over the next few months. You still have to reply to your aunt over her offer to loan you the family tiara.'

Kitty and Matt had set their wedding day for Christmas Eve at the ancient St Saviour's Church in the town. Ever since they had become engaged, her grandmother, aided and abetted by Mrs Craven, had been consumed by wedding fever.

There had been constant talk of bridesmaids, tulle, flowers and cake. Kitty had been hoping for a simple ceremony without any fuss. Matt's first wife, Edith, had been killed during the Great War. Their baby daughter, Betty, had also perished in the same air raid. She knew Matt was of the same mind as herself about keeping the service small and intimate.

For now, however, she did not wish to provoke yet another argument about her intentions. She had arranged to call for Matt and Bertie the dog, just before lunch, and she would drive them all to the beach for the day. She had a rather nice new bathing suit and the day looked set to be as hot as yesterday.

———

Matt telephoned the police station in Torquay shortly after breakfast and passed on the information that Kitty had discovered to the inspector. He wished he could have attended the reading of Sir William's will at Palm Lodge. It would be interesting to discover if Sir William had made any changes to his bequests or if he had discussed any planned changes with his solicitor.

When he had visited Palm Lodge himself a few months previously he recalled that it had been a large Victorian-style villa. It was somewhat gloomy with dark, heavy furniture and old-fashioned drapes and Turkish carpets. Many of the fixtures and fittings had been inherited from Sir William's late parents.

Now, having met Lady Lettice Winspear, he suspected that the lodge was furnished to Sir William's tastes rather than that of his wife. He wondered what Elspeth thought of the décor. If the house was to be Henry and Padma's, perhaps they might redecorate. He would have given a great deal to be a fly on the wall there this morning.

Instead, with Bertie snoozing sounding in the shade beneath the apple tree in the garden, he decided to go for a swift round of golf at the club next to his house. A speedy nine holes would be just the ticket before Kitty arrived at lunchtime for their beach trip.

His housekeeper agreed to keep an eye on the dog while he set off to walk the short distance to the club at Churston. It was another fine and sunny morning, and the course was already quite busy.

'I say, Captain Bryant, are you going around on your own? Fancy a spot of company?' Matt turned around to see a casual acquaintance approaching him. Mr Turner was a retired bank manager who he had shared a round of golf with before.

'It would be a pleasure. I'm just playing a quick nine holes before lunch,' Matt explained.

'Just the ticket. The old heart has been a bit off just lately, so my doctor said to avoid the full eighteen holes for a spell.' Mr Turner's beam split his round, ruddy face.

They teed off and fell into step as they strolled across the course towards the first green.

'Haven't seen you for a few weeks. I expect the old detective stuff has been keeping you busy, eh?' Mr Turner remarked jovially.

'Just a little. I've also been away in Yorkshire for a wedding.' Matt waited while his companion selected his club and took his next shot.

Mr Turner peered hopefully towards the green. 'Lovely part of the world.'

They made their way amicably around the first few holes exchanging chit-chat about the weather and the game.

'Bit of a shocker what's happened over at Oldway, eh?' Mr Turner remarked as he collected his golf ball from the hole on the fourth tee.

Matt wondered for a moment if his golfing companion had heard of his involvement in the case. However, knowing Mr Turner, he thought it unlikely. The man was not known for being particularly nosy or for gossip.

'Indeed. Did you know Sir William at all, sir?' Matt asked.

Mr Turner scratched the side of his nose with the pencil he was using to mark his score card. 'Oh yes, he was a customer at the bank for many years. We were also members of a couple of the same clubs.'

Matt lined up his club for the putt and holed out. 'May I ask what your opinion of him was, sir?'

Mr Turner placed his score card and pencil back in his pocket. 'Well, between ourselves, I'm not surprised someone saw him off. He could be very charming when you first met him, but the man was a dreadful bully. It was wicked the way he used to speak to his sister.'

'His sister? You mean Elspeth? I've met her a couple of times.' Matt was careful to keep his tone casual.

'Good-looking gel when she was young, and smart too. You've got to like a woman with a bit of spark.' Mr Turner stood at the side of the green, a wistful expression on his face.

'You've known Miss Winspear for some time, then, sir?' Matt marked his own score card then retrieved his ball.

'What? Oh yes, years. Elspeth should have been married. She was engaged a couple of times, I believe. Nothing came of it though. William saw to that. It suited him to have Elspeth at home, dancing to his tune.' Mr Turner shook his head.

Matt shouldered his bag of clubs and they set off to the next tee. 'What about Henry Winspear? He's recently returned from India.'

Mr Turner set down his bag and placed his tee and ball ready to make his shot. 'Henry was always rather wild. One of those fellas who can't settle to anything. Rather think he left the country under a bit of a cloud. Something about financial irregularities, if I recall.'

Matt's eyebrows raised at this revelation. He waited for Mr Turner to finish his shot before continuing the conversation.

'I rather gathered there was no love lost between the brothers.' He set up his own tee and selected a club.

'I say, good shot, my boy. No, Henry hated William, always did – right from when they were boys. I always thought he was rather jealous of him, especially after William was knighted. Services to manufacturing or some such nonsense. Fella made his money from glass. Anyway, Henry was always after a loan for some scheme or other and William would send him away with a flea in his ear. He used to tell me all about it when he called in at the bank.'

They collected their bags and set off along the course. Matt took it slowly, allowing for his companion's more sedate pace.

'Do you know Lady Winspear at all, sir?' Matt asked when they reached Mr Turner's golf ball, which lay just shy of the green.

The older man gave a cackle of laughter. 'Ah, the fair Lettice. Not much that's ladylike about her, I'm sorry to say. She was appearing in some third-rate revue-type show in the provinces when William took up with her. His first wife was a lovely soul. Died young, pneumonia. Tragic.'

'I had heard that Lady Lettice was an actress before her marriage. There's quite an age gap between them,' Matt said, waiting while Mr Turner decided which club would serve him best to reach the green.

'Actress, my eye. I don't think there was much acting going on in the kind of shows she appeared in. She must be at least thirty or forty years his junior. Silly old fool and William was smitten with her.' Mr Turner frowned. 'At least he *was*.'

Once Mr Turner had made his shot and his ball was safely on the green, Matt picked up on his companion's last comment.

'You said he *was* smitten? I take it you think something had changed between them?' He tried to phrase the question delicately.

Mr Turner waited until Matt had taken his shot. 'Yes. The last time I saw William was just after he and Lettice had come back from Paris, maybe a week or so ago. They had some Russian dancers staying with them. I was making conversation as you do and joked about Lettice enjoying the dance exhibitions.' A crease formed on the older man's brow. 'His mood changed straight away. Became quite surly and short and said that she was enjoying them rather too much. I thought to myself, oh, the cracks are appearing now.'

They turned their attention to their game and putted out.

Matt marked his score card. 'I had heard a rumour that Miss Winspear was courting.'

Mr Turner's bushy grey eyebrows rose in mild amusement and his eyes twinkled. 'Good for Elspeth if she is. William wouldn't have approved but perhaps she may be luckier now he's no longer around.'

'Of course, Henry is married too now.' Matt set up his tee at the next green.

'Yes, an Indian woman, used to be Henry's housekeeper. Another annoyance for William. He was the most dreadful snob and that knighthood made him worse. He always wanted people to think he was a member of the gentry instead of a glass manufacturer who got lucky.' Mr Turner shook his head. 'No, I wasn't surprised when I heard about his murder. I was just surprised no one had done it sooner.'

TEN

Kitty called for Matt promptly after lunch with a wicker picnic hamper strapped to the boot of her car. Another bag contained a blanket, towels and bathing things was stowed on the rear seat, leaving just enough space for Bertie.

'You look rather pleased with yourself,' she remarked as Matt secured his dog on the rear seat beside the bathing things.

Privately she thought he looked quite dashing in his open-necked shirt and smart, ivory-coloured linen jacket. The dimple quirked in his cheek as he smiled at her.

'That's because I happened to run into a chap on the golf course this morning who gave me quite a lot of information on the Winspears.'

Kitty shot him a glance before returning her attention to putting her car in gear. 'Really? Do tell.'

Matt took the journey along the coast road to Goodrington Sands to tell her everything that he had learned from Mr Turner. She pulled her car to a halt at the side of the road near the path leading to the beach.

'How very interesting. Clearly Sir William was not a very popular man in any sphere of society,' Kitty said as she busied herself with undoing the buckles on the leather straps that secured the picnic hamper to the rear of her car.

'No, Mr Turner remarked that Sir William was equally unpopular with some sections of the business community. He could be quite ruthless when chasing monies owed and yet was not a prompt payer himself.' Matt collected the bag containing their beach things and unfastened Bertie's leash.

'That doesn't make a happy combination,' Kitty said.

Matt handed her Bertie's leash and relieved her of the picnic hamper so he could carry it to the sands along with their towels. Kitty walked alongside him as they looked around for a spot offering some shade from the red-hot heat of the afternoon sun. The beach was fairly crowded with the blue sea glittering temptingly in the sunshine.

Bertie had his nose down as he pulled forward, eager to start tunnelling on the coarse red sand.

'Over there.' Kitty indicated a vacant spot where the sand seemed firmer and the beach less busy. There was also a very handy spar of wood so they could secure Bertie's lead and a spot of shade where he could rest once he had completed his excavations.

Kitty spread out the blankets and prepared the towels. They hired two deckchairs and settled down for a leisurely afternoon. Kitty had already donned her bathing suit beneath her simple, pastel-coloured cotton sundress before driving to collect Matt. She unfolded her Japanese-style umbrella to provide more shade and arranged their things on the sand.

After a refreshing dip in the sea and a delicious picnic tea Kitty was feeling suitably refreshed. She had just finished packing away the remains of their sandwiches into the hamper when to her astonishment she spotted a red-faced young police constable making his way across the beach towards them.

'Begging your pardon, sir, miss, but are you Captain Bryant and Miss Underhay?' The perspiring constable stood unhappily before them, and Kitty thought she recognised him as the one who had been present at the interviews at the mansion.

'Yes, we are. Is there a problem, Constable?' Kitty asked, more than a little alarmed that a policeman had tracked them down at the beach. 'Is it my grandmother? The hotel? My car?' A series of potential disasters ran through her mind.

'No. miss. Please don't be alarmed. I was sent by Inspector Greville. He telephoned to the Dolphin and the young lady at the desk said as you had come here to the beach. When I got here the deckchair attendant pointed me in your direction.' The boy's tone was apologetic.

'The inspector? Why? Has something happened?' Matt exchanged a worried glance with Kitty.

'He's asked me if you could present yourselves at Palm Lodge as soon as possible. That's why I've come to find you.' The constable looked rather unhappily at his sand-covered boots.

Kitty's pulse speeded and she wondered what had occurred. The reading of the will had been scheduled to take place that morning. Perhaps the inspector was poised to make an arrest and required them to corroborate some piece of evidence. Or perhaps something even worse had transpired.

'We shall come immediately. Could you give me the directions as I'm not certain of exactly where the house is situated?' Kitty was glad that her bathing suit had dried in the summer heat and she could replace her sundress without feeling too damp.

While the constable gave her directions, Matt left the beach to change in a nearby bathing hut. His knitted, dark blue bathing costume was made of heavier material and was still wet from their dip in the sea. He returned quickly though, and they made their way off the beach, only pausing to ensure that Bertie had a drink of fresh water before loading Kitty's car.

The constable had already set off back to Palm Lodge on his

bicycle. 'That was unexpected. I wonder what's occurred?' Kitty said as she attempted to tidy her hair with the aid of the driver's mirror. Much to her annoyance she saw that the tip of her nose looked pink from the sun.

'I don't know, but I'm willing to wager it must be something important for the inspector to send one of his men to find us at the beach.' Matt took his place beside her as she started the engine.

Palm Lodge was only a few minutes' drive away from the sands. Lying further inland, the house stood in an elevated position on a street with several other Victorian villas. It was built of grey local stone and lay back from the road behind a high wall. Like the other houses around it, a gabled turret was at one end.

Kitty swung her little car in through the open, wrought-iron gates and up the gravel drive to the front of the house. The inspector's black police car was already parked there alongside another sportier-looking motor car that Kitty was also familiar with.

'That's Dr Carter's car,' she said as she stopped the engine and opened the driver's door.

'Oh dear, that doesn't bode well.' Matt untied Bertie's leash and they made their way to the front door of the lodge.

A pale-faced maid in a black uniform opened the door at their ring and after checking their names, stood aside to allow them entry.

'If you'd care to come with me, sir, miss, I'm to take you through to the back of the house. The policeman is expecting you.'

Kitty followed Matt and Bertie along a rather gloomy hallway filled with dark landscape pictures and sporting prints. As they neared the end of the hall a door opened, and Elspeth appeared. She too looked pale and her eyes were rimmed with red as if she had been crying.

'Thank you, Tilly, I'll take Captain Bryant and Miss

Underhay to the inspector.'

The girl scuttled away, a relieved look on her face.

'Miss Winspear, whatever has happened?' Kitty asked. Somewhere in the distance she thought she could hear a woman sobbing and the sound of voices.

'I'm afraid there seems to have been the most terrible accident.' Elspeth wrung her hands together in distress.

She turned sharply on her heel as if too distressed to say any more. They followed her through a large and untidy sitting room out onto a broad flagstone terrace that ran all along the rear of the house. Below the terrace, set in an emerald-green lawn, Kitty could see the bright blue waters of a swimming pool. Around the edge on the one side, near a small wooden building, a group of men were huddled around a dark shape.

'The inspector is down there.' Elspeth indicated the group.

Bertie pulled on the leash in Matt's hand, clearly eager to be off exploring this new and exciting space. It seemed that Elspeth was too upset by whatever had occurred to say anything more.

Kitty and Matt hurried along the path to the pool. As they drew nearer, one of the men straightened and advanced towards them.

'My apologies for disturbing your afternoon, Captain Bryant, Miss Underhay, but I thought it would be helpful to have you here.' Inspector Greville shook hands with Matt and tipped his hat to Kitty.

'What's happened, Inspector?' A queasy sensation rolled around inside Kitty's stomach, and she slightly regretted the sausage rolls she had eaten earlier.

'Our Russian friend Mr Ivan Bolsova appears to have met with an unfortunate and fatal accident at the pool.' The inspector inclined his head in the direction of the group at the side of the water. 'Dr Carter is there now.'

'And does the doctor think it was an accident, sir?' Matt

asked.

'Mr Bolsova was fully dressed when he was found in the water and his sister says that he couldn't swim. There is also an unexplained injury to the back of his head.' The inspector's mouth set in a grim line.

A shiver danced along Kitty's spine at the implications. Ivan had obviously not gone into the pool for a dip on a hot day. It seemed from the sound of it that someone may have hit him on the head to ensure he could not escape from a watery death.

Dr Carter approached the group, his black medical bag in his hand. 'Miss Underhay, Captain Bryant, good afternoon.' He beamed at them as Bertie sniffed at his trousers.

'Poor Ivan.' Kitty shuddered. 'We watched him dance last night at Oldway and he was so fit and full of life.' She recalled Ivan in his white flowing shirt, a lock of dark hair falling on his forehead as he had bobbed up and down in the Cossack dance. Her gaze strayed beyond the doctor's portly figure to where they were placing a sheet over the dancer's body.

Matt placed a reassuring arm around her waist.

'Yes, it's a terrible thing,' the doctor agreed cheerfully. 'It looks as if someone bashed him over the head and into the water he went. I'll know more when I get him back and have had a poke around.'

'Have you any idea, sir, what might have been used to strike him?' Matt asked.

The doctor glanced at Inspector Greville. 'Plenty of stuff inside that pool house there. The door was open; apparently, it's kept unlocked and there are all kinds of things inside, tennis racquets, bowls. I'd suggest your men take a look and see, Inspector.'

They walked together slowly back along the gravel path back towards the house while Ivan's body was collected and moved.

'When was he discovered?' Kitty asked. She still felt quite

shaken.

'Earlier this afternoon, not long after lunch.' Inspector Greville combined with Matt to shield Kitty from the sight of Ivan's body being transported past them on the path.

'And no one saw or heard anything, sir?' Matt asked.

The inspector shook his head. 'Mr Morley, the family solicitor, and I were here this morning for the reading of Sir William's will. Obviously, Mr Bolsova and his sister were not party to that event so had been out until lunchtime. They returned to the house shortly after myself and Mr Morley had taken our leave. The family then had lunch and it was a little time afterwards that Mr Bolsova was noticed in the water.'

Kitty wondered what had happened during the reading of the will – if the contents had been as the Winspear family had expected and if there was any connection between that event and Ivan's death.

'Did Mr Morley know anything of Sir William's intention regarding a change to his will? Or was the existing will a fairly recent one?' Kitty asked.

The inspector cleared his throat. 'The existing will was made shortly after Sir William's marriage to Lady Lettice, some two years ago. However, a draft will had been recently drawn up on Sir William's instructions with new provisions. I believe it was this one that Sir William probably intended to sign at his next meeting with Mr Morley.'

The inspector turned to instruct his constables and Kitty took a seat on the low stone garden wall. Her gaze was drawn back towards the Japanese-style building at the side of the swimming pool. She wondered why the inspector had sent for them with such urgency. He must have something in mind that he wished them to do.

Matt perched on the wall beside Kitty. Bertie flopped down at his feet with a sigh. 'This case has taken a nasty turn,' he observed.

'First Sir William and now Ivan.' Kitty pondered on what the link could be between the two murders.

There had been plenty of motives for any of the occupants of Palm Lodge to kill Sir William, but it was less clear about the potential reasons for murdering the Russian dancer.

Inspector Greville finished talking to the constable and came to join them. He took his cigarette case from his pocket and offered it to Matt and Kitty. When they both declined, he took out a cigarette for himself and lit it.

'This is a bad business.' He took a pull on his cigarette and blew out a long stream of pale smoke. 'Two murders in twenty-four hours in the same household.'

'Why Ivan?' Kitty mused. 'Did he know something? See something?'

The inspector sighed. 'My guess is that he may have known who killed Sir William. The murderer obviously wished to prevent him coming forward.'

'Then it must have been something he either saw on the afternoon Sir William was killed or something he heard or worked out afterwards.' Matt's brow crinkled as he thought about the problem.

'But it must have been something he discovered after the reading of the will or otherwise he could have spoken to the inspector this morning. Unless of course he made the mistake of trying to blackmail the murderer.' Kitty looked at her fiancé.

'From the conversation you overheard yesterday evening I'd surmise that money was not far from Ivan's mind at any time.' Matt's tone was thoughtful.

Kitty thought this was probably true. 'Yes, Natasha did sound rather sharp when she pointed out that Lettice would be a very wealthy widow. You were about to tell us the contents of the will. I assume, Inspector, that Lady Winspear is now very wealthy?' Kitty looked at Inspector Greville.

'The will itself had few surprises. Small bequests for some

charities and long serving members of staff. Palm Lodge is entailed to Henry Winspear as expected. Lady Winspear inherits the money and a substantial property in London and the controlling shares in Sir William's businesses.'

'And Elspeth Winspear?' Kitty asked. 'What did she receive?'

Inspector Greville finished his cigarette, dropping the butt to the floor and extinguishing it with the toe of his shoe. 'Basically nothing. The right to continue living at Palm Lodge if she remained a single woman and an annuity of fifty pounds a year to be paid from the estate.'

'That's appalling. Poor Elspeth. She was hoping for a much more generous annuity.' Kitty was shocked by Sir William's lack of provision for the woman who had been managing both his personal and business affairs for years.

'I suppose it must diminish her motivation for murdering her brother if she does not benefit financially from his death,' Matt said.

'Or increased it if she had nothing to lose and Sir William was poised yet again to ruin another relationship for her,' Kitty pointed out.

'Henry Winspear was also none too pleased. Remember he said that he was expecting to receive money left by his mother, money that Sir William had been managing? Well, that was left to a local charity instead. Financially Henry has done almost as poorly as Elspeth,' the inspector said.

'And what were the changes to the will that Sir William intended to make then? Was there anything there that favoured Elspeth or Henry?' Kitty asked.

Inspector Greville's eyes took on a flinty look. 'Lady Lettice was to receive a small annuity only. The London townhouse and the shares in the business were instead to go to a distant cousin. The rest was unaltered. Mr Morley also indicated to me privately that Sir William had raised the question of divorce.'

Kitty's eyes widened in surprise. 'Lady Lettice then had a great deal to lose if Sir William had gone ahead with his plans. I wonder if she was aware of his intentions.'

'Which is one of the reasons I would like your assistance, Miss Underhay, when I speak to Lady Winspear, Natasha Bolsova and Miss Winspear. A woman's perspective would be very useful.' The inspector looked more intently at Kitty. 'I know that I can rely on your discretion in these matters.'

'Thank you, I'm flattered, Inspector. By the way, who discovered the body?' Kitty couldn't help but feel pleased that the inspector had asked her to assist. Usually, because there were no female police officers, the wife of one of the constables might be asked to stand in if a lady needed to be searched, or if the questions might take a delicate turn.

'One of the kitchen maids. She was taking some rubbish outside and looked out over the grounds and saw something dark in the pool. She took a closer look, realised it was one of the guests and started screaming her head off. The gardener went and fished him out while the housekeeper telephoned for us.' The inspector's moustache quivered as he blew out a sigh. 'Miss Bolsova is very distressed, as you can imagine.'

Kitty nodded. The connection between Ivan and Natasha on the dance floor had been palpable. For her brother to be murdered in such a way was truly shocking.

The inspector looked at Matt. 'Captain Bryant, your expertise would also be valuable. After my meeting with Mr Morley this morning, it seems to me that Sir William may have wished to discuss some of his concerns with you when he arranged the meeting at the country club.'

'Kitty and I would be delighted to assist you, sir.' Matt spoke for both of them, the corners of his mouth quirking upwards when he looked at Kitty for approval.

Her fiancé was well aware of her delight at being properly included in the investigation for once.

ELEVEN

Matt was deep in thought as they accompanied the inspector back towards the house. He knew that Kitty was both pleased and flattered to be fully included in the police investigation. However, he strongly suspected that her grandmother would hold a very different view of the matter.

There was also the element of risk. Kitty's life had been in danger more than once over the last twelve months. The continued menace of Esther Hammett, the sister of the man who murdered Kitty's mother, was something else that he knew bothered Mrs Treadwell and Kitty. While Kitty would undoubtedly be an asset to this investigation, he wondered if it was sensible for her to become more involved in the case.

Two people had been killed in two days. He had to hope that the culprit would be captured swiftly before anyone else became a victim.

The inspector led them into the back of the house through the rear door to the scullery and kitchen. A young maid, her eyes red from crying, was seated before the range, blowing her nose noisily on a large grubby cotton handkerchief. A half-drunk cup of tea in a thick white cup was at her elbow and the cook, a stout lady enveloped in a blue floral pinafore, stood beside her.

'You'd best pull yourself together, young Winnie. Here's the police come to talk to you.' The woman patted the girl's skinny shoulder with an awkward floury hand that left a mark on her black dress.

The maid looked up at the inspector and promptly dissolved into a louder bout of sobbing.

'I don't know as you'll get any sense out of her. Proper shook her up, it 'as,' the older woman said. Her tone was not unkind, more resigned, as if used to dealing with the girl regularly.

'Miss Winifred Popplewell?' the inspector asked.

'That's her, Winnie, she's the maid of all the work. Helps me in the kitchen, she does, scrubbing and cleaning and such.' The cook spoke for the maid, who appeared unable or unwilling to answer the inspector's question.

'Thank you, Mrs...?' The inspector turned to the older woman.

'Mrs Lithgo. I'm cook here, have been for the last ten years,' the woman answered promptly.

'Thank you, Mrs Lithgo – and Winnie? How long has she been employed here?' The inspector had taken out his book and was busy taking notes.

Matt was engaged in preventing Bertie from entering into the heart of the kitchen to investigate for himself the scent of roast chicken coming from the larder.

'A few months, she come here straight from school,' Mrs Lithgo confirmed.

Matt guessed that Winnie must be of a similar age to Dolly, Alice's younger sister. It was little wonder that the girl was so upset.

'Does Winnie have any family?' the inspector asked.

His enquiry increased the rate of sobs coming from the maid.

'No sir, she come from the orphanage and lives in.' Mrs Lithgo replied.

Kitty knelt down beside the girl and took her hand in hers. 'Please don't worry, Winnie, everything will be all right.'

The volume of the sobs dropped to a noisy sniffle punctuated by hiccups. 'I don't want to be in no trouble, miss. I don't want to be sent back.' The girl lifted a tear-streaked face to Kitty.

'Now, who would do something like that? You'm not in no trouble, young Winnie. You just tell the policeman and this nice young lady what they wants to know,' Mrs Lithgo said fiercely.

'It must have been the most awful shock for you,' Kitty said. 'Tell us what happened when you stepped outside the house.' She glanced at the inspector.

Matt could see that Kitty's warm and sympathetic nature was having a soothing effect on the young girl and he waited for her response.

The girl gave another sniff and commenced her tale. 'Mrs Lithgo asked me to take out the peelings from where she'd been preparing the potatoes ready for dinner later on. There's a pig bin where we puts things, see.' She hesitated and looked at the cook for confirmation.

'What time was this?' Inspector Greville asked.

'It would be getting on for half past two. We was going to have a cup of tea then before we got on with the rest of the dinner preparation,' Mrs Lithgo said. 'Winnie here can't tell time, so I have to keep an eye on things.'

Tears trickled miserably down the girl's thin cheeks at the cook's words and she gave a small nod to confirm this.

'What happened then?' Kitty asked gently as she addressed the girl.

'It was such a nice day, and the kitchen was really hot so I puts the peelings in the bin over yonder.' The girl paused to wave a red, work-roughened hand in the direction of what Matt assumed must be the bins.

She wiped her nose with her handkerchief and continued. 'It was nice to get a breath of air and I was looking forward to five minutes' sit-down and a cup of tea. I set off back and stopped just for a second to look out over the gardens. Just for a few seconds though, I swear that were all it were.' The girl looked at Mrs Lithgo.

'Well, you weren't gone outside for very long. The kettle weren't even boiling when I heard the commotion,' the cook confirmed.

'Then what happened?' Kitty asked.

'I seen something in the pool, floating like on top of the water. I thought, now, what's that, then? That don't look right. I goes a bit down the path as I were a bit worried and then I sees him. The Russian man afloating all still atop the water. I couldn't help it miss. I screamed for help and the gardener, Mr Brown, he comes arunning and leans over to catch a hold of him to pull him out the water.' Winnie's hands were trembling.

'I heard Winnie scream so I runs outside. I didn't know what had happened. Whether it were that fool chauffeur playing a prank on her or if she'd hurt herself.' Mrs Lithgo pursed her lips indignantly. 'When I saw what was happening then, I got her inside the house and Mrs Tillett, the house-keeper, sent for you.' Mrs Lithgo looked at the inspector.

'You didn't see anyone else outside, near the pool or the pool house?' Kitty asked.

The young maid shook her head. 'No, miss, not a mortal soul, not till Mr Brown come running from around the front of the house.'

Kitty straightened up and looked at the inspector. The girl's evidence was very clear.

'Thank you, Winnie, that was most helpful.' Inspector

Greville closed his notebook and returned it to the inside breast pocket of his jacket.

'Yes, and please don't worry, Winnie, you are not in any trouble. We are very grateful for your help. I'm sure Mrs Lithgo here will look after you now. Put all of this from your mind,' Kitty said kindly as she followed the inspector out of the kitchen and through to the rear hall of the lodge. Matt and Bertie followed behind.

———

'Thank you, Miss Underhay, that was most kind of you.' Inspector Greville gave her an approving smile as they passed through the green baize-covered door separating the service part of the house from the family rooms.

The inspector led them along the hall to the front of the house until they reached a partly open oak door. 'Lady Winspear has graciously said that I might use Sir William's study,' he explained as they entered a large square room.

The walls of the room were covered in an ornate and old-fashioned wallpaper, heavily decorated with peacocks and flowers in shades of dark green, purple and mustard. A large mahogany kneehole desk dominated the centre of the room. A button-backed office chair was behind it, upholstered in a similar shade of dark green leather. Around the room a few other chairs, similarly upholstered but less imposing in nature, stood before a low bookcase.

A couple of wooden filing cabinets were also in position, overlooked by the rather ugly and moth-eaten head of a long dead stag, which regarded Kitty with cold unseeing eyes. An imposing portrait of the late Sir William in his younger years dominated the space above the stone fireplace. The desk was clear except for a blotting pad with fresh paper, an ornate brass inkstand, a few carved wooden boxes and a black Bakelite telephone.

Kitty could easily picture Sir William seated behind the desk giving his orders to Elspeth. Despite the heat of the day the room was cool, and Kitty was relieved to take a seat at the side of the room to rest for a moment while the inspector made arrangements to interview the Winspear household once more.

Bertie settled down at Matt's feet and was sleepily watching the proceedings as they arranged themselves in their chosen seats. Inspector Greville settled himself behind the desk in the late Sir William's seat and dispatched a constable to fetch Natasha Bolsova.

Kitty was a little surprised that the girl felt well enough to be interviewed after the inspector had remarked on how devastated Ivan's sister had been at the news of his murder. However, when Natasha entered the room, head held high and eyes flashing, she saw she had been mistaken in her judgement. Natasha was not distressed, she was furious.

The girl took a seat on the chair in front of the inspector and crossed her long, slender, silk-stockinged legs. She took out a silver cigarette case and then waited until Matt stepped forward and offered her a light for her small dark cigarette.

'Well?' she demanded, looking at Inspector Greville. 'You are searching for whoever did this?'

Inspector Greville leaned back in his seat and surveyed the dancer. 'I can assure you, Miss Bolsova, no stone will be left unturned in the quest to find your brother's murderer.'

Natasha's eyes flashed again as she took a pull on her cigarette. 'What kind of place is this? First Sir William and now Ivan. Even in Russia this would not happen in this way. I knew Ivan's death was not an accident.' Her accent had grown more pronounced as she spoke.

'When did you last see your brother, Miss Bolsova?' Kitty asked.

The girl half turned her head as if suddenly realising that Kitty was there. 'We spend the morning down by the seaside and come back to the house for lunch. Lady Winspear, she was busy with her family this morning with the reading of the will.' She shifted her gaze to the inspector who retained his bland expression under the dancer's scrutiny.

'I take it that everyone dined together at lunchtime?' Kitty asked. The girl hadn't directly answered her question, which was interesting.

Natasha shrugged her slender, silk-clad shoulders. 'Of course, although the atmosphere at the table was not so nice. I think the reading of the will had caused some problems.' She gave another shrug.

'And then what happened?' Inspector Greville took over the questions once more.

'After lunch, I have a headache. I think from being outside this morning. The heat was strong and the sun on the water.' For the first time the girl's voice wavered. She paused and took another pull on her cigarette before continuing. 'I decide to go to my room and lie down. Ivan said that he intended to sit downstairs and read the newspapers. That is it. That is the last time I saw him.' She looked around for an ashtray and Matt leaned forward once more to proffer her a jade-green marble one from the side table next to Kitty.

'Do you know where the other members of the household were intending to go?' Inspector Greville asked.

Natasha's shoulders rose slightly once more. 'Lady Lettice said that it was too hot, and she was upset after the morning, she said she was going to sit in the drawing room and listen to the radio. Elspeth was annoyed by this, I think.'

'What made you think that, Miss Bolsova?' the inspector asked.

Natasha's red, heavily lip-sticked mouth curved slightly. 'She was muttering about needing to make arrangements and sorting out business things for Sir William's affairs. Lady Lettice told her to just get on with it then and walked away. I think Elspeth came in here.'

'And Henry and Padma Winspear?' Inspector Greville asked.

Again, the girl gave a faint humourless smile. 'They had their heads together, plotting something. I do not think they were happy after the will reading. I do not know where they went after lunch was finished.'

'Had your brother had any arguments with any member of the household? Was there anyone who bore any ill will towards him that you know of?' Kitty had wondered when the inspector would ask that question. They already knew that the late Sir William had not been fond of the dancer.

'No, I do not think so. I am sure some of them would prefer Ivan and I not to be here. Henry Winspear, he was making allegations, hinting about Ivan and Lady Lettice. Elspeth too, but I think perhaps they are jealous.' Natasha finished her cigarette and extinguished it in the ashtray. 'You will find who killed Ivan, Inspector?'

Although phrased as a question, Kitty thought it sounded more like a command.

'You may be assured, Miss Bolsova, that we shall endeavour to arrest whoever did this as quickly as possible,' Inspector Greville reassured her. 'Will you be remaining here at Palm Lodge for the immediate future?' he asked.

'I do not know. I am feeling very unsafe. First Sir William and now Ivan, who will be next? Lady Lettice has asked me to remain, and I am told the hotels are full so...' She broke off.

'Thank you, Miss Bolsova, and my condolences once more on your loss.' The inspector nodded to the constable who had remained standing in front of the study doorway. 'We shall, of course, keep you informed of any progress in the case.'

Natasha rose and left with the constable, her head held high and her back ramrod straight.

'I suppose we'd better have Lady Lettice next.' Inspector Greville looked at the notes that he had been busily making throughout the interview with Natasha.

'Yes, it should be interesting to discover if she was in the drawing room. If that was the room we walked through to get outside, then she may have had a view of the garden,' Kitty suggested.

Inspector Greville assented and dispatched the constable once again to find Lady Lettice.

Lettice made her entrance clad in an elegant, black crepe de chine dress with her bright blonde hair neatly coiffured and a tragic expression on her face.

'Oh, Inspector Greville, what a terrible thing to have happened. Poor dear Ivan, so talented. Such a dreadful accident happening so quickly after the death of my darling William.' She produced a delicate lace-edged handkerchief, which she held to her nose as she subsided gracefully onto the seat in front of the desk.

Kitty saw Matt's eyebrows raise.

Inspector Greville cleared his throat and made a show of flipping through the pages of his notebook.

'I'm afraid, Lady Lettice, that it seems Mr Bolsova's death was not an accident.'

Lettice's eyes widened and she pressed her handkerchief more firmly over her mouth. 'Ivan was murdered? But why?'

'May I ask, Lady Winspear, when you last saw Mr Bolsova?' Inspector Greville asked.

Lettice's brow crinkled. 'I'm not sure. I think it was shortly after lunch. Elspeth was being a dreadful nuisance about wanting me to deal with some of William's affairs. I mean, my husband is barely cold, and she was annoying me. I told her she knew more than I about such matters so she could deal with them. I mean, it's not as if she has anything better to do with her time now. Anyway, I decided to go to the drawing room and listen to the radio. I thought it might help me relax. You know, take my mind off things, everyone was being so beastly after the will reading this morning. Ivan popped his head in to see if I was all right. He was so sweet in that way.' She paused as if reflecting. 'And then he said he intended to go to the library.'

'And that was the last time you saw him? What time was this, Lady Winspear?' Inspector Greville asked, his pen poised above his notebook.

'I don't know, probably about two o'clock, maybe later.' Lettice dabbed at her nose once more with her handkerchief.

'I believe the drawing room offers a view across the terrace to the pool and the lawns?' Inspector Greville remarked mildly. 'You didn't hear or see anything untoward? Or anyone outside in the gardens? The windows are open, I notice, with the heat?'

Lettice's cheeks pinked. 'No, nothing. I had the radio, on remember,' she replied quickly, then she appeared to pause. 'No, wait, I did hear something and when I glanced outside, I saw Padma crossing the terrace.' She settled back in her seat, the faint traces of a smug smile at the corners of her lips.

'You witnessed Mrs Padma Winspear on the terrace? At what time?' Inspector Greville's tone sharpened.

'Not long after Ivan left to go to the library. I didn't look at a clock.' Lettice gave a careless shrug.

'You were unaware of any ill feeling towards Mr Bolsova from any of the other members of your household?' The inspector asked.

'Henry and Padma do not appreciate the arts and Elspeth, I think, would have preferred Ivan and Natasha to have left, but nothing notable.' Lettice smoothed the material of her dress complacently. 'Ivan and Natasha were my guests, and I am entitled to invite whoever I wish to my home.'

'Although now I suppose it's Henry and Padma's home,' Kitty said mildly.

Lettice turned a furious gaze in her direction. 'I suppose so, technically yes.'

'Are you aware, Lady Winspear, that your husband was unhappy with your friendship with Mr Bolsova, and there were rumours circulating about the nature of your relationship?' Inspector Greville looked at Lettice.

She jumped to her feet. 'How dare you? My husband was killed only yesterday and now you are accusing me of improper behaviour.'

The inspector appeared unmoved by her histrionics. 'Please take a seat, Lady Winspear, I am not accusing anyone of anything. However, I do need to know the true nature of the relationship between you and Ivan Bolsova. A relationship that had apparently troubled Sir William so much that he had consulted Mr Morley about the possibility of a divorce.'

Kitty watched as the colour drained from Lettice's face leaving only two red, angry spots on her cheekbones.

'No, that can't be true. He wouldn't have...' She sank back down on her chair.

'You were unaware of his intentions?' Inspector Greville asked.

Kitty thought he looked a little like a predatory moustachioed cat eying a tasty little mouse.

'Of course. Ivan and I were close, yes, we had similar interests. Ivan admired me and William was a very jealous man. My tango lessons had caused some friction between us, but I never suspected for one moment that he was so concerned.' A tear rolled down her cheek. 'My poor darling William. I would have reassured him.'

She dashed the tear away with the back of her hand and turned in her seat to face Matt who was watching the proceedings with Bertie's head resting on his knee.

'Is that why you were there yesterday? Had he asked you to spy on me?'

Matt straightened indignantly, disturbing the dog. 'Certainly not. Sir William was well aware that I do not handle divorce cases. He had merely said to me that he wished to ask my advice on something. He did not say anything more than that.'

'So you are saying, Lady Winspear, that you were unaware of Sir William seeking advice about a possible divorce and that he had been contemplating changing his will to effectively disinherit you.' Inspector Greville's voice cut across the room, drawing Lettice's attention back in his direction.

'I had no idea at all. I knew he was consulting his solicitor, but I had thought it was in regard to Henry and nothing at all to do with me.'

Kitty couldn't help but feel that Lettice's protests were all a little hollow and somehow unconvincing. She could also see that the woman was scared.

'Thank you, Lady Winspear.'

Inspector Greville indicated the interview was concluded and the constable escorted Lettice from the room.

TWELVE

'Do you believe her, sir?' Matt asked once Lettice had gone.

'Quite frankly, no. I think she was having some sort of liaison with the Russian chap and that was why Sir William intended to change his will. Everyone has hinted as much and her ladyship said her husband was a jealous man. I suspect she had a pretty good idea about it too. All that "poor darling William" was rather overdone, don't you think?' Inspector Greville dropped his pen down on the desktop and sighed. 'It certainly gives Lady Winspear quite a motive for removing both her husband and possibly her lover.'

'If Ivan knew what she'd done, you mean?' Kitty asked. 'From what I heard of his conversation with Natasha, the implication was that he was interested in Lettice for her money. He could have attempted to blackmail her.'

'Except that Lettice was with Elspeth when Sir William was killed, and Ivan was allegedly with his sister,' Matt reminded them.

'True, and there are plenty of others in this house who may have wished to see Sir William dead. Although I'm not certain what their motive would be for murdering Ivan, unless they thought he knew they were the murderer.' Kitty had hoped that during the interview with Natasha and Lettice some clue would have emerged to either clear them or point the finger of guilt more firmly on one of the other members of the household.

'Indeed. I think the next person we should see is Mrs Padma Winspear, since Lady Lettice says she saw her on the terrace shortly before Ivan's body was discovered.' Inspector Greville looked at his constable once more and the man hurried off in search of Padma.

Kitty settled back in her seat and waited for the third member of the Winspear household to appear.

Padma's expression was resigned, even somewhat sulky as she entered the room. She was dressed in a light-blue linen two-piece, with no sign of mourning for her deceased brother-in-law. She took her place in front of the desk and rested her hands composedly in her lap.

'How may I help you, Inspector?' she asked.

'Mrs Winspear, may I ask when you last saw Ivan Bolsova?' Inspector Greville had reclaimed his pen and was poised once more to continue taking notes.

'At lunchtime. I heard him say that he intended going to the library when Henry and I were leaving the dining room.' Padma looked to Kitty as if she had thought about and prepared her answers ready for whatever the inspector might ask of her.

'I see. Where did you and your husband go after lunch?' Inspector Greville asked.

'I had a letter to post so I walked to the end of the lane. There is a box there. It was very hot, so it took me longer than I had anticipated. My husband went to our room as he had some documents that required his attention.' Padma looked almost bored by the conversation.

Inspector Greville duly noted her response in his book. 'Are you aware of anyone in the house having had any kind of quarrel or bearing ill will towards Mr Bolsova?'

Padma shook her head. 'No, not at all. I think Elspeth felt, and I agreed, that with Sir William's death perhaps it was unseemly for Ivan and Natasha to continue residing here, but Letty said that the hotels are all full as it's the height of the summer season.'

Matt cut in before the inspector could ask the next question. 'Why would it have been unseemly, Mrs Winspear?'

Padma blushed. 'Well, it was pretty common knowledge, I think, that Lettice and Ivan were having a romantic liaison. His attentions towards her after William's death, Inspector... you must have noticed that for yourself?'

Inspector Greville's moustache twitched at this apparent confirmation of his earlier suspicions but he refrained from answering Padma's question. 'When you returned from posting your letter, Mrs Winspear, which way did you come back into the house?'

Padma's colour deepened, and for the first time since she had entered the room, Kitty saw the woman's composure crack. 'I'm not quite sure. Oh yes, I was going to enter through the front door but then I thought I might as well go around the back as the French doors on the terrace would be open.'

Before the inspector could question Padma further about why she had decided to walk the long way round on a hot afternoon, there was a sharp knock on the study door. One of the constables from the pool stood in the doorway, his face shining with suppressed excitement.

'Begging your pardon, sir, but I think we've got something.'

Kitty realised that in his gloved hand he was holding a croquet mallet. To her horror she noticed the head of the mallet was streaked with a dark red substance and a few strands of hair.

Padma obviously noticed the mallet at the same time and her complexion turned grey. The inspector jumped up from his chair and hurried to the door, taking the constable out into the hall with him. Kitty heard the rumble of male conversation from just beyond the doorway.

'Oh my goodness.' Padma swayed on her chair and Kitty hurried towards a large glass decanter she had noticed standing on a brass tray nearby. She pulled out the stopper and sniffed; having determined that the amber contents inside the decanter were brandy, she poured a glass for Padma and pressed it into her hand.

'Do take a sip,' she urged.

Bertie ambled forward to investigate the sudden bustle of movement as the girl took a reluctant but reviving taste of the drink.

'Was that...? Was that mallet used to kill Ivan, do you think?' Padma raised troubled dark eyes towards Kitty.

'It did look as if it may have been the weapon,' Kitty said cautiously.

'What a grisly discovery. Natasha said Ivan had been murdered. She said there was no way that he would have slipped and fallen into the water. His balance was too good,' Padma murmured as colour began to return to her cheeks.

Matt looked at Kitty. 'Forgive me, Mrs Winspear, I realise this must all be a dreadful shock, but are you surprised that Ivan has been murdered?' he asked.

Padma shook her head. 'No, I don't think so, at least... I am explaining this badly. His death is shocking, why would anyone wish to murder him? From that point of view, I am shocked. There is no reason why someone would kill him. But, as Natasha said, it seemed too much of a coincidence that it could have been an accident. He was young and very fit. How could he simply have just drowned in the pool? He was not a strong swimmer, he told us that himself a few days ago when we were by the water, but he wouldn't have drowned.'

She took another drink from the glass, almost without thinking, and coughed when the fiery liquid reached the back of her throat. 'Thank you, I think I am recovered now.' She returned the glass to Kitty as Inspector Greville re-entered the room.

'My apologies, Mrs Winspear, for my constable's thoughtlessness.' He assessed her with a quick glance and took his seat once more behind the desk. 'Now, I think you were telling me why you decided to return to the house via the terrace at the rear rather than through the front door?'

Padma's colour deepened and Kitty noticed the woman clutching her hands together where they were resting on her lap.

'I did not wish to disturb the house by ringing the bell as I know Lettice prefers the front door to be kept locked. The French windows were open so I thought I would go around to the back of the house.'

'How did you enter the house, Mrs Winspear? Lady Lettice said she saw you cross the terrace yet you didn't enter through the drawing room.' Inspector Greville's eyes narrowed as he waited for the woman to reply.

'No, I, well, I could hear the radio and knew Lettice was in there and I didn't wish to speak to her. She had been quite unpleasant since the reading of the will and she and my husband had exchanged words. I had no desire to get dragged into their quarrel, it's all quite tiresome. The French door to the library was also open so I entered the house through there.'

'Did you see anyone besides Lady Winspear when you returned? Anyone in the grounds or outside the house?' The inspector asked.

'Lettice was in the drawing room with the radio on, listening to some play or other. She was standing near the French doors. I didn't know if she was on her way out or had just come in. Or she may have simply been trying to get some air. The library was empty, and I didn't notice anyone in the gardens but then I didn't really look.'

Kitty thought Padma sounded flustered and a little defensive.

'And where did you go then, Mrs Winspear?' The inspector asked.

'I was on my way upstairs to see if Henry had finished dealing with his correspondence. I thought he might care for a cup of tea. I hadn't reached the landing when I heard a dreadful commotion. The maid, screaming about a body. I turned right around and hurried back down to see what had happened.'

Kitty waited for her to finish before asking, 'When you reached the hall, who did you see?'

Padma frowned. 'Lettice had already gone out to the terrace, I think, Elspeth was in the hall, she was terribly out of breath. Natasha came down the stairs a moment after me and we all went outside.'

'And your husband, Mrs Winspear?' the inspector asked.

'Oh, I think Henry must have followed Natasha. He was at the back of the group when we went out onto the terrace.'

Kitty raised her brows as she looked at Matt. It seemed strange to her that Henry had not responded more swiftly. Perhaps they needed to check with Natasha if Henry had followed her downstairs.

'Thank you, Mrs Winspear, you have been most helpful.' Padma rose and was halfway out of the room before the inspector had finished speaking.

'I take it that the croquet mallet is our weapon, sir?' Matt asked as soon as the door had closed behind Padma.

'Undoubtedly. The constable found it a short distance away from the pool house. It had been pushed deep inside some laurel bushes.' Inspector Greville rested his pen down on the blotting pad. 'I've arranged for it to be sent to Dr Carter just to dot the Is and cross the Ts.'

'It speaks of a spur-of-the-moment crime with the killer using whatever was to hand, unlike Sir William's murder, which seemed to have been executed with some degree of planning. After all, the arrow was taken along with the fabric from Lady Winspear's dress and presumably an idea of luring our victim to the grotto,' Matt suggested.

'I wonder why Ivan went down to the pool? He had said he was going to the library,' Kitty asked.

Matt scratched his chin. 'To meet someone where they couldn't be overheard perhaps?' he suggested.

Kitty was turning everything they had just heard over in her mind.

'Will you excuse me for a moment, Inspector?' She jumped to her feet and hurried out of the room. Once in the hall she looked around trying to work out the geography of the house.

At the end of the hall at the rear was the drawing room, which overlooked the gardens and the pool. On the opposite side was the library, which she presumed also offered a view of the gardens. The study was at the front of the house, near the front door. She tried various other doors and discovered a compact dining room and a dark and repressive billiards room.

She walked down the hall and opened the door to the library. The room was not as large as she had expected and was furnished in the same rather fussy old-fashioned style as the rest of the house. There was a small French door, which was open, onto the terrace.

Kitty stepped outside and looked at the view. She could see the pool and the pool house more clearly from this angle than from the drawing room. She walked back into the hall deep in thought and met one of the maids as they were making their way along the passageway carrying a tray.

'Excuse me, I was looking for the bathroom.' Kitty had decided this would provide good cover for her to understand the layout of the house.

'There's one just along here, miss,' the maid assured her, and went to move away.

'This is such a lovely house, the rooms at the back have a magnificent view of the gardens. I expect Sir William and Lady Lettice must have their rooms on the back of the house?' Kitty said.

The girl goggled at her in mild astonishment for a minute. 'Well, there's Mr and Mrs Winspear and Miss Bolsova's rooms what has a view of the gardens. The best rooms though is on the front of the house. Miss Elspeth and Lady Lettice is on the front, as they gets more sun.'

Kitty thanked her and the girl darted off back to her duties. Satisfied with her answers, Kitty returned to the study to discover that Matt and Inspector Greville had been joined in her absence by Henry Winspear.

It seemed that Henry had taken it upon himself to seek out the inspector rather than wait to be sent for.

'Now, look here, Inspector. I won't have it. My wife was traumatised after her interview. She tells me that the Russian chap was murdered, hit over the head and knocked into the pool. To show a delicate woman like Padma a hammer dripping in blood, it's most ungentlemanly.'

Kitty slipped into the room quietly while Henry bellowed at Inspector Greville.

'Mr Winspear, please do take a seat.' Inspector Greville signalled to the constable to return to his post at the door.

'It's a disgrace, that's what it is. I shall telephone the chief constable.' Henry's face was mottled puce with rage and small pieces of spittle flew from his mouth as he waved his hands at the inspector.

'If you will take a seat, Mr Winspear, I can bring you up to date with what has been happening.' The inspector's voice took on an authoritative tone and he indicated the chair in front of the desk.

For a moment Kitty thought Henry might refuse, but the

constable took a step forward again and Henry subsided sulkily into the vacant seat.

'I am very sorry, sir, if you feel that your wife was in any way distressed during her interview. I can assure you that Miss Underhay here took great care to ensure that Mrs Winspear was cared for. My constable has already been reprimanded for his lack of tact in drawing my attention to his discovery. However, this is a murder investigation, sir, and it is clear that Mr Bolsova's death must be connected to that of your brother.' Inspector Greville picked up his pen once more.

'Well, and what are you doing to catch whoever murdered them?' Henry demanded.

'I can assure you, sir, that no stone will be left unturned until the miscreant is captured,' the inspector told him. 'Now, sir, perhaps I might ask you a few questions just to establish where everyone was earlier this afternoon when Mr Bolsova was killed?'

Henry grunted a reluctant assent.

'I believe you last saw Mr Bolsova at lunchtime. What happened after lunch?' The inspector's pen was poised once more over his notebook.

Henry gave an exasperated sigh. 'I'm sure you've heard this from my wife already. Lettice and Elspeth were bickering over something or other and Lettice said she was going to the drawing room. Elspeth wanted to sort out some things from William's papers. I felt this was something I should have taken on, but she insisted. I had some correspondence to deal with of my own, so I left her to it and went upstairs. Ivan said he was going to the library and Padma had a letter to post.'

'And was this the last time you saw Mr Bolsova?' Inspector Greville asked.

'Yes, well. I went upstairs and realised I'd left my spectacles in the library, so I went back to get them. The room was empty.

I looked out through the French door and saw Bolsova walking down to the pool house.'

The inspector leaned forward in his chair. 'What time was this?'

'I don't know. Sometime around two probably.' Henry scowled at the policeman.

Kitty couldn't believe that Henry had waited until now to reveal something so important.

'Did you see anyone else?' the inspector asked.

'No one. Lettice had some dashed radio play going on in the drawing room and I didn't hang around. I just collected my spectacles and went back upstairs. I didn't come down again until I heard all the racket from that girl screaming. By the time I came down everyone was milling about.'

Inspector Greville's moustache twitched. 'I see, thank you, sir, that's most helpful.'

Henry stood and glowered at the inspector once more before making his exit, still muttering under his breath.

Bertie heaved a loud sigh as the door closed with a bang.

'Well, that was interesting,' Inspector Greville remarked. 'Pins the time of the murder down quite tightly. Winnie must have only just missed seeing the murderer.'

'The same could be said for Padma Winspear if we assume that she is not the killer. It looks as if whoever murdered Ivan must have been already down in the pool house waiting for him. The ground is quite open otherwise and anyone could have seen them,' Kitty said.

'It was quite a risky business,' Matt agreed, 'but then, so was Sir William's. The grotto is a popular spot and there were plenty of people about at Oldway when he was killed.'

'Whoever our murderer is it's clear they were desperate.' Inspector Greville looked down at his notes. 'One more to see. Let's have Elspeth Winspear in and see what she has to say for herself.'

THIRTEEN

Kitty hoped the interview with Elspeth wouldn't take too long. She was starting to feel quite uncomfortable now in her knitted bathing suit under her frock. She also really wanted another restorative cup of tea or coffee and a bun. Perhaps that was why Inspector Greville was so partial to food. Investigating murders definitely gave one an appetite.

Elspeth entered the room dressed in a dove-grey dress, which looked a little too warm for the weather. Kitty could only assume she had decided to wear it as a mark of respect for Sir William.

'Miss Winspear, my apologies for keeping you waiting. I'm sure you realise that there is a lot for us to do if we are to discover who is responsible for the murders of your brother and Mr Bolsova,' Inspector Greville explained as Elspeth took her place in front of the desk.

Elspeth gave a stiff nod of her head to acknowledge the inspector's greeting. Her eyes were red-rimmed, and she looked tired.

'We are trying to establish where everyone was within the

household prior to Mr Bolsova's death and when he was last seen alive,' Inspector Greville explained.

'Of course, I understand. I shall do my best to assist you.' Elspeth took out a small white handkerchief and dabbed quickly at her nose. 'This has all been such a dreadful shock especially so soon after yesterday and William's murder.'

'May I ask when you last saw Mr Bolsova?' The inspector had his notebook at the ready to take down her answer.

'He returned to the house for luncheon with his sister. I think they had been out sightseeing while the reading of my brother's will was taking place. Which I have to say was quite thoughtful of them. After lunch I suggested to Lettice that she might care to assist me in sorting out some of William's business affairs. There is such a lot to be done. Of course, she refused and took herself off to the drawing room.' Elspeth heaved an exasperated sigh. 'Natasha said she had a headache and she intended to rest. Henry had his own correspondence to deal with and Padma was going to post a letter. Most unwise, I thought, with this heat but then I suppose she is more used to it than any of us. Ivan had said to everyone that he was going to the library to read the newspapers but of course he didn't.'

The inspector paused in his note taking to look at Elspeth. 'I'm sorry, may I just clarify that. You say he didn't go to the library, Miss Winspear?'

Elspeth met his gaze. 'No, he went into the drawing room with Lettice. I had come in here ready to make more telephone calls to business associates of William's. I realised I needed to check with Lettice what she wished me to say if any of them wanted to make a donation in my brother's memory or if she wanted floral tributes only. I came back along the hall, and I saw Mr Bolsova slip into the drawing room. Then I heard laughter. Well, I could hardly interrupt. That she could be so blatant with my brother barely cold.' Elspeth's mouth pursed in disapproval.

Kitty's eyes widened at this piece of information. Lettice certainly hadn't mentioned that Ivan had been to see her in the drawing room. She had only said that he had popped his head in to speak briefly to her.

'What did you do then, Miss Winspear?' Inspector Greville asked.

'What could I do? I'd already had one argument with Letty over her refusal to assist me with William's affairs. I had no wish to walk in on some kind of amorous liaison and cause yet another upset. I returned to this room and started to sort out William's correspondence. I intended to tackle Lettice again at teatime.' Elspeth indicated the wire tray on the desk in front of the inspector where bundles of papers were neatly stacked.

'I see. You don't know of any disputes within the household? Anyone who may have wished to harm Mr Bolsova?' Inspector Greville asked.

Elspeth appeared to consider for a moment. 'Well, I personally felt it was highly inappropriate given my brother's death that Natasha and Ivan should continue to remain in the house, but of course the hotels are all full at the moment as it is the height of the season as you know, and the weather is so good. I know my brother agrees with me on the matter, but our hands are tied. Lettice was insistent that they stay. Anyway, I don't know if it is my imagination, but I received the impression during lunch that things were strained between Ivan and his sister.'

This too was news to Kitty and everyone else in the room.

'Was there anything in particular that you think gave rise to this belief?' Inspector Greville asked as Kitty leaned forward in her seat, eager to hear Elspeth's reply.

The lines on the older woman's brow deepened as she thought about her answer. 'I don't know if anyone else saw or heard anything but as we entered the dining room, Ivan went to assist Natasha with her chair, and she actively moved away from him. Then when they were seated, I was on Natasha's other side, he muttered something to her, and she glared at him. All through lunch she paid him no attention even when he tried to include her in any conversation between himself and Lettice. Henry and his wife were seated opposite Ivan so they may have observed something.'

'I see.' The inspector was scribbling rapidly in his notebook.

'In fact, I really think that Natasha's headache was perhaps an excuse not to spend more time with her brother,' Elspeth said thoughtfully.

'Did you see anyone else between the time you returned to the study and when the alarm was raised?' The inspector asked.

'Only Padma. She'd been out along the lane to post her letter and I heard the gravel crunching on the drive as she returned. I looked out and I remember feeling annoyed, thinking she would ring the doorbell and I'd probably have to go and open the door as the staff would all be busy. I looked out though and she'd disappeared so I assume she must have entered through the drawing room or library windows instead.' Elspeth sighed. 'I must say, Inspector, I'm very concerned. My brother was brutally murdered yesterday at the country club, and now Ivan in the grounds of my home. I feel very unsafe. What if this lunatic is targeting members of the household for some reason? I don't think I shall sleep easily in my own bed tonight.' Her generous frame shivered dramatically.

Inspector Greville's moustache twitched. 'I have arranged to have one of my constables remain here at the house. I presume you have no idea of any person who might hold such a grudge against your family?'

'Well, that does make me feel a little easier knowing we have some protection in the house. And no, I don't know of anyone who might wish to harm us.' Elspeth's expression indicated that she found this supposition ridiculous.

'Yet your brother was known to have upset several people in his business dealings,' the inspector remarked casually.

'Really, Inspector, business is business. I agree there were some who felt aggrieved by actions my brother had taken but none I'm certain that would go so far as to murder him.'

'I see. Thank you, Miss Winspear. I wonder if we might trouble you for another tray of tea?' the inspector asked as Elspeth went to take her leave.

'Certainly, I'll ask the staff to bring one through.' She nodded to Kitty and Matt and left the study.

The inspector leaned back in his chair and heaved a gusty sigh. 'Well, there we go. Once again it seems as if no one in this house can tell the complete truth. There are always these little bits of information that are withheld or forgotten.'

'On purpose or accidentally?' Kitty asked.

'Sometimes maliciously,' Matt said, and Bertie grumbled an agreement.

'And one of them killed Sir William and Ivan. I cannot see how or why an outsider would have committed either crime. I suppose we have ruled out the man Matt discovered had been stealing a few months ago?' Kitty reached out a hand to fuss the top of the dog's head as he placed his nose on her knee.

'Moved abroad, we checked after Sir William's murder,' the inspector said.

Kitty was grateful to see that the tea trolley when it arrived was provisioned with slices of fruitcake. Her picnic lunch seemed hours ago and it was still a few hours until dinner.

She had just taken a sip of tea and consumed a finger of cake when the doorbell rang.

'Who is that?' Matt had risen to cross to the window that overlooked the driveway. He shushed Bertie who had instantly begun to bark at the sound of the bell echoing along the hall outside.

'There's a taxi parked outside and some fellow on the front step with a large suitcase,' Matt said.

Kitty immediately went to look as one of the maids opened the front door to the stranger. There was the sound of voices in the hall.

Inspector Greville finished his piece of cake and opened the study door to step into an argument.

'I have invited David to stay. He is my friend and with poor William dead and now Ivan I need protection. What if I am next?' Lettice glared at Henry who looked as if he were prepared to toss the stranger back out through the front door.

'The house now belongs to Henry and he should have been asked before you fill the place with more of your undesirable friends and protegees,' Padma snapped as she backed up her husband's position.

Kitty noticed in the centre of the dispute, the new arrival was a good-looking dark-haired man in a light linen suit.

'I may have whoever I choose to stay at my home.' Lettice turned on her sister-in-law. 'You have no right to tell me who I may or may not invite.'

'I say, I really don't wish to cause a bother. Lettice darling, if it's a nuisance I can go back,' the stranger suggested.

Elspeth waded into the dispute, holding up her hand to prevent further discussion. 'Our apologies, Mr...'

'David Fairweather,' the man obliged.

'Mr Fairweather. I'm so sorry, you must think us all frightfully rude. I'm not sure if you are aware but we are somewhat at sixes and sevens here. My brother, Lettice's husband, was killed yesterday, murdered, and now this very afternoon it seems another man has also been killed in our gardens.'

'Lettice told me when she telephoned me this afternoon. I was staying nearby so I threw a few things in a case and came as soon as I could. I'm an old friend of Letty's,' David explained. 'She said she was terrified by everything that had happened.'

Lettice gave a dramatic sob and attached herself limpet-like to his arm. 'Thank you for coming here so quickly. I'm so frightened, David darling. I shall feel much better now you are here. Elspeth, please go and sort out a room for David. One of the best rooms at the front. Now, do come through.' She bore her friend away in triumph, leaving Padma, Henry and Elspeth fuming powerlessly in her wake.

'The nerve of that woman.' Elspeth looked as if she was about to burst into tears.

'Heaven only knows how many more of her so-called friends she intends to invite to stay.' Henry's face was red with fury.

'May I suggest, sir, that Mr Fairweather remains for the time being,' Inspector Greville suggested. 'However, I will speak to Lady Winspear and point out the lack of wisdom in inviting any more guests until the investigation is concluded.'

'Yes, thank you, Inspector,' Henry grumbled as if suddenly becoming aware that Matt, Kitty and the inspector had all just witnessed the altercation in the hallway.

'I suppose that I had better speak to the housekeeper. I just hope Lettice realises the difficulties one has with staff. They were already upset when they heard about William and then after this afternoon, well, it wouldn't surprise me if some wished to give notice. You know what they're like. The house is all upside down and good servants are hard to find.' Elspeth frowned unhappily and set off towards the servant's door.

Kitty and Matt withdrew back to the study where they discovered that Bertie had taken advantage of their absence by helping himself to the last few slices of fruitcake – something which caused Inspector Greville's moustache to take on a dejected air when he noticed the now empty plate.

'That was quite a turn-up for the books,' Matt remarked as he chastised the unrepentant Bertie.

'Yes, I wonder where the obliging Mr Fairweather has come

from and if he has an alibi for yesterday.' The inspector looked thoughtful.

'He certainly arrived very promptly,' Kitty said. It seemed Lettice hadn't wasted any time in securing another admirer

'His arrival has definitely put the cat amongst the pigeons.' Matt finished his cup of tea.

'The reaction of the others to Mr Fairweather's unexpected arrival was interesting. I dare say we shall learn more shortly. Anyway thank you both for interrupting your afternoon to assist.' The inspector looked at Kitty and Matt. Kitty surmised that this was their cue to leave.

'It was our pleasure. That was all very interesting.' Kitty rose and slipped her hand into the crook of Matt's arm as he tightened his hold on Bertie's leash.

'I shall of course keep you informed of any progress in the case.' Inspector Greville walked with them to the front door.

'If we can be of further assistance then you know where to find us, sir,' Matt said.

'Oh, I shall, I assure you.' The inspector watched them from the step as they clambered into Kitty's car, raising his hand in a farewell wave as she drove away.

FOURTEEN

Alice woke Kitty the following morning with a cup of tea and a look of eager enquiry on her narrow face.

'I've heard as there was another murder yesterday,' her friend said as she slid the tea tray onto the bedside table next to Kitty.

'Yes, that's right, the Russian dancer Ivan Bolsova has been killed. Inspector Greville sent a constable to the beach to find us yesterday afternoon.' Kitty sat herself up in bed and rubbed the sleep from her eyes. It seemed that it hadn't taken long for news of the murder to reach Dartmouth.

'The inspector telephoned the hotel after you and Mary told him as you'd gone to Goodrington for a picnic with Captain Bryant.' Alice set out two cups, one of delicate porcelain for Kitty and a thicker plain cup for herself.

Kitty scooted over and patted the rose-coloured satin coverlet to invite Alice to sit down beside her. 'How did you hear there had been a murder?'

Alice blushed as she concentrated on pouring them both a cup of tea. 'Dr Carter's car was seen parked at Palm Lodge next to your car and the police motor. It don't take long for word to get around as you know, miss.' She added milk to the cups with a generous hand.

Kitty accepted her cup from Alice and settled herself against her pillows before telling her friend of yesterday's events. The maid listened attentively, her eyes wide with astonishment.

'Oh dear, miss, they sounds a rum lot at that house.' Alice shook her head in disbelief. 'Although, I think I might have heard that name somewhere recently,' she said, frowning when Kitty told her about David Fairweather's unexpected arrival at the house.

'It's clear that he's someone that Lady Winspear knows very well, or she would not have asked him to stay, especially at such a delicate time. I mean, her husband and her lover both dead within hours of one another.' Kitty savoured her tea.

'She doesn't sound like a lady that likes to be without a gentleman friend.' Alice gave Kitty a meaningful look.

'I don't think she's much of a lady. Oh dear, now I sound like Mrs Craven. Lettice was an actress before she married Sir William.'

Alice clicked her fingers. 'Of course, that's it, miss. That's where I know that Mr Fairweather's name from. The touring company at Babbacombe. They'm performing at different theatres with a modern play. I went the other week with our Dolly, I'm sure as he's the one who played the lead. His name was on the playbill. Good-looking with dark hair?'

'Well, it sounds as if he could be the same man. It would account for how Lettice knows him if they worked together at some point,' Kitty mused. There had been something theatrical about his entrance and the way he and Lettice had greeted one another.

Alice's eyes sparkled. 'He could have killed Sir William and that Russian dancer all for the love of Lady Winspear so they could get their hands on the money.'

'Inspector Greville will be checking out his alibi for both murders, I'm certain of that.' Kitty smiled at her friend's enthusiasm.

Her smile faded as she recalled that she was about to have very little free time to continue assisting with the investigation. There was far too much to do at the hotel. Even worse, one of the first things she needed to do was to apologise to Mrs Craven after her outburst on Sunday.

———

Matt had barely finished his breakfast when there was a ring at his door. A volley of barks from Bertie sounded the alarm. The murmur of voices in the hall reached him as he folded the morning newspaper.

'Begging your pardon, Captain Bryant, but there's a lady and gentleman here to see you. I've shown them into the sitting room.' His housekeeper didn't look very impressed by his unexpected visitors.

She offered him a cream embossed card. To his surprise, he realised that Henry Winspear was the person waiting in his sitting room.

'Thank you, could you bring a tray of coffee through, please,' he asked, and after straightening his tie, he went through to greet his guests.

Henry Winspear was standing in front of the fireplace as he entered the room. Matt discovered that it was not Padma who had accompanied Henry, but Elspeth.

'Mr Winspear, Miss Winspear.' Matt shook hands with them both and took a seat on one of the black leather armchairs as his housekeeper entered and deposited a silver tray onto the chrome and glass coffee table.

'May I offer you both a drink?' Matt picked up the tall silver jug and poured himself a cup while waiting to see if either of his guests wished to join him.

'Thank you, Captain Bryant, that would be most kind.' Elspeth looked quite dreadful. Her complexion showed a lack of sleep.

'Not for me, thank you.' Henry declined as Matt passed one of the modern angular cups to Elspeth so she could add her own cream and sugar.

'Now, how can I assist you both?' Matt asked once he had stirred his drink and settled back to enjoy his coffee.

Elspeth exchanged a glance with her brother. 'I took the liberty of finding your address from William's files. I, that is we... well, we thought you might be able to advise us.'

Matt was instantly on his mettle. 'I see. What sort of advice do you require?'

Henry began to pace back and forth between the fireplace and the French window. 'To be perfectly frank, Captain Bryant, we're very worried. Our brother is dead and now this Russian chappie has been killed actually at our home. The connecting character in all of this, although it pains me to say so, is Lettice. And now she's invited this other gigolo fellow to stay at the house too. We need help to find out more about him and about Lettice.'

'You see, Captain Bryant, we wish to challenge the will. Who is this David Fairweather anyway?' Elspeth blurted out, interrupting her brother.

Henry glared at his sister.

Matt set his cup down on the saucer. 'You think this David Fairweather may have been involved in the murders? To prevent Sir William from changing his will to disinherit Lady Lettice?'

Colour climbed in Elspeth's cheeks, and she smoothed the pale blue linen skirt of her two-piece with a shaky hand. 'It would make sense. I think she knew William intended to change his will and she wanted the money. Letty is terribly fond of money.'

'And Ivan Bolsova? Where do you think his death fits this scenario?' Matt's curiosity was piqued.

'Well, he had clearly discovered something and now this Fairweather chappie is on the scene he had to go,' Henry blustered.

'So what do you expect me to do?' Matt was intrigued. The Winspears seemed determined that the blame for the murders should be attached to David Fairweather with the motive of benefitting Lettice. He had to discover if there was any real reason for this – or was it just because Lettice had inherited all the money?

'There has to be some evidence to prove Fairweather could have murdered William and Ivan.' Elspeth looked hopefully at Matt.

'I would imagine that Inspector Greville will look at Fairweather's alibi for both murders.' Matt picked up his cup and took another sip of his coffee.

'The police! Pah!' Henry Winspear paused in his pacing, his face florid and ruddy with frustration. 'We need someone on our side who'll dig deep. Lettice has inherited a fortune. A fortune, I tell you. All of William's business interests, and his private monies.'

'It's just not fair! All the years I've worked for William. I've run his office, dealt with his businesses, run the household. I always thought at the very least he would leave me with a good annuity so I could have some independence. The servants have received larger bequests. Then for Letty to have everything while she carries on treating me like dirt.' Elspeth fumbled in her pocket for a handkerchief. 'And she's so smug. She's not even sorry that William is dead.'

Henry gave an embarrassed cough as his sister burst into

tears. He patted her on the shoulder. 'There, there, Elspeth, pull yourself together.'

'What's even worse,' Elspeth said as she wiped her nose, 'is that I don't feel safe. What if I'm next on that man's list? I keep looking over my shoulder all the time. The atmosphere in the house is simply horrid.'

'The Russian girl has taken to her bed. That doesn't really help matters, makes more work for the servants.' Henry twiddled his hands behind his back.

Matt finished his drink and placed his cup and saucer back on the tray. 'You realise that I cannot hinder the police investigation in any way. Inspector Greville is in charge of the enquiry and you both are also under investigation until whoever killed Ivan and Sir William is caught.'

'Of course, of course.' Henry sounded impatient.

'The same goes for Miss Bolsova and Mrs Padma Winspear. I must tell you both now that if you want me to work on the investigation that you will all need to be completely honest with me.' He looked keenly at both of them.

Elspeth was the first to drop her gaze.

'Stands to reason. We've nothing to hide.' Henry turned on his heel and walked towards the fireplace, his back to Matt for a moment.

'And if Lady Winspear and Mr Fairweather are innocent? What then?' Matt asked.

'They won't be. They can't be. There has to be something.' Elspeth put her cup and saucer back on the tray with some force. 'Please, Captain Bryant.'

'Mr Winspear?' Matt wanted to be certain that Henry and Elspeth were both on the same page.

'Do whatever you need to do,' Henry responded gruffly. 'I shall meet all your fees.'

Elspeth rose to stand next to her brother.

'Very well. I'll look into Mr Fairweather and his connection with Lady Winspear but I will also need to ask you and the other household members more questions, as I am sure Inspector Greville will be doing also,' Matt warned as he escorted his guests into the hall.

Bertie began barking once more as soon as he heard Matt in the hall.

'Miss Underhay will also be assisting me in my enquiries at times.' Matt opened the front door to see Sir William's chauffeur-driven, dark blue Rolls Royce parked outside his house.

'Very well. Whatever it takes to bring our brother's murderer to justice,' Elspeth said as Henry shook hands with Matt.

Matt was thoughtful as he closed the front door behind the Winspears. They had certainly seemed keen to blame Lettice or David Fairweather, but he knew they had both been less than honest with Inspector Greville.

It didn't seem to have occurred to the Winspears that if Lettice and Fairweather were innocent then another member of their household must be the killer. Kitty would be interested to learn about the visit. Was their request an attempt to divert suspicion from either of them? He wondered if Padma was aware of Henry and Elspeth's plans.

The kitchen door opened, and Bertie came charging into the hall, clearly disappointed to have missed the visitors. His ears flopped as he padded into the sitting room after Matt and sat down in front of the French doors to gaze mournfully out at the garden.

Matt sat for a moment considering his next moves before picking up the telephone and placing a call to the police station. He wanted to make the inspector aware of his visitors sooner rather than later.

Several minutes later, after an interesting conversation with

Inspector Greville, Matt replaced the receiver for a moment while he considered his course of action. Satisfied that he had the inspector's blessing to take the Winspears on as clients, Matt picked the black Bakelite receiver up once more and dialled the number to connect him with the Dolphin Hotel.

FIFTEEN

Kitty was having a very trying morning. After her morning catch-up with Alice, she had taken breakfast with her grandmother before returning to her hotel duties. By mid-morning she had uncovered a knotty issue in the accounts, dealt with an awkward but influential guest and managed to break two of her fingernails on the drawer of her desk.

The telephone conversation with Matt put her in a slightly better humour. She passed on the information Alice had given her about David Fairweather.

'Alice said she and Dolly had seen him in a performance recently?' Matt asked.

'Yes, near Babbacombe somewhere. She said it was a small touring company that regularly played local theatres, halls and playhouses,' Kitty confirmed.

'That's very interesting. It would certainly explain his connection to Lettice if they knew one another from her acting days.' There were rustling sounds from Matt's end and Kitty assumed that he was probably taking notes. 'I'll make some telephone calls to track down the company.'

Kitty sighed with frustration as she regarded the pile of

correspondence still sitting in a wire tray on her desk. She wouldn't be able to do anything to assist the investigation until all of that had been dealt with. 'I wish I could help.'

'Don't fret, old thing, the information you've just provided is really helpful. I'll telephone you if I learn anything else.' He rang off after arranging to meet her for dinner that evening.

Kitty had just picked up the first letter from the pile when there was a tap on her office door and Dolly, Alice's younger sister, entered the room. Although just turning fifteen, Dolly was a bright girl and had proved a valuable addition to the hotel staff. Now, however, her usually smiling face looked anxious.

'I'm sorry to disturb you, Miss Kitty, but Mrs Treadwell said please could you come upstairs for a moment.' Dolly's tone was apologetic.

Kitty set the letter back in the tray. 'Very well. Did Grams say what she wanted me for?'

Dolly shifted awkwardly from foot to foot. 'I believe she has Mrs Craven with her, miss.'

Kitty groaned. 'Thank you, Dolly. I'll go right up.'

The girl slipped away, and Kitty braced herself in preparation to visit her grandmother's salon and make her peace with Mrs Craven. She checked her hair in a small pocket mirror and reapplied her pale pink lipstick before taking the stairs to the next floor.

'Here you are, Kitty darling, I'm so pleased you could join us for your break.' Her grandmother gave her a meaningful look when she entered the salon. Mrs Craven was installed on the armchair opposite her grandmother dressed in a lilac floral summer dress complete with her favourite diamond brooch and pearl necklace.

Her slightly smug expression told Kitty that she knew exactly why Kitty had been sent for and it wasn't just to take her morning tea break with her grandmother. Kitty suppressed a sigh and greeted her grandmother with a kiss on her cheek.

'Good morning, Mrs Craven.' Kitty took a seat on the sofa while her grandmother poured her a cup of tea.

'Kitty.' Mrs Craven inclined her head somewhat coldly in Kitty's direction.

Mrs Craven was obviously not about to make Kitty's apology easy. Kitty consoled herself with the thought that at least there were jam tarts on the trolley to compensate for the large slice of humble pie she was about to swallow.

Her grandmother fixed her gaze on Kitty.

'Mrs Craven, I believe I may have offended you when I saw you on Sunday. I am so sorry if you were upset by anything I said.' Kitty did her best to sound sincere even though she had no regrets at all about the content of anything she had said. It was merely the delivery of her message that had been rather unfortunate.

. Kitty knew her old adversary well enough to know that Mrs Craven would milk the situation as much as possible.

'I have to say, Kitty, that I was very distressed. I know that your grandmother has raised you to have much better manners when addressing your elders.'

Kitty suspected that the older woman had been tempted to add 'and betters' to the end of her sentence but had thought better of it at the last minute.

'You are correct; indeed she has, Mrs Craven.' Kitty flashed an apologetic smile in her grandmother's direction. 'Again, I can only apologise if you felt I was rude. It was not my intention to distress you.' Her apology given once more, Kitty consoled herself with a jam tart.

'Well, I suppose I shall overlook it this time, Kitty, but I do wish that you would consider before you speak.' Mrs Craven eyed her with disapproval as Kitty dropped pastry crumbs on the front of her dress.

'Of course,' Kitty agreed meekly as she carefully removed the pastry flakes from the delicate pink floral fabric of her dress.

Mrs Craven appeared suitably mollified by Kitty's apparent penitence. 'Have the police made any headway on capturing Sir William's murderer? I heard there had been another death at Palm Lodge yesterday. An accident of some kind involving that dancer.' She eyed Kitty over the rim of her china teacup.

'I don't believe an arrest has been made just yet. Inspector Greville does have several lines of inquiry to follow.' Kitty waited to see if Mrs Craven would expand on whatever she might have heard about Ivan's death.

'What happened to the dancer? Russian, wasn't he? Well, I suppose he was Russian, one never knows these days. So many people claim to be refugees or from exotic locales, especially when they work in the theatre. You know how these theatricals are. Untrustworthy.' Mrs Craven helped herself to a tart, having pronounced judgement on the whole of the acting profession.

'He was discovered floating in the swimming pool.' Kitty took a sip of her tea.

'Oh dear, I wonder what his dance partner will do now?' her grandmother asked. Kitty had taken care only to give her the bare minimum of details when they had breakfasted together, playing down her involvement in the investigation.

'Natasha was Ivan's sister as well as his dance partner so it will probably hit her very hard.' Kitty wondered how Natasha was feeling now the first shock of Ivan's murder was wearing off. Yesterday her anger had seemed to dominate over her grief.

Matt had said that the Winspears had complained that she had taken to her room. It might be that Natasha too thought Lettice or David was responsible for Sir William and Ivan's deaths. Or perhaps like Elspeth, the girl just felt unsafe staying at Palm Lodge. With her brother dead, she might believe she could also end up as a victim.

It was too aggravating that she was trapped here at the Dolphin taking morning tea with Mrs Craven when she could be out and about asking questions.

'I suppose I really should pay Lady Lettice a condolence visit. Not that I am very well acquainted with her, not really the kind of person I would be acquainted with, but Sir William and I served on many of the same committees. I would hate anyone to think I wasn't showing proper feelings towards his widow,' Mrs Craven mused before popping the last bite of her jam tart into her mouth.

'If you would like me to accompany you, I could drive us in my car,' Kitty offered. Mrs Craven was always quick to tag onto Kitty's investigations. Now was an opportunity to turn the tables.

She watched and tried not to smile as an array of emotions passed across Mrs Craven's face. She knew the older lady strongly disapproved of Kitty driving but she was clearly torn about having company for the visit.

'That sounds like an excellent idea. I'm sure you can be available later today, can't you, Kitty?' her grandmother asked, smiling benignly at her.

She suspected that Grams knew she was dying to go back to Palm Lodge to poke about but was choosing to believe that Kitty was trying to make amends to her friend for her rudeness on Sunday.

'Oh, I wouldn't wish to inconvenience anyone. I can easily ask Mr Potter to take me.' A worried frown creased Mrs Craven's brow.

'Nonsense, I wouldn't dream of it. Not when I have a car at my disposal. I shall call and collect you. Would three thirty suit you?' Kitty asked smilingly.

Mrs Craven obviously sensed she was defeated on this occasion. 'Very well, three thirty but you must drive carefully, Kitty. None of this haring around that you young people are so fond of.'

'I'm sure that Kitty will be the model of decorum,' Kitty's grandmother assured her friend, a touch of asperity in her tone.

'Well, I had better get back to work then if I am to be ready in time. I shall see you later, Mrs Craven.' Kitty kept her face straight until she was safely outside the room before allowing a huge grin to appear.

She might have had to apologise to Mrs C but she had managed to secure a little free time to go poking around at Palm Lodge.

Kitty took a sandwich lunch at her desk to ensure she had completed all her office tasks for the day before setting off to collect Mrs Craven. Her grandmother's friend lived in one of the newer, detached houses that had been constructed near the top of the town, not far from the Naval College.

Mrs Craven must have been watching out for her from the large bay window at the front of her house. As Kitty pulled her little red car to a halt outside Mrs Craven's house, the front door opened and the lady herself appeared.

She carried a large bunch of sweet peas and roses, which she had obviously cut from her garden. Kitty hopped out to open the passenger door for her and to stow the flowers carefully on the back seat of the car.

'You are quite sure about this, Kitty? I can still telephone Mr Potter and ask him to drive us.' Mrs Craven fussed with her white leather handbag.

'I couldn't possibly let you disturb Mr Potter when I'm right here with my car.' Kitty smiled brightly at her.

Mrs Craven reluctantly accepted Kitty's assistance to enter the car and took her place on the passenger seat. Kitty resumed her own seat and started the engine, ready to drive back down into the town to take the ferry across the river.

She hid a smile as Mrs Craven squeaked and clutched at her handbag as she drove onto the ferry. Within a few minutes they were driving off at Kingswear and up the hill towards Paignton.

The weather was still warm but there were more clouds in the sky today and the air felt muggy and close. Kitty drove carefully along the lanes past the fields and across the common before taking the turn along the coast road leading to the town.

Mrs Craven was not apparently in the mood to chat. Instead, she was preoccupied with flinching every time Kitty overtook a bicycle or horse and cart, and with holding on to the brim of her hat.

As they neared the town, Kitty turned inland towards Palm Lodge. She drove along the street and through the gates to pull to a stop near the Winspears' front door. After assisting Mrs Craven from the car, she collected the flowers from the rear seat, and they approached the entrance together.

'Have you visited here before, Mrs Craven?' Kitty asked as they waited for someone to answer the doorbell.

'One or two times. Sir William would sometimes host the committee meetings here. His sister, Elspeth, usually acted as his hostess. Lady Winspear was often away either in London or Paris, not that I think she would have been interested in our charitable ventures. It strikes me, Kitty that this may a good opportunity for us to do some sleuthing. Heaven knows that Inspector Greville needs all the help he can get.'

Kitty barely suppressed a groan. She had almost forgotten how much Mrs Craven loved to feel that she was assisting in an investigation.

'I'm sure that the police have everything in hand.' Kitty hoped Mrs Craven would see reason.

'Just follow my lead, Kitty.' Mrs Craven ignored her hint and pasted on a bright social smile as they heard footsteps approaching inside the house.

The door was opened by the maid Kitty had spoken to the day before. Mrs Craven gave their names, explained the purpose of their visit and asked for Lady Winspear. The girl stood aside and allowed them in before showing them down the long and gloomy hallway to the drawing room.

'Please take a seat. I'll tell her ladyship as you'm here.' The girl vanished leaving them alone.

Despite the French doors standing open, the air in the room was stuffy and the scent from a vase of pink roses and white lilies on one of the occasional tables was overpowering. Kitty wondered over to the window and looked out towards the swimming pool where Ivan had been discovered only yesterday afternoon.

A shiver ran along her spine, and she turned away to join Mrs Craven who had seated herself on one end of the dark green, overstuffed, velvet-covered sofa.

'Mrs Craven, Miss Underhay, thank you for calling.' Elspeth Underhay entered the room first.

The grey dress had been replaced with a pale blue, linen two-piece with a narrow black armband. The woman still looked pale and unwell.

'Not at all, my dear. I must confess I was shocked when I heard that poor William had been murdered. I simply had to call and pay my respects. How are you, my dear? And poor Lady Winspear?' Mrs Craven asked.

Elspeth took a seat on one of the armchairs. 'Oh, you know, bearing up as one must under such horrid circumstances. You have heard no doubt of the death yesterday of one of our guests?' She glanced at Kitty as she spoke.

'Yes, Kitty told me. My dear, how terrible.' Mrs Craven reached over and patted Elspeth's hand. 'Sir William was so well thought of in the business community. I cannot conceive of why anyone would do such a terrible thing. And as for that poor Mr Bolsova, his sister must be distraught.'

'Yes, well, Natasha has taken to her room,' Elspeth said.

The door to the drawing room opened once more and

Lettice appeared dressed in a diaphanous, floaty, pastel pink summer dress, her short blonde curls immaculately styled and no sign of distress on her well made-up face.

'My dear Lady Winspear.' Mrs Craven rose to greet her. 'Sir William and I worked together on many charity committees. I simply had to call to pay my condolences. I am so very sorry for your loss.'

Elspeth made the introduction to her sister-in-law.

'Thank you, it's most kind of you to call, Mrs Craven. No doubt Miss Underhay and Elspeth have told you what happened here yesterday?' Lettice sat neatly on the edge of one of the smaller occasional chairs.

'They have indeed. It's all so very shocking. I've brought a few flowers from my garden, which I gave to your maid to arrange. I thought it might lift your spirits a little in the light of these terrible misfortunes.' Mrs Craven reinstalled herself on the end of the sofa.

'That really is very good of you,' Elspeth said.

'It must be awful for Sir William's brother too. I mean only being back in England for such a short time and now this.' Mrs Craven shook her head and tutted.

'I think Henry and his wife are bearing up quite well. After all, they had not seen dear William for quite a few years. Henry and William were not terribly close. I must confess that with William's death and then Ivan's, it has all been quite terrible. I don't know what I would have done if I didn't have the support of one of my dear friends.' Lettice dabbed the corner of her dry eyes with a dainty handkerchief.

'Oh, I'm sure, my dear, and of course Elspeth here will be a rock for you, I'm certain. Sir William would have been lost without her.' Mrs Craven smiled at Elspeth.

'We would all be lost without Elspeth,' Lettice agreed.

Kitty didn't think Lettice's words had any genuine warmth in them and from Elspeth's sour expression it seemed that she was not prepared to assist her sister-in-law the way she had aided Sir William.

'It must be so difficult for you, my dear, having poor Miss Bolsova staying here after her brother's tragic death,' Mrs Craven said.

'Indeed, dear Natasha, she is quite bereft, as am I. She is staying in her room and refusing to see any of us.' Lettice immediately appeared mournful, and Kitty saw Elspeth roll her eyes when she thought Lettice wouldn't see her.

Mrs Craven nodded her head sympathetically. 'I take it that the police have not yet arrested anyone for the murders?'

'Oh, the police. What good are they?' Elspeth rose from her seat and paced about the room in front of the windows as if unable to contain her feelings.

'I'm sure they are doing their best.' Lettice dabbed at her eyes once more. 'Though who would want to harm my poor dear husband or Ivan, I have no idea.'

Elspeth gave an audible snort.

Kitty was relieved when the drawing room door reopened, and a maid entered with a tea trolley. The atmosphere in the room was distinctly frosty between Elspeth and Lettice.

'Mrs Craven, Miss Underhay, would you care for some refreshments? The weather is so very muggy today and hot.' Elspeth took over the trolley and began to dispense drinks. 'I think Henry and his wife may join us,' she said as she handed a cup to Mrs Craven.

'Oh goody,' Lettice muttered.

'Will your *friend*, Mr Fairweather, also be coming down for tea?' Elspeth emphasised the word friend as she poured herself a drink.

'David is in the library learning his lines ready for his new play. I hope he remembers it's teatime, he gets so absorbed when he is preparing for a performance,' Lettice explained to Mrs Craven.

'Your friend is an actor, then?' Mrs Craven took a sip of her tea and eyed Lettice over the brim of her cup.

Elspeth gave another audible snort, which she hastily converted into a cough when Lettice glared at her.

'David has appeared in many performances. He played Hamlet, you know, and his company have been touring locally. You may have seen them at one of their productions.' Lettice selected a biscuit from the trolley and nibbled daintily at the edge.

As she spoke, David Fairweather entered the room looking very dapper in a smart, ivory-coloured linen suit.

'David, I was just telling Mrs Craven about your new play.' Lettice beamed as Mr Fairweather helped himself to a cup of tea from the trolley.

'Are you interested in the arts, Mrs Craven?' he asked as he took a seat near to Lettice.

Mrs Craven nodded. 'I attend a great many performances. Music is my great love though, I am very fond of opera.'

Kitty observed the scene from her seat near Mrs Craven. David Fairweather certainly appeared to be very personable.

'Have you known Lady Winspear long, Mr Fairweather?' Kitty asked.

David turned to smile at her, displaying a row of perfectly white teeth. 'Letty and I go back a long way. We were in repertory theatre together a few years ago.' He turned his smile towards Lettice. 'Then Letty changed company and we lost touch for a little while. The next thing I knew she was Lady Winspear.'

'How nice that you met up again. Was that when your company was touring locally?' Kitty asked.

'I ran into David in London of all places. I had just come out of Selfridges, and I walked right into him. We caught up over a cocktail at the Ritz and I've followed his career with interest ever since. He is wonderfully talented, and you know that I love to support the arts.' Lettice smiled complacently at Kitty.

'Lettice has agreed to back my new play,' David announced before crunching into a biscuit.

Kitty wondered how Matt's enquiries were progressing. It seemed to her that David Fairweather might very well be their man. With Lettice's husband and her lover removed and Letty herself now a wealthy widow, that had to be a good motive for murder.

'Oh, give me strength,' Elspeth muttered as her teacup crashed down on her saucer. She rose from her seat and left the room.

As Elspeth made her exit, she passed Henry and Padma Winspear entering the room.

'Miss Underhay and...' Henry Winspear advanced towards Kitty to shake her hand.

'Mrs Craven was a colleague of Sir Williams. They served on many charity committees together. Mrs Craven is a former mayoress of Dartmouth.' Kitty made the introduction. 'Mrs Craven, may I present Henry Winspear and his wife, Mrs Padma Winspear.'

'I felt compelled to call and express my condolences when I heard about Sir William, and Kitty here very kindly offered to bring me,' Mrs Craven said.

'Thank you, that's most kind.' Padma peered inside the teapot and immediately tugged on the embroidered bell pull at the side of the fireplace. 'I'll just send for some more hot water. By the way, what was wrong with Elspeth? She seemed upset.'

'Well, I'm sure I don't know. We were talking about David's new play, and she stormed out.' Lettice gave a careless shrug of her shoulders.

The maid re-entered the room, carrying a tray with a fresh pot of hot water, more cups and a tiered stand with sandwiches.

She replenished the trolley and removed the used crockery before leaving.

'So, what's this play about?' Henry asked, looking at David.

'Oh, it's simply marvellous. It's by a new playwright and it's an exploration of modern themes. It's so good of Lettice to offer to support us.' David beamed at Henry.

Kitty watched as Henry's already florid complexion turned a deeper shade of puce. 'Very good of her,' Henry growled, fixing Lettice with a flinty glare.

Lettice, however, appeared to be quite impervious to the Winspears' disapproval. 'There is already talk of an agent coming to watch the opening night. This could make David a huge star. We have already set up some meetings that could lead to opportunities in film. You never know, I may even make a return to the stage myself.'

Padma passed her husband a cup of tea. 'How nice.'

Kitty didn't think that either Padma or Henry thought it was at all nice that Lettice appeared to already be spending Sir William's money on David Fairweather. Or that she seemed to be contemplating resuming her acting career.

'You must have been planning this for a while?' Padma continued, looking at Lettice.

'Well, we'd discussed it of course, but *you* know, Henry, how William could be a bit of an old fuddy-duddy sometimes. Now though, well, the play is already to go, and the theatres are available that we want in order to make this a huge success.' Lettice looked like the cat who'd got the cream.

Kitty thought Henry was about to have a stroke. Padma rushed over to her husband's side. 'Come, darling, let us take our tea out on the terrace for a moment. Perhaps some air...' She steered Henry out through the French doors onto the terrace.

Audible muttering floated back inside the drawing room of, 'Dashed gigolo.'

SIXTEEN

Lettice and David both seemed happily impervious to the Winspears' disapproval.

Mrs Craven cleared her throat. 'I suppose you won't be able to organise Sir William's funeral until after the inquest. You will let me know the details when you have them, won't you?'

'Oh yes, of course. I think Elspeth will have everything in hand as soon as we are allowed. I've been so distressed that I've had to leave everything to Elspeth to arrange. She is very friendly with the local clergy.' Lettice smirked at the last part of her statement.

'I suppose Miss Bolsova will have to organise her brother's funeral too when the police allow it to go ahead. Does she have any family in this country?' Mrs Craven asked.

Lettice gave another shrug. 'I really don't know. Ivan never mentioned anyone to me. Poor Natasha is hoping to move to a nearby hotel when a suitable room becomes available. I think she is finding it difficult staying here after what happened to darling Ivan. He was such a talented dancer.' Lettice gave a delicate shudder and raised her handkerchief to her face.

'Letty darling, please don't distress yourself. You've been a perfect angel to Natasha. The police will soon catch whoever murdered Sir William and Ivan.' David held Lettice's hands in his.

'Oh, David, I am so glad that you're here with me. I feel so terribly frightened. Suppose whoever did this comes after me next?' Letty's eyes widened with fear as if the implications of recent events had just registered in her mind.

'Is there anyone you think might wish to harm you?' Kitty asked.

Lettice shot a glance in the direction of the terrace. 'It has to be someone here who killed Ivan and William. I know they are William's family, but you must have seen how they treat me. They all hate me, you know, even more so after the will reading yesterday morning. I know they are trying to convince the police that I murdered William.' A sob broke free from Lettice's throat.

'Surely that can't be the case if you were with Elspeth like you said,' Kitty reasoned.

'I know, I *was* with her. Well, most of the time I was with her. I did have to visit the bathroom during that wretched tennis match, but I was only gone for about ten minutes before the end.' Lettice's lower lip set in a mutinous line.

'Letty darling, please don't take on so. I'll stay with you for as long as you need. You'll be perfectly safe, I promise,' David assured her.

'I would never have hurt William, never. I know people think that's not the case as there was a big age gap between us, but William was so good to me.' Lettice fished out her handkerchief once more and blew her nose daintily.

'And yet I understand he was considering divorce?' Kitty said. She wasn't taken in by Lettice's poor little me act. She had seen too many hotel guests tell her and her grandmother the most blatant lies in order to secure a discount on their stay.

This procured a fresh flood of tears from Lady Lettice.

'That was just a silly misunderstanding. William was a proud man and jealous. He completely misunderstood the relationship between myself and Ivan. He would have changed his mind once I explained everything, I'm certain.'

'There, there, Letty darling,' David Fairweather consoled her and glared at Kitty.

'I am so very sorry for your loss, my dear. Sir William did many good things for the local community. Kitty, I think we should take our leave.' Mrs Craven stood and gathered her handbag and light cotton gloves. 'Now, please don't forget to let me know the funeral details when everything has been arranged. Elspeth has my address, I'm sure.'

Lettice sniffed and dabbed at her eyes. 'Of course, Mrs Craven. Thank you for calling, I do appreciate your support. Miss Underhay.' She gave Kitty a stiff nod of her head.

Kitty followed Mrs Craven out into the gloomy hallway where a maid met them to take them to the front door. It was something of a relief to be outdoors once again despite the muggy air.

'Well, that went quite well I think, despite your tactlessness, Kitty.' Mrs Craven waited at the passenger door of the car for Kitty to open it for her.

'Sometimes you have to ask a direct question if you are to get an answer. I was rather tired of Lady Winspear's playacting,' Kitty grumbled as she opened the door and assisted Mrs Craven into her seat.

She walked back around the nose of her car and paused with her hand on the driver's door. At first, she wasn't certain what had caught her attention, but then she realised that stealing through the trees near the end of the drive, she could see a familiar female figure.

Before she had the opportunity to do anything, the woman had vanished from sight. Kitty climbed into the driving seat and placed her key in the ignition. She could have sworn that the figure she had just seen was Natasha, but what was the Russian girl doing creeping around in the shrubbery?

'We had better set off back to Dartmouth. I have a bridge club meeting at my house this evening and I must make sure my maid has prepared everything. Now, do drive carefully, Kitty,' Mrs Craven instructed as Kitty reversed her car, ready to set off back along the driveway.

'I'm always careful, Mrs Craven.' Kitty drove slowly along the gravel drive to the gates looking for any sign of Natasha but saw no signs of life except the squirrels playing in the trees.

———

Matt had spent his day making enquiries amongst David Fairweather's theatre company. He discovered that they were currently boarding in Torquay in preparation for the opening of a new play.

The lodging house was one often used by theatrical people and was situated at the back of the town in a quiet street of tall, thin terraced houses. He had left Bertie in the reluctant care of his housekeeper and made his way to the lodgings on his trusty Sunbeam motorcycle.

He had managed to procure the address after telephoning the various theatres and playhouses from a playbill. After leaving his motorcycle at the curb, he approached the white-washed house. The front door – the blue paint sun faded and slightly peeling – stood ajar. A printed notice in the window proclaimed 'no vacancies'.

Matt pressed the bell at the side of the open door and a loud buzzing noise sounded inside the house. After a few moments, the sound of shuffling footsteps could be heard on the decorative tile flooring.

'Can I help you?' A generously built, middle-aged lady clad

in a voluminous navy-blue apron and slippers stood in the doorway.

'I hope so, I'm looking for the Newhampton Strolling Players. I was told they were boarding here.' Matt gave the landlady his most beguiling smile.

The woman sniffed and folded her arms across her bosom. 'Press, am you?'

'I had been hoping to speak to David Fairweather as I gather that he is the company's leading man, but I understand he has been called away, so perhaps another member of the company might be available?' Matt dodged the question as he had no wish to reveal he was a private investigator at this point. It also struck him that masquerading as a journalist might prove useful.

'Who is it, Ma?' a younger female voice called out from behind the woman.

The woman turned her head to reply over her shoulder. 'There's a chap here asking for the Players.'

'One minute,' the voice answered.

A few seconds later, there was the sound of heels and the older lady was joined by a glamorous young woman in a rather daring pale yellow frock. She seemed to be around Kitty's age with bobbed brown hair and bright, inquisitive eyes.

'Hello, I'm Doris Loveday, the Players' leading lady.' The girl held out her hand.

'I'm charmed to meet you, Miss Loveday. Matthew Bryant, I called hoping to speak to some of the group. I was telling this lady that unfortunately I heard David Fairweather had been called away?' Matt shook the girl's hand and raised his hat.

'Are you from the press? About the new play?' the girl asked excitedly. 'You'd better come inside. It's all right, Ma, I'll see to this gentleman.' She chivvied the older woman away and led Matt into a small parlour beside the front door.

'You mustn't mind Mrs Tonks, Ma we all call her, she's very protective of us. Looks after us like a mother,' Doris said.

The room was homely in an old-fashioned style with china Staffordshire dogs either side of the clock on the mantelpiece. A large aspidistra stood in a blue glazed pot on a table near the window and a battered upright piano was in the corner of the room.

Doris seated herself on one end of the floral, chintz-covered sofa and patted the vacant space next to her in invitation. Matt took a seat on one of the bentwood dining chairs instead, earning a pout from Doris's full ruby lips.

'Well, Matthew Bryant, how can I help you?' the girl asked.

She took out a cigarette and inserted it in a black holder shaped like a panther and looked at Matt for a light.

Once he had obliged her, he came to the reason for his call. 'I had hoped to speak to David Fairweather. I understand that he is your leading man?'

Doris blew out a thin stream of smoke and resumed her pout. 'Leading man and director of the Players. He's away on business at the moment securing us the funds for our next tour.' She eyed Matt curiously.

'I see. I think I heard that Lady Lettice Winspear is to be your next backer?' Matt connected the dots and decided to risk a guess at David Fairweather's business connection with Lettice.

Doris smirked. 'You have done your homework. Yes, Lady Winspear has agreed to fund our next run. David sent a message this morning to say rehearsals for the new play will start in the next few days.'

'Do you know Lady Winspear?' Matt asked.

Doris flicked some glowing embers from the tip of her cigarette into a large plain glass ashtray. 'She came to a few performances of our last play. She's known David for an absolute age. They used to be in the same company a few years ago, but then Letty's ship came in and she married the money.'

'Have you heard about Sir William Winspear's recent death?' Matt was curious about how and when all of this had come about. Had Sir William known of Lettice's intention to invest in David Fairweather's theatre group?

Doris licked her lipsticked lips. 'Somebody murdered the old boy, didn't they? That's what it said in the newspaper and then on Monday David got a telephone call mid-afternoon from Letty. He packed a bag and called a taxi, saying Letty needed him to stay at her house for a while.'

'Do you know where Mr Fairweather was on Sunday?' Matt asked.

Doris's gaze sharpened. 'Here, are you from the police?'

Matt shook his head and tried disarming the girl with a smile. 'No. I am involved with the case, however.'

Doris stubbed out the remains of her cigarette in the ashtray. 'What kind of involved?' she asked suspiciously.

'I work as a private investigator and have been engaged to assist with the case. I don't know if Mr Fairweather told you that a second person connected with Sir William and Lady Winspear has been killed?' Matt decided he would be better to come clean. Doris did not appear to be the kind of girl to be easily fooled.

She leaned back in her seat and gave Matt an assessing look as if deciding if she could trust him. He reached into his pocket to find his card case and handed her one of his cards.

'Hmm, I don't know. I don't want any bother from the police. If Ma, our landlady, thinks we might be caught up in any kind of scandal she'll have us all out. She keeps a respectable house, and these are really good lodgings.' The girl bobbed her head towards the partially closed door of the parlour.

'I assure you that I am very discreet, and it would be better to talk to me than to have a uniformed constable come calling,' Matt assured her.

'That's true,' Doris conceded. 'David was with us here on Sunday. We finished our run of the last play on Saturday night, so we had a bit of a bash afterwards. So come Sunday morning none of us were exactly feeling bright and breezy. It was such a hot day that we all went down to the beach for sea bathing and had fish and chips for supper at the café near the harbour. David was with us all day.'

'And yesterday?' Matt asked.

Doris's brow creased in concentration. 'On the morning, David had a note from Lady Winspear saying that something terrible had happened to her husband. She said not to worry, it would all be all right and that at least now David could go ahead with the plans for the play.' Doris gave a slight shrug. 'He read it out to us and, well, I suppose you might think it callous, but we were all quite chipper. An ill wind blowing us some good, you might say.'

Matt assumed Lettice must have sent the note as soon as she had been made aware of her legacy from Sir William.

'And on the afternoon?' he asked.

'We had lunch all together at one of the cafes on the seafront. Then I went off with one of the girls to do a spot of shopping. David said he planned to call in at the hall we were going to use for rehearsals. We don't usually get the luxury of rehearsal time. We generally learn the new play on a morning while we're putting the other one on of an evening. This was different though. David had said now we were having backing that he could get London agents interested in us. We might even get spotted for a movie.' Doris's eyes lit up at the thought. 'I'd just come back here when Ma said as Lady Lettice had telephoned David. She wasn't very pleased. She guards that telephone like a hawk, and we aren't supposed to make or receive any personal calls on it. I met him in the hall, and he had his bag all packed. That was when he told me what had happened, and he was going to stay with Letty.'

'I see.' There might just have been time for David to have killed Ivan and then returned to the lodging house, but it would have been a tight squeak. Besides which, Matt couldn't really see a motive for the actor to murder Ivan.

'You don't think it was David who killed Letty's old man, do you?' Doris asked in a laughing tone. 'For one thing he hates the sight of blood. We did a play last season and even the stage blood made him queasy. He could no more kill anybody than fly to the moon.'

'That's good to know, Miss Loveday. You've been most helpful,' Matt assured her.

'Call me Doris, please. Who was the other person you said had been killed?' The girl asked curiously.

'I expect it will be in the newspapers later today. It was a man called Ivan Bolsova, a Russian dancer, who was also under Lady Winspears' patronage.' Matt stood, ready to leave.

Doris's face paled. 'He has a sister that he dances with? Natasha?'

Matt's interest was caught by the actress's reaction. 'Yes, that's right. Do you know them?'

'They came to see the performance once with Lady Winspear. I think David was a little put out. I suppose he thought that the Winspears might not fund our play if they were already supporting them. That's truly shocking, he was a good-looking bloke, that Ivan.' Doris was clearly shaken by his revelation.

'One last thing, Miss Loveday, do you know if Mr Fairweather has a romantic connection with Lady Winspear?' Matt asked.

The actress's mood changed and she laughed. 'David is a good-looking man, all the ladies like him. There was a rumour that he was married at one time, but no one knows for sure. I doubt that Lady Winspear is backing us solely out of the good-ness of her heart though, let's put it like that.' Doris winked.

'If you think of anything else that might be relevant to the case, you have my card, so please get in touch.' Matt tipped his hat once more to the girl and let himself out of the lodging house. He was certain that Doris had been taken by surprise that Ivan had been murdered.

David Fairweather however seemed to have a strong alibi for Sir William's murder. It was possible that he could have killed Ivan, but it seemed extremely unlikely at the moment. The real puzzle seemed to be Lady Winspear. Could Lettice have somehow murdered Sir William and then Ivan? Or were Elspeth and the other Winspears trying to divert suspicion from themselves by leading a trail to her?

SEVENTEEN

Kitty felt quite exhausted by the time she had returned Mrs Craven to her home. The older lady had spent the entire return journey proposing various theories about who could have murdered Sir William and Ivan Bolsova. Each theory had been more far-fetched than the one before.

The information they had gleaned during their visit seemed to indicate that now neither Lettice nor Elspeth had an alibi for Sir William's murder since they had been apart for a period of time. Kitty guessed that Lettice's claim of ten minutes was probably more likely to be twenty, which could give either woman time to get to the grotto, stab Sir William and get back to the terrace tea room at the mansion if the match had ended. It was tight but doable.

If Elspeth was so keen to point the finger at Lettice, then surely she would have told Inspector Greville this. The only reason Kitty could determine about why she hadn't done so was that she must have had something to hide herself.

Kitty secured her car in the shed where she garaged it and walked slowly back along the riverside embankment towards the Dolphin. The atmosphere was oppressive, and the sky held a faintly yellow tinge, a sure sign of the approach of thunder. Even the air smelled of heat, dust and stagnant river mud from the low tide.

As she entered the wood-panelled lobby of the hotel she saw Dolly deep in conversation with Mary, the receptionist. Relief appeared on the expressions of both girls as she walked towards the desk.

'Oh, Miss Kitty, I'm glad to see you back,' Mary spoke first.

Alarm spread through Kitty. She had only been gone for a few hours. 'Why? What's happened? Whatever is wrong?'

''Tis your grandmother, miss. She didn't want us to telephone Palm Lodge to fetch you back, but she's took a bit of a funny turn.' Dolly looked anxiously at Mary as if for reassurance that they had done the right thing.

Kitty thought she might faint. 'Where is she? What happened? Has the doctor been sent for?' Her words tumbled over one another in her anxiety. If anything happened to her beloved Grams, she didn't know what she would do.

'She's lying down in her room, miss. Our Alice is with her, and the doctor has been. She's a bit better now,' Dolly hastened to reassure her.

Kitty didn't stay to listen to anything further. Instead, she hurried to the stairs and took them two at a time in her haste to reach her grandmother. She needed to see her for herself to find out what was wrong. Thank heavens for Dolly and Alice.

Her heart pounded and she was out of breath as she rushed into her grandmother's salon and went straight to the bedroom. The pastel pink curtains had been closed and the room was bathed in a soft rosy half-light.

'Grams darling, what's happened?'

Alice was seated at the bedside and rose as Kitty entered the room. Her grandmother was lying in bed, propped up on a pile of pillows, her face as pale as the white cotton linen.

'It's nothing, my dear. Just a bit of a queer turn,' her grandmother attempted to reassure her as Kitty took Alice's place on the chair beside the bed.

Kitty's heart was still pounding with fear as she took her grandmother's hand in hers. 'What happened?' She directed the question to Alice who was busy straightening the rose-coloured satin cover on the bed.

'Mrs Treadwell was working downstairs, miss, with Dolly in the office. She stood up to go and get some of the ledgers and our Dolly said as she went all giddy like and fell down.' Alice bit her lip and looked anxiously at the pale figure in the bed. 'Dolly thinks as she might have banged her head on the edge of the table as there was a right thump, and it took a bit for her to come to. Mary rung for the doctor straight away and Mickey helped us to get her up here.'

'A lot of fuss over nothing,' Mrs Treadwell protested weakly from the bed.

'Has the doctor been?' Kitty asked.

'Yes, miss. He came right quick as he were down the road at the cottage hospital when his wife got a hold of him. He said as she needed to rest, her blood pressure was a bit high, and she's got a bump on the back of her head.' Alice twitched the corner of the cover into place.

'Oh, Grams.' Kitty squeezed her grandmother's hand. 'I knew you were doing too much.' She felt horribly guilty. The hotel was at its busiest at the moment and she really had no business disappearing to play detective while leaving her grand-mother to cope with it all, no matter how much her Grams insisted.

She had to face facts. Her grandmother was not a young woman and she had worked hard all her life. Kitty had never known her grandfather; he had been killed in an accident involving a horse and cart when her own mother had been a young girl. Then Elowed, Kitty's mother, had vanished when Kitty herself was small.

Her grandmother had run the hotel and raised first Kitty's mother and then Kitty alone. Over the last twelve months they had finally found the remains of Kitty's mother and laid her to rest. The price for discovering what had happened to Elowed after she had vanished had however come at a heavy cost.

Kitty's own life had been put at risk on more than one occasion. Even now, Esther Hammett, the sister of her mother's murderer, was still at large and making threats against Kitty.

'Nonsense, darling. It was just the heat. It gets so stuffy in that office. I stood up too quickly,' her grandmother tried to reassure her. 'A day or two resting and I shall be as right as rain. Alice and Dolly have taken very good care of me.'

'I should have been here.' Kitty compressed her lips together to try and stop herself from crying.

'I shall be perfectly all right when I have rested. Do stop fussing, Kitty dear. Now, you and Alice can go, and I shall close my eyes and rest for a spell.' Her grandmother's voice took on the stern note that Kitty knew meant there would be no further discussion on the matter.

She kissed her grandmother's soft cheek and followed Alice out of the bedroom into the lounge.

'What did the doctor say exactly?' Kitty asked Alice in a low voice as she closed the bedroom door behind her. She knew her grandmother well enough to know that she would play down any kind of illness.

'He said as he thought it might have been the heat and standing up quick like. She caught her head on the edge of the desk when she fell so he was more bothered about that really,' Alice said.

'The doctor told you her blood pressure was high?' Kitty took a seat on the edge of the sofa.

'Yes, miss. When he tested it, he said as the pressure were up a bit but that could have been because of the fall. He said as she is to rest, and he'll call again tomorrow to check on her.'

Alice fiddled with the hem of her white starched apron. 'Don't you be blaming yourself none for this, Miss Kitty. 'Tis the heat what's done it. It's been enough to make anyone feel bad today.'

Kitty gave her friend a wan smile as a tear escaped to run down her cheek. 'I should have been here though, Alice. Grams does far too much for someone her age.'

'You'd best not let her hear you say that.' Alice took a seat next to Kitty and gave her a quick hug. 'Skin you alive, she will.'

Kitty put her head in her hands. 'Seriously, Alice, what am I to do? Grams needs me here. She is relying on me to take over the hotel completely at some point and with the wedding and helping Matt with his cases...'

For a moment everything seemed to overwhelm her. Was she being selfish to not want to be a hotelier all her life? Much as she loved the Dolphin, sometimes the weight of the responsibility and family history was too much. It closed in on her, making her feel as if she was drowning.

Her marriage was planned for Christmas Eve at the old church of St Saviour's in the centre of town, but she and Matt had not even determined where they were to live afterwards, or how Kitty would continue to manage her responsibilities at the hotel.

'Now then, Miss Kitty, don't you go borrowing trouble. Everything will sort itself out, you'll see. I'll go and fetch you a nice cup of tea while you go and wash your face.' Alice jumped to her feet and bustled to the door, a determined expression on her face.

'You're right. Thank you, Alice. I really don't know what I should do without you.' Kitty sniffed and fished about in the pocket of her dress for her handkerchief.

By the time Kitty heard the jingle of crockery on the trolley outside the door of her grandmother's apartment, she was feeling much more herself again. There was a light tap on the door and Alice entered with the tea things accompanied by Matt and Inspector Greville.

'Alice has told us about your grandmother. Is she all right?' Matt asked as he greeted her with a kiss on her cheek. She realised that he could probably tell from her eyes that she had been crying.

Inspector Greville removed his hat as Kitty assured Matt that her grandmother was recovering.

'Alice says that the doctor has seen her and says she just needs to rest,' Kitty said.

'It'll be this infernal heat.' Inspector Greville mopped his brow with a white, slightly grubby cotton handkerchief. 'It's enough to make anyone feel bad,' he grumbled as he took a seat in the bay closest to one of the open windows.

Matt took the chair opposite and looked out across the river. 'It looks as if a storm is coming. I thought I heard a rumble of thunder earlier.'

'Let's hope it reduces this blooming heat. Stifling it is, out there.' The inspector brightened when Alice set a cup of tea in front of him and placed a small plate of biscuits on the table.

'I'd just pulled up outside the hotel when I saw the inspector parking his car further down the street so I thought it would be a good idea if we caught up and compared notes,' Matt explained as Alice set a cup in front of him.

'Of course. I accompanied Mrs Craven this afternoon to call on Lady Winspear. Mrs Craven knew Sir William from her charity work.' Kitty smiled gratefully at Alice and told them what she had learned during her visit.

Alice smiled back and slipped quietly out of the room.

'So, either Lady Lettice or Elspeth Winspear could have killed Sir William by the sound of it now. Lady Lettice for the money if he intended to change his will and divorce her, and Elspeth if he planned to send another potential suitor packing or if she had grown tired of being at her brother's beck and call.

She believed he was leaving her a good annuity.' Inspector Greville stirred an extra spoon of sugar into his cup.

Matt told them the results of his interview with Doris. 'It seems very unlikely that David Fairweather is involved. At least, definitely not in Sir William's murder.'

'But he could still be working with Lady Lettice, if she murdered her husband and then persuaded this Fairweather chappie to kill Ivan Bolsova,' the inspector mused as he helped himself to biscuits.

'Possible but unlikely, I'd say, sir. Fairweather has no transport so it would have been difficult in the time for him to have gone to Palm Lodge and back.' Matt picked up his cup.

'Elspeth could have committed both murders,' Kitty reminded them. 'And I'm not at all certain about Natasha. Why was she creeping around the grounds at Palm Lodge? She definitely didn't wish to be seen.'

'Do you think she could have been meeting someone?' Matt asked.

Kitty frowned. 'It's a possibility but I didn't see any sign of anyone else.'

'How are your enquiries progressing, sir?' Matt asked.

Inspector Greville's moustache drooped. 'Slowly, I'm afraid. We've been following up some potential witnesses from Sunday to try and confirm any of the Winspears' alibis. As you can imagine it's been a tricky job. I sent men to re-interview members of the country club who had indicated they had been in the right vicinity of the park, or who had confirmed that they knew any of the party.'

'Were these the people who were originally questioned as they left the country club on Sunday?' Kitty asked. She presumed the police must have narrowed it down somehow. It would have been impossible to trace and question everyone who had been there that afternoon.

'Yes, my constables had a set of questions that they asked

everyone as they left. We are now busy following up with anyone that appeared to have anything useful to tell us. That's what I was doing when Captain Bryant saw me. I had just been to talk to a lady who had seen Mrs Padma Winspear hurrying towards the mansion from the direction of the grotto around the time Sir William was killed.' The inspector sighed deeply as he took the remaining biscuit from the plate.

'Padma Winspear appears to be entering the frame quite a lot,' Kitty observed.

'Indeed, she does. Her alibi and that of her husband is certainly not substantiated for when Sir William was killed, and she was on the terrace at Palm Lodge at around the time Ivan Bolova was murdered.' Inspector Greville examined his biscuit and took a bite from the edge.

'She may have resented how Sir William treated her and that he wouldn't give any money to Henry,' Kitty suggested. Her mind was busy exploring possible motives for Padma.

'She may have thought Henry would benefit financially from Sir William's death. He inherits the house after all and expected to get a substantial lump sum from money Sir William's mother had left. She might have thought he would naturally get Sir Williams shares in his businesses too.' Matt set down his cup. 'Or it could be that Padma and Henry are in this together.'

'But then why would they murder Ivan?' Kitty asked.

'I suppose he could have seen or heard something when Sir William was killed so they could have murdered him to prevent him from speaking out and pointing the finger at them. Or of course Ivan may have tried his hand at a spot of blackmail.' As Matt spoke, a long, low growl of thunder sounded outside the window.

A shiver ran along Kitty's spine at the ominous sound. 'The storm is closing in.' She glanced out at the still busy embankment.

'I should get back across the river. I'd like to speak to the Winspears again. Captain Bryant, may I offer you a lift? If this rain comes it will be most uncomfortable riding your motorcycle.' Inspector Greville finished his tea and set his cup down on its saucer.

The first large spots of rain hit the leaded panes of the bay window as he spoke, splashing hard and fast like bullets into the weathered and pitted glass.

'Thank you, Inspector, that would be most kind. I can leave the bike here until tomorrow.' Matt looked at Kitty who nodded her agreement.

'Of course. I'll ask Mickey to place a cover over it when the rain eases.' Water was cascading down the glass now and she was forced to pull the windows to, to prevent the water from splashing inside onto the sills.

'Let's hope this cools the air a little,' the inspector said as he shook hands with Kitty and redonned his hat ready to face the elements outside.

'I'll telephone you later, darling. I hope your grandmother is feeling better soon.' Matt gave Kitty a quick farewell kiss before following the inspector to the door.

She saw the men out and returned to her grandmother's bedroom door. A quick peep inside reassured her that her grandmother was sleeping peacefully, undisturbed by the noise of the storm.

Kitty wished she could have accompanied the inspector back to Palm Lodge. There were all kinds of questions buzzing in her mind that she would have liked to ask the Winspears. Instead, she tidied up the tea things and went back downstairs to her office ready to finish her day's work.

EIGHTEEN

Inspector Greville had parked his police car further along the rapidly emptying street.

'Hop in, Captain Bryant.' The inspector leaned across to open the passenger door. The thrum of the rain on the metal roof and body of the car was deafening and water poured down the windscreen like a waterfall.

'What a deluge.' Once inside the car Matt brushed the rainwater from his shoulders while the inspector caught his breath.

Even with the windscreen wipers turned on, it was hard to see as the rain was coming so quickly. The street was completely empty of people now as everyone had taken cover from the storm.

'We had best give it a minute before we head for the ferry,' the inspector suggested.

'Yes, I think so, sir,' Matt said as another loud crack of thunder rent the air. 'Are you intending to go straight to Palm Lodge?'

Inspector Greville's moustache twitched, and he glanced across at Matt, his eyes twinkling. 'Why, do you fancy coming along?' he asked.

'If you would have no objection?' Matt was curious to know how the Winspears would respond to Inspector Greville's questions now their alibis had all been challenged.

'Not at all.' The inspector put his car in gear and, taking advantage of a lull in the downpour, set off for the ferry crossing.

Unsurprisingly, the ferry was virtually deserted and only one other vehicle joined them on the somewhat choppy journey across the river. Matt glanced back across the water to the Dolphin. He hoped Kitty's grandmother would make a swift recovery from whatever had caused her to faint. He knew his fiancée would be worried sick over her beloved Grams.

The question was bound to arise about the future of the hotel and Kitty's role in its management. He knew that Kitty had no appetite to be tied into a full-time role managing the hotel, especially with their wedding only a few months away. They had yet to even decide where they would live after their marriage since crossing the Dart late at night would not be ideal for Kitty. It was certainly a conundrum.

The rain continued as they drove through the sodden countryside towards Palm Lodge. Thunder growled intermittently overhead, and streaks of lightning flashed across the smoke-grey sky. Some of the side roads had begun to flood with puddles of red sandy water washed out of the fields and Matt was relieved when they finally arrived at the Winspear's house.

Despite the early evening gloom, the front of the lodge was in darkness. Rain dripped from the trees and gurgled down the drainpipes while a lone crow cawed overhead. Matt straightened his hat and followed the inspector to the front door of the house. He was glad of the stone canopy, which at least prevented the worst of the rain from pouring down the back of his neck.

There was no answering ring inside the house when the inspector pressed the bell. 'Power must be out,' Inspector

Greville observed as he raised the large black ring knocker in the centre of the door and rapped sharply instead.

After a few minutes, the door was finally opened by a flustered-looking maid. 'I'm so sorry, sir, the bell isn't working. Please come in.' She let them inside and took their wet coats and hats before showing them along the hall to the drawing room.

The storm had done little to cool the air and with the windows of the house now closed against the rain, the air was both gloomy and oppressive. The scent of roses, lilies and sweet peas hung heavy and cloying in the air.

'Inspector Greville and Captain Bryant to see you, sir, miss.' The maid announced them to Henry and Padma Winspear who it seemed were the sole occupants of the room.

Henry looked up from his newspaper. 'Inspector, Captain Bryant, any news of an arrest yet?'

Padma was seated near the window; skeins of embroidery silk lay across her lap as if she had been sorting them out. She looked at her husband and Matt thought he saw a flicker of fear cross her face.

'I believe we are making progress, sir,' the inspector responded smoothly. 'I'm pleased you are both here. There are a few anomalies that have arisen during our investigation, which you may be able to assist me with.'

Henry set aside his paper. 'Certainly, Inspector, how can we help you?'

Inspector Greville took a seat on the armchair nearest to the chimney breast where he could see both Padma and Henry. Matt placed himself discreetly on a low stool in a corner of the room.

'I wonder if I might check a few things with you both, concerning your statements on Sunday?' Inspector Greville took out his notebook and began to flick back through the pages. 'I think, Mr Winspear, that you and your wife were together sitting in the Italian gardens at the time of Sir William's murder?'

'Yes, that's correct. It was dashed hot and there was a seat near the roses with plenty of shade. That's right, isn't it, Padma?' Henry looked at his wife for confirmation.

'Yes, we went to the garden and sat on a bench.' Padma agreed.

Matt thought the woman looked quite nervous now and she didn't meet the inspector's gaze.

'Are you sure of that, Mr Winspear? You and your wife were together all afternoon in the garden until you went up to the terrace of the house for tea?' Inspector Greville asked.

The room had grown darker, and it was hard to read Henry's expression in the poor light.

'Yes. That's what I said.' Henry sounded belligerent.

'I'm just checking, sir, because I have a witness that states that they saw Mrs Padma Winspear approaching the mansion from the direction of the grotto at around the time Sir William was killed.' The inspector's voice took on a stern note.

Just as he finished speaking there was a pop and the lamp on the side table next to Henry suddenly came on, throwing his face into bright relief. Matt thought he looked like a naughty boy who had been caught red-handed stealing apples.

'Well, I think your witness must have been mistaken.' Henry's face grew ruddier as he blustered.

'Please forgive me, Mr Winspear, but your wife's appearance, being a foreign lady, is quite distinctive, and my witness is a lady who has met your wife before.' The inspector looked at Padma.

Padma was frozen in place, her dark eyes wide and frightened as she returned the inspector's gaze.

'I suggest, Mrs Winspear, that you tell me the truth,' Inspector Greville said firmly.

'Henry... I...' Padma looked at her husband as if for guidance but any thought he had of aiding his wife seemed swiftly quelled by the expression on the inspector's face.

'You had better tell him what happened,' Henry muttered.

'Mrs Winspear?' Inspector Greville had his pen poised over his notebook.

'I didn't kill William. I swear I didn't. I only wanted to talk to him. We were sitting in the garden like we said. Henry had nodded off and I saw William walking towards the grotto so I thought I would go after him.' She glanced miserably at Henry. 'I thought it would be a chance to see him alone without Lettice or Elspeth always being there.'

'Was anyone accompanying Sir William when you saw him walking towards the grotto?' Inspector Greville asked.

Padma shook her head. 'No, no one.'

'What did you want to talk to him about?' the inspector asked.

'I was angry with him. He had been so rude to me, and he wouldn't listen to my husband or give him any help at all. It seemed to amuse him, having us be dependent on him. Like some puppet master pulling our strings and making us beg for crumbs from his table. I knew that money was left for William and Henry in their mother's will and Henry had never received his share. I intended to ask him for it.'

'Padma!' Henry's voice held a note of warning.

'I wanted to tell him that I would not put up with his rudeness towards me anymore either. That he was a foolish man to treat his only brother this way.' Padma's voice trembled. 'I walked down to the grotto but when I got there...' Her voice broke, and she swallowed. 'He was already dead. Someone had stabbed him with the arrow from the archery demonstration. I panicked. I thought I would be accused of his murder, so I hurried back to Henry and hoped no one had seen me.'

'My wife told me what had happened, and I advised her to

say nothing. We thought it best.' Henry raised his chin defiantly.

'Had you arranged to meet Sir William at the grotto?' Matt asked.

Padma shook her head vehemently. 'No. I thought he was going to stay at the tennis match with Elspeth and Lettice. I was surprised to see him walking in the garden. I thought perhaps he had argued with Lettice over Ivan or had sat in the sun too long and wanted to cool off.' A tear rolled down her cheek and she sniffed. 'I didn't think I would find him dead.'

'Did you see anyone in the grotto apart from Sir William?' the inspector asked.

Padma dried her eyes with a delicate handkerchief. 'I didn't see anyone, but I had the feeling that I wasn't alone. I panicked and dropped a scrap of material that Letty had torn from her dress near Sir William's body. I had it in my handbag at the time and I thought it would throw suspicion on her instead of me. I was so panicky and frightened, I ran out of there as fast as I could. It was horrible.'

Matt wondered that he and Kitty hadn't seen Padma but there were a couple of paths that led towards the grotto, and it was entirely possible that she had taken a different route. It also explained the mystery of how the material from Lettice's frock had arrived in the grotto.

Henry rose from his seat and crossed the room to comfort his wife, placing a reassuring hand on her shoulder. 'Is there anything more, Inspector? My wife is very distressed.'

Inspector Greville cleared his throat. 'Yes, sir, I'm afraid there is. Mrs Winspear was seen on the terrace here at Palm Lodge around the time Ivan Bolsova was murdered.'

'And?' Henry exploded. 'Good grief, man, what are you implying? That because my wife was outside that she could have killed Bolsova and my brother? Poppycock.'

Padma was visibly shaking. 'I saw nothing at all that afternoon. I never even looked down the garden, I was too busy trying to avoid Letty because I didn't want another argument. Why would I murder Ivan?'

'Perhaps he saw you take the arrow from the table after the archery display?' Inspector Greville suggested.

'I didn't take the arrow. It was still on the table. If anyone might have taken it, I'd think it was Natasha. She was the one who kept stroking it, admiring the feathers. Henry, make him stop saying these things.' Padma looked at her husband.

'I think, Inspector, my wife and I have said all we wish to say on this matter. Come, Padma, my dear.' Henry helped his wife from her seat and guided her from the room with his arm around her waist.

Matt glanced at his wristwatch. It would be dinnertime shortly and he wondered if any of the other residents at the house would make an appearance. The interview with Padma and Henry had certainly been interesting. It seemed as if Padma Winspear certainly could have killed both Sir William and Ivan.

'Inspector Greville, Captain Bryant, I do apologise. I've just returned home, and the maid said you were in here. Will you join us for dinner?' Elspeth Winspear entered the room looking flustered and sounding breathless. Her mouse-brown fringe was damp and her cheeks rosy from exercise.

'Thank you for your kind offer, Miss Winspear, but I'm afraid we must decline the offer of dinner. We were just clarifying some points with your brother and sister-in-law that had arisen from our investigation. I wonder, Miss Winspear, if you could spare us a few moments too?' Inspector Greville asked.

Elspeth looked at the large ornate porcelain clock on the mantelpiece and perched herself on the edge of the sofa. 'I suppose so, Inspector. I do really need to change for dinner though. I got rather damp dashing from the motor in all this rain.'

'Of course, this will only take a moment of your time, I'm certain. Miss Winspear, On Sunday, if I recall, you said that after the archery demonstration you accompanied Sir William and Lady Lettice to the tennis match?' Inspector Greville made a great show of referring to his notebook.

'Yes, that's right.' Elspeth fidgeted on her seat.

'Then Sir William slipped away shortly before the end of the match?' the inspector asked.

Matt could see that Elspeth was discomfited by the – so far at least – innocuous questions. 'Yes, that's correct. He made some excuse about having to check on something.'

Inspector Greville flicked over a couple of pages as if reading the contents. 'And you and Lady Lettice remained together until you both went up to the terrace at the mansion for tea and were informed shortly afterwards that there was a problem.'

The colour in Elspeth's cheeks deepened. 'I think so, yes.'

'Are you quite certain that you and Lady Lettice were together the whole time?' Inspector Greville fastened his gaze on Elspeth.

'Well, I, well... perhaps not the whole time.' Elspeth's cheeks were now dark crimson and her chin wobbled.

'Lady Lettice has already admitted that she left the match shortly before Sir William in order to visit the bathroom. She claims she was gone for a short time and then rejoined you at the terrace later as the match had ended.' The inspector's tone was stern.

'Yes, well, Letty did say she needed to pay a visit. I didn't think it was important, she was only gone for a short time.' Elspeth looked at Matt as if seeking support for her omission.

'How long would you say Lady Lettice was gone before she returned to the mansion?' Inspector Greville asked.

'I don't know. Perhaps twenty minutes or so. She said there had been a queue for the toilet and then she had been diverted by a group coming up from the cricket match.' Elspeth sounded close to tears.

'Why on earth didn't you tell us this before?' the inspector asked. 'Why were you providing Lady Lettice with an alibi when you must have realised that she could have killed your brother? You must see how this appears, Miss Winspear?'

Elspeth appeared to visibly shrink under the full force of the inspector's glare. 'I was upset when William was killed. I wasn't thinking straight.' Her lips quivered. 'I felt that it was all my fault.'

Matt exchanged a glance with the inspector as Elspeth collapsed into noisy sobs.

'Why would you feel as if your brother's death was your fault?' Matt asked.

'Because, because... it was me who suggested that he go to the grotto,' Elspeth wailed.

'You? But why, Miss Winspear?' Inspector Greville's brow creased into a frown.

'I knew he was suspicious about Letty and Ivan, that they were having an affair. I knew that he had contacted his solicitor and then you arrived, Captain Bryant. Earlier, while everything was being set up for the archery demonstration, I'd overheard Letty and Ivan arranging an assignation at the grotto. At least that's what it sounded like.' Elspeth sniffed miserably and scrubbed at her eyes with her handkerchief.

'What exactly did you hear, Miss Winspear?' Matt asked.

'I heard Ivan say something like "when?" – and Letty said during the tennis match, meet at the grotto, she would get away.' Elspeth sniffed. 'I thought if William saw them together then that would make everything so much easier. So, I told him that he should go to the grotto during the match to find out the truth about Letty. As soon as Letty said she was paying a call to the powder room, he set off after her. It was me, I sent him to his death instead. Then I thought if I told you any of this you might

think that I'd made it up. That it was me who had killed him.'
She broke down into a fresh bout of sobbing.

Inspector Greville's moustache twitched as he frantically
scribbled notes in his book. 'I still don't see why you would not
have told us all of this, Miss Winspear, especially if you believe
that Lady Lettice murdered Sir William.'

'I didn't know what to do and then when I thought about it,
I wasn't sure if she could have been away long enough. Everything seemed so confused. I wondered if I had been mistaken
and it was Ivan who had murdered William but then Ivan was
killed, and I don't know anything anymore,' Elspeth finished
miserably.

The door to the drawing room opened and Lettice
appeared, dressed in a short, black, silk evening gown trimmed
with silver thread. 'Good heavens, Elspeth, whatever is the
matter?' Her eyes rounded when she saw her sister-in-law's
distressed state.

'You must excuse me, Inspector.' Elspeth seized her opportunity and bolted from the room.

'Inspector Greville, Captain Bryant, whatever is going on?
Don't tell me you have come to arrest poor old Elspeth?' Lettice
strolled over to one of the side tables and took the lid off an onyx
box to help herself to a cigarette. She inserted it into a small
black holder and looked to the two men for a light.

Matt duly obliged her as a distant growl of thunder rolled
around the room. The lamp flickered and went off, once more
casting an eerie gloom over the room.

'We may be moving closer to an arrest, but not necessarily
Miss Winspear,' Inspector Greville affirmed.

NINETEEN

Lady Lettice's immaculately painted brows lifted slightly as she arranged herself on one of the old-fashioned armchairs. 'An arrest at last. That would be wonderful. It's quite frightening, Inspector, having one's husband and a houseguest murdered. I keep wondering if I might be the next victim.' She gave an elaborate shiver.

Matt wished that Kitty was there. She wouldn't be very impressed if it transpired that Lettice was the murderer and all the action at Palm Lodge was taking place without her. As it was there would be a lot of information to share with her later.

There was another crackle and the lamp on the side table flickered back into life once more. 'Oh, thank heavens the power is back again. Let's hope it stays on this time, it's such a nuisance when it goes out.' Lettice reclined back gracefully in her seat and blew out a thin plume of smoke.

Inspector Greville's eyes narrowed. 'I'm afraid that I need to ask you some more questions, Lady Winspear.'

Lettice gave a small careless shrug. 'Of course, Inspector, although I really don't know what more I can tell you. It is almost time for dinner too.' She glanced at the elaborate clock on the mantelpiece.

'Lady Winspear, all through this investigation you have been less than frank with your responses to my questions. I would urge you to think very carefully about any of the answers you give me now,' the inspector warned.

Lettice leaned forward to knock some of the ash from the tip of her cigarette into a large onyx ashtray. Matt noticed her hand trembled although she maintained an assumed air of casual indifference. 'Heavens, that sounds alarming. I assure you, Inspector, I really do have nothing to hide.'

The inspector rose and moved closer to stand over Lady Winspear, forcing her to look up if she wished to meet his gaze. 'Then perhaps you can tell me about the conversation you had with Ivan Bolsova at the archery display, just hours before your husband was killed. The one concerning the grotto?'

Lettice took a pull at her cigarette before answering and Matt wondered if she was stalling for time to think of a response.

'I don't recall a conversation.' She fidgeted in her seat.

'Then I suggest you try, Lady Winspear, or I shall arrest you right now for the murder of your husband and Mr Bolsova.'

The ice in the inspector's voice combined with the threat drew a shocked gasp from Lettice.

'Ivan wanted to meet me away from the others. He was in love with me and wanted me to leave William. I had already told him it was impossible. While they were setting up the archery, he asked me to meet up with him one last time. I suggested the grotto during the tennis match. I thought it would be more private there. Here at the house, there is always someone listening in or lurking about.' Lettice pressed her free hand to her temple. 'Then, when William was killed, I was terrified. I thought that Ivan must have killed him so that we would be free to marry. I didn't know quite what to do or what to think. The conversation between us was private or so I thought – yet from what you say, Inspector, someone must have overheard our plans.' She looked up at the inspector. 'Obviously they could be the murderer. After all, Ivan is dead now too.'

'Letty darling, are you all right?' David had entered the room dressed ready for dinner and seeing Lettice looking distressed, immediately rushed over to reassure her.

'Oh, David, the inspector thinks that I might have murdered William and Ivan. You know that's not true.' Lettice sobbed and clung onto David Fairweather's arms. 'I'm so frightened.'

'I suggest, Inspector, that unless you have firm evidence to charge Letty with these terrible crimes, you leave the house. You can see how upset she is.' David threw out his chest as he stood protectively in front of Lettice.

The inspector's eyes narrowed. 'I have some more interviews to conduct so I shall return tomorrow. In the meantime, Lady Winspear, I suggest you avail yourself of legal advice.' The inspector collected his hat and nodded to Matt.

Matt took his cue and followed the inspector out to his car.

'I'm surprised you didn't arrest her, sir. She admitted lying about her alibi and she set up the meeting at the grotto where her husband was killed,' Matt said as they reached the car.

The rain had now ceased, and the air smelled of wet earth.

'I was tempted to, believe me. Wretched woman. But a good barrister would have her off the hook in no time. It's all circumstantial. I could make just as good a case against Mrs Padma Winspear if not better. Elspeth too.' Inspector Greville scowled at the blank frontage of Palm Lodge as he opened his car door.

'You are not afraid that one of them might abscond?' Matt asked as he slid onto the passenger seat.

'I have a man still watching the house.' The inspector gave a thin smile. 'Discreetly, of course.'

———

'It sounds as if I have missed all the excitement again,' Kitty remarked as she listened to Matt's account of the events at Palm Lodge. He had telephoned her as soon as he had arrived back at his house. She wished she could have been present to see and hear everything for herself.

'How is your grandmother faring?' Matt asked.

Kitty sighed. 'She's resting at the moment. She insists that she is perfectly all right, and that it was simply the heat that overcame her.'

'Inspector Greville intends to return to the Winspears again tomorrow. He wants to speak to Natasha Bolsova again. He mentioned that he was awaiting some information from London about the Bolsovas,' Matt said.

'I wonder what that could be? Something from the Russian embassy perhaps?' Kitty could only surmise that the inspector must have discovered something new about Ivan and Natasha that had required further investigation.

'He didn't elaborate, but we may know more in the morning.'

'Will you accompany him back to Palm Lodge?' Kitty asked. She wished she could go along to Palm Lodge with the inspector. It certainly seemed as if Lady Winspear or Padma might be the culprit. Henry and Elspeth's suspicions might prove well placed if it were to be Lettice after all – even though it seemed that David Fairweather's alibi was sound. Still, it seemed to Kitty that there were a good many holes in the case for Lettice's guilt.

'I have not yet been invited.' Matt's chuckle rumbled in her ear. 'Perhaps the inspector will wait until he has made his arrest before informing us of the outcome.'

Kitty smiled. 'You have a point. We are not so indispensable that Inspector Greville cannot manage a case without us. Something my grandmother has reminded me of on several occasions now.'

She talked to Matt for a little longer before replacing the receiver. The storm from earlier had cleared the air a little. Despite the open windows, however, her grandmother's drawing room still felt quite warm. Kitty walked over to the window and looked out. The embankment below was still deserted from where everyone had taken shelter from the storm.

The cobbles gleamed wetly in the dull evening light and the only sounds were the rushing water of the river and the stray cries of the gulls circling in the estuary. A shiver ran along Kitty's spine, and she tried to shake off the prickly feeling that she was being watched.

She moved back slightly behind the curtain and peered out to try and see what had triggered the sensation. Further along the path she thought she detected a movement, someone, a man, quickly moving out of sight into one of the side streets.

Kitty moved away from the window, rubbing at the goose-flesh that had appeared at the tops of her arms. This was ridiculous. Her imagination was playing tricks on her. She stepped back and ventured another quick peek outside. The wet street remained empty.

'Kitty darling, are you cold?' Her grandmother had come out of her bedroom and was eying her curiously.

'No, not at all, a little cool air would be most welcome. Should you be out of bed just yet?' Kitty hurried across the room to her grandmother.

'I woke up and was bored. If I lie in bed too long, then I shall not sleep tonight.' Her grandmother took her arm and permitted Kitty to steer her to the sofa.

'At least sit and rest here instead,' Kitty urged. Her grandmother still appeared pale, and she didn't want her to have another fall.

'I feel perfectly all right now, my dear. Even my headache has dissipated.' Mrs Treadwell settled back on the sofa with a sigh and allowed Kitty to help her put her legs up.

'Even so, you must be careful.' Kitty fetched a lightweight paisley shawl from her grandmother's bedroom and spread it over her legs.

'Kitty dear, do stop fussing. Now, come and sit down, I wish to speak to you.' The expression on her grandmother's face sent a shiver of apprehension through Kitty's body.

She took a seat on a nearby armchair and braced herself, wondering what it was that her grandmother wished to say.

'I have been giving a great deal of thought recently to what should happen with the management of the Dolphin on your marriage to Matthew.' Her grandmother held up her hand to silence her when Kitty went to speak. 'Now, I discussed all my thoughts with your Great-Aunt Livvy when I went to Scotland. I should like to share them with you now so that you may discuss them with Matthew and see what you think. I had not intended to spring it upon you quite so suddenly, but I can see that today's little tumble has concerned you.'

'Grams, of course I am concerned about you.' Kitty interjected.

'It seems to me that you will never be wholly content with remaining simply as a hotelier. As Matthew's wife he will quite rightly have the first call on your time and your place must be at his side. Especially if your union is blessed with children.' Her grandmother paused and smiled at Kitty. 'Naturally you will wish to reside in his house and I'm sure that you can see that it would not be practical for you to keep crossing the river at all hours of the day and night.'

Kitty swallowed. 'Are you saying that you no longer wish me to run the hotel?'

'No, not at all, darling. The Dolphin is your inheritance. I do however think that you cannot manage the hotel from a distance. Not if you are in sole charge, which is what I intend. I wish to step back and hand over the reins. This tumble today has reminded me that I am not as young as I was, something

Great-Aunt Livvy also kept telling me. I shall of course keep on this suite and continue to reside in the Dolphin.'

'Then what are you proposing?' Kitty was confused.

'If you, and of course, Matthew, are agreeable, I propose that we employ a full-time manager for the hotel. You would naturally oversee them and could arrange your hours and remit to suit. If you are willing to give up your suite of rooms here, then they could be accommodated within the hotel. I, of course, would still be on hand if needed.' Her grandmother scanned her face with anxious eyes.

Employing a manager for the Dolphin wasn't something Kitty had considered. She could see that it would make good commercial sense if they managed to get the right person for the post.

'I see, I hadn't thought about a manager. Are you certain this is something you would wish to do?' Kitty asked. She tried to imagine the Dolphin without her grandmother's firm grasp on the helm.

'I have considered all the other possibilities, darling. Matthew is not a man who would wish to take on the Dolphin. He has a restless streak in his nature as well you know. His mother may be a bit of a witterer, but even she acknowledges that he has never settled in one place for long. After the life he has led, I do not feel that he would be satisfied with running this place and it may cause problems between you if you are too tied down with responsibilities here.'

Kitty nodded slowly. She knew that her grandmother was telling the truth. The period Matt had spent in Torbay had been the longest time he had ever settled anywhere. She believed the death of his wife and child had contributed to the air of restlessness that always surrounded Matt. However, she also recognised in him a kindred spirit as the same urge to move and change also called to her.

Much as she loved the Dolphin and could never imagine it

not being in the family in some way, it also oppressed her. The weight of responsibility of being the next generation to maintain it pressed upon her.

'Your mother, had she lived, would obviously have inherited but no doubt your father would have run the place into the ground or drunk all the profits.' Her grandmother gave a scornful sniff.

'Grams!' Kitty rebuked her but smiled as she did so. There was still no love lost between her errant father and her formidable grandmother. She also had to acknowledge that there was a note of truth in her gram's assessment of Edgar Underhay.

'Discuss the idea with Matthew, and if you are agreeable then I shall start the ball rolling. It would be good, I think, to have this sorted out before your wedding at Christmas. No doubt you and Matthew will be happy to have the matter settled.' Her grandmother leaned over and gave Kitty's hand a reassuring pat.

———

Kitty spent a restless night turning over her grandmother's proposition in her mind. She wanted to be certain of how she felt about the idea of a manager before raising it with Matt. Not that she was concerned about how he would receive the news. She knew he would only want her to be happy. At least if she were no longer solely responsible for the Dolphin then she was free to move to Churston to reside with Matt at his home there.

Her grandmother seemed much improved and in cheerful spirits when they breakfasted together.

'Will you discuss my idea with Matthew today?' her grandmother asked as she finished her boiled egg.

'Yes, I intend to telephone him shortly.' Kitty applied more marmalade to her toast.

Her grandmother eyed her shrewdly. 'I know my suggestion came as a bit of a shock to you yesterday, darling, but please do not make a worry of it. I just want you and Matthew to have a happy life together without feeling the burden of the hotel.'

Kitty smiled to reassure her. 'I know, Grams, and I appreciate it. It was simply a surprise, that's all, and I was concerned about your health.'

Her grandmother returned the smile. 'Well, as you can see, I'm perfectly well, so do stop fretting.'

Kitty finished the last few crumbs of her toast. 'I will, I promise.'

She left her grandmother to finish her breakfast and headed downstairs to her small office behind the reception area. She calculated she should have just enough time to telephone Matt before Dolly arrived to start work.

Kitty had barely taken her seat behind her desk when the black Bakelite telephone in front of her rang.

'Captain Bryant for you, miss.' Mary transferred the call to her.

'I was just about to telephone you,' Kitty said as the call connected.

'I hope I'm not disturbing you at work, old thing, but there have been developments overnight with the Winspear case,' Matt explained.

Kitty was instantly on the alert, all thoughts of asking his opinion of her grandmother's plans for the Dolphin put aside. 'Oh, what has happened. I do hope no one else has been killed?'

Matt's chuckle rumbled in her ear. 'No, nothing so drastic. I thought you would like to know that Inspector Greville has arrested Natasha Bolsova.'

'Natasha!' Kitty had thought the day might bring an arrest from what Matt had told her yesterday, but Natasha had been quite low on the list of suspects compared to Padma and Lettice. 'What happened?'

'I'm not entirely certain. Henry Winspear telephoned early this morning to inform me that he and Elspeth had decided to dispense with my services as the inspector had arrested Natasha.' Matt's tone held a note of wry amusement. 'I think Henry hoped I would not send him an invoice for any work done already on the case.'

'But something must have happened surely for the inspector to act? Was it something to do with the information he was expecting from Scotland Yard?' Kitty could see that Natasha had opportunity to kill Sir William and Ivan, but why?

'Inspector Greville told me that he had set a man to discreetly observe Palm Lodge and its occupants. You said yourself that you thought you saw Natasha behaving oddly in the grounds of the house,' Matt said.

'Yes, when I thought I saw her acting furtively as Mrs Craven and I were leaving the other day, when she was thought to be in her room.' Kitty was intrigued. Natasha had certainly given the impression that she hadn't wished to be noticed that afternoon while hiding in the shrubbery.

'Well, according to Henry Winspear, the household had all retired to bed last night when there was the most frightful commotion in the early hours of the morning. The man the inspector had set to keep a watch on the house saw someone climbing out of the window of Sir William's study at the front of the house.'

'Climbing out?' Kitty interrupted.

'Climbing out. He rushed over to apprehend the person and it transpired that Miss Bolsova was attempting to leave the house along with all of Lady Winspear's jewellery,' Matt said.

'Natasha tried to steal Lettice's jewels?' Kitty was bewildered.

'Naturally, all the ensuing noise and commotion woke the household. I understand from Henry that Natasha bit the constable on his hand in her attempt to escape.' There was a distinct hint of laughter as Matt recounted this part of the tale.

Kitty blinked in astonishment. 'Then is Natasha under arrest for just the robbery or is she also accused of the murders? I assume Inspector Greville must have arrested her for the murders as well, if Henry and Elspeth feel that they are no longer in need of your services.'

'Henry said that when they checked the house it seems that a quantity of the household silver was also missing, and some of Padma's jewellery. Natasha's clothes were already gone, and her room emptied. When you saw her that afternoon it seems she had been concealing various items amongst the trees to collect later, in order to make good her escape. I can only suppose that the inspector believes that robbery was her motive for killing Sir William. There was a considerable sum in banknotes in her possession taken from the house safe.' Matt's tone was more sober as he told Kitty the last part of the tale. 'Those have been returned.'

'But why would she kill Ivan? He was her brother. Did he know of the planned robbery, do we think? Or did he find out his sister's plans and threaten to tell Lettice? Has she done this before and Sir William found out? Is that her motive for killing him?' Kitty's mind whirred as she tried to fit the pieces together.

'I don't know. Perhaps the inspector might tell us soon. I wonder if she has confessed?' Matt mused.

Kitty thought that was highly unlikely. 'I can't see Natasha willingly placing her neck on the block, can you? Theft is one thing, but murder is a beast of a different order.'

'I agree. Listen, I'll let you get back to work, darling. Are you free for an hour at lunchtime?' Matt asked.

As she eyed the large pile of invoices in the wire tray on her desk waiting for her attention, Kitty decided she would definitely be ready for a spot of lunch with Matt by the time she had worked her way through all of them.

'Lunch together sounds lovely. I have something I wish to discuss with you too.' Kitty was keen to hear his thoughts on her grandmother's unexpected proposition.

'That sounds ominous.' His chuckle tickled her ear, calling a smile to her lips.

'I'll tell you everything at lunch.' She finished the call and sat for a minute contemplating her work with an unseeing eye. Her mind was still digesting everything Matt had just told her about the case.

'Good morning, Miss Kitty. How's your grandmother today?' Dolly's cheerful face appeared at the office door, ready to start work.

'She is much better, thank you,' Kitty assured her.

With Dolly installed on the wooden office chair beside her, taking notes and filing, Kitty began her work. The morning passed quite quickly, and Kitty had little time to allow her concentration to wander back to the curious events at Palm Lodge.

TWENTY

By the time Matt rapped on Kitty's office door to escort her out to lunch she and Dolly had worked solidly through the morning. They had even taken their morning tea break at the desk while they worked.

The mildly cooling effects of yesterday's storm had completely worn off and it had grown quite warm inside the tiny office.

'Dolly, I'm going out to lunch with Captain Bryant. Make sure you take your full hour and leave the office door ajar to allow some air to circulate in here. I'll ask Mary to keep an eye on things while we are gone,' Kitty instructed as her young workmate stretched in her seat to ease her back.

'Very good, miss.' Dolly beamed happily at her as Kitty collected her straw hat and joined Matt in the lobby.

'I thought we would walk down towards the park and take some lunch at the tea room near the river. There seems to be a little more breeze nearer the water,' Matt said as Kitty rested her hand lightly on the crook of his elbow.

'That sounds lovely. It's so hot and stuffy in my office, it's no wonder that Grams fainted yesterday,' Kitty agreed as they stepped outside onto the bustling embankment. The sun glinted on the river and the waterway was busy with pleasure craft.

They made their way through the crowds of holidaymakers towards the small green recreation area and iron bandstand near the boat float. The tea room was busy, and they had to wait for a few minutes while a table was found and cleared ready for them.

'Gosh, it's still so horribly sticky today,' Kitty said as she took her place opposite Matt. All the other tables were full, and the young waitress looked hot and harassed as she darted about carrying laden trays of tea and sandwiches.

'The storm didn't do much to cool things down,' Matt said as he opened his menu. They gave the girl their order for a pot of tea and crab sandwiches then settled down in their seats.

'I telephoned Inspector Greville just after I called you,' Matt said, glancing around the tea room.

'Oh really? What did he have to say? Has Natasha been charged with the murders?' Kitty asked. She was curious to know if the inspector had any evidence to prove the girl had killed her brother and Sir William. She also wanted to know what the motive was if Natasha were the guilty party.

'Not as yet, but I gathered that it would merely be a matter of time. I think the inspector is under some pressure to resolve the case quickly. Henry has probably carried out his promise to involve the chief constable.' Matt paused while the waitress set their order down in front of them.

Kitty lifted the lid of the silver metal teapot and stirred the contents. 'What else did he say?'

Matt set the tea strainer over the top of one of the white china cups. 'Inspector Greville said that he had received information from London and Paris that potentially linked Natasha and her brother to several notable jewel thefts. Apparently, all of the robberies occurred shortly after the Bolsovas had performed at the houses concerned or after they had stayed with the families.'

Kitty poured the tea through the strainer and then transferred the strainer to the next cup. 'It sounds as if Ivan was involved in those thefts, then, as well as Natasha?'

'It would seem so.' Matt added milk to their tea once Kitty had set the strainer aside.

Kitty frowned. 'Why then would Natasha murder her brother? I can see that if Sir William had found out their secret and threatened to expose them, then either Natasha or Ivan could have murdered him to prevent exposure. That seems so unlikely though.' She paused to stir her tea. 'But what motive would she have to then kill Ivan?'

Matt shrugged. 'Perhaps he was tired of the game and wanted to stop and marry Lettice. He may have wanted his share of the proceeds. Natasha would have been without a partner then and would have lost a fair amount of money.'

Kitty nibbled at her sandwich and considered Matt's suggestion. She supposed he could have a point, but she thought there had been real affection between Natasha and Ivan. The girl had certainly appeared genuinely distressed after his death.

'Anyway, enough of the case for now. What did you wish to discuss?' Matt asked as he sipped his tea. 'You sounded very serious this morning when I called.'

Kitty explained her grandmother's proposition. 'She suggested we discuss the matter to see what you thought of the idea.'

Matt's eyebrows lifted slightly. 'What really matters is how you feel about it all, old thing. Obviously it would be wonderful if you were based full-time with me at the Churston house, but I know what the Dolphin means to you and your family. Would you be content with such an arrangement?'

Kitty sighed. 'You know how much I would love to live with

you at Churston. In many ways I'm delighted that Grams's idea seems to be a solution.'

'I sense a but coming.' Matt smiled at her.

'I suppose that I do feel rather guilty. Grams has devoted her life to the Dolphin, to building it up as a business, and I suppose I feel as if I'm being terribly ungrateful that I don't have the same desire to run it full-time in the same way that she has.' She gazed at Matt, hoping he would understand what she meant.

'Darling, you know that I only want what will make you happy. Your grandmother feels the same way.' He took her free hand in his and gently squeezed her fingers. Her emerald and diamond engagement ring sparkled in the sunlight. 'In many ways, your grandmother had little choice in devoting herself to the Dolphin. She was widowed when your mother was young and then she had you to bring up. Hiring a manager with you to oversee them sounds like a sensible solution to me.'

'Thank you.' She returned the pressure on his hand. 'I know I'm being silly really. I have no desire to tie myself to the Dolphin even though it is my home. I suppose the changes that our marriage would bring just suddenly struck me. Grams deserves to enjoy herself a little after all the hard work she has put in over the years. It will seem very strange however having her step back completely.'

Matt grinned and raised his teacup. 'Do you think she will step back?'

Kitty laughed and picked up her own cup. 'I suspect she may find it more difficult than she thinks to let go.'

He chinked his cup against hers. 'To positive changes at the Dolphin and happy times ahead for us.'

'To us.' Kitty returned his toast and sipped her tea. 'Does that mean that when the new manager is in post that I can come on more cases with you?' she asked.

Matt grinned at her, the dimple flashing in his cheek. 'I suspect that I would have difficulty in stopping you.'

Kitty smiled back demurely. 'Absolutely.'

They finished their lunch and set off back along the embankment towards the hotel. Kitty's mind was more at ease now that Matt had approved her grandmother's plan. It was quite exciting to have settled what had been her biggest concern. She could devote herself more fully now to choosing a wedding dress and deciding whether to take up her aunt's offer of the family tiara to secure her veil.

'I had better reclaim my motorcycle and return home or Bertie will have created havoc in my absence,' Matt said as they arrived at the front door of the hotel.

'At least you only had to make one journey here by bus. Do let me know if you hear any more about the case,' Kitty said as she prepared to return inside to her work.

'I will, I promise.' He kissed her cheek, and she entered the cooler air inside the wood-panelled lobby of the hotel.

Dolly had also just arrived in the lobby from the direction of the kitchens and Kitty guessed she had probably taken her lunch break with Alice. Mary looked unusually flustered as they approached the desk ready to return to work in the small office behind the front desk.

'Is everything all right, Mary?' Kitty asked. The girl was usually quite unflappable. 'Is Grams all right?'

'Oh yes, Miss Kitty. I'm sorry. It's been quite busy the last ten minutes or so. The telephone was ringing and then there was a problem with one of the guests in room nine.' Marry apologised. 'And to top it all, miss, just afore you comes back, there was a right to-do outside the hotel. A little lad fell in the river. They fetched him out all right, thank goodness. His mother said he'd over-balanced feeding the ducks.'

While Kitty was listening to Mary, Dolly opened the door to the office a little wider, ready for them to resume the day's work. Her startled shriek sent Kitty hurrying to the office door with Mary hot on her heels.

'Don't you get going in there, Miss Kitty,' Dolly cautioned fiercely as she barred the door preventing her from entering. 'Mary, call to the kitchen and ask Mickey to come. He was just finishing up his lunch as I come away.'

'Dolly, whatever is the matter?' Kitty asked as Mary hastened to the telephone to contact the kitchen and ask for the hotel's maintenance and security man.

Dolly's face was paper-white apart from a rosy spot of high colour on each cheek. The girl trembled as she placed herself firmly in Kitty's way. ''Tis horrid, miss. A nasty sort of practical joke as somebody as done.'

'Dolly!' Kitty managed to push past her assistant as Mickey arrived, slightly out of breath from his race along the corridor.

Kitty's eyes widened in shock when she saw her desk. When they had left for lunch, they had stacked a pile of envelopes ready for the post on one side of the desk. The tray with the remaining bookings and invoices was placed sorted and ready to be dealt with on their return on the other side.

Now the wire tray contained something else: the decapitated and decaying remains of a large grey river rat. The severed head lolled to one side, regarding her with black cloudy unseeing eyes. Kitty's stomach rolled and her recently consumed lunch threatened to make a reappearance.

She stepped back out of the office into the slightly cooler air of the lobby. Mary hurried forward to offer her a chair.

'I told you not to go in,' Dolly remarked, a note of reproof in her voice. 'I knows as how you don't like rats.'

Kitty pretended to ignore the muttered choice curses that escaped from Mickey as he surveyed the grisly scene.

'Hold there, Miss Kitty, Miss Dolly, I'll fetch a sack.' He strode away, a grim set to his lips.

Kitty sucked in a breath. The sight had momentarily given her quite a turn.

Mary too looked pale. 'What a nasty thing. I swear Miss Kitty, I weren't gone from the desk for more'n a couple of minutes sorting out those guests and seeing if they had fetched that little lad safe out the water.' The girl's lips quivered.

'It's quite all right, Mary. This is not your fault. I believe someone has been waiting for just such a moment to play a dirty trick like this.' Kitty hastened to reassure her receptionist as Mickey returned wearing thick leather gloves and carrying a brown hessian sack.

'I'll have it gone in a minute, Miss Kitty. Let's hope as it hasn't done no damage to your papers,' Mickey said as he stepped inside the office.

A shudder ran through Kitty. She didn't really fancy having to check the pile of paperwork for damage after a decayed rat had been resting on them.

A minute later, Mickey emerged from her office. The hessian sack now bulged ominously. ''Tis done, miss Kitty. There isn't too much damage, I don't reckon. There was a card left with the creature. I think as you ought to let the inspector know about it.' Mickey inclined his head towards her desk.

Kitty swallowed hard, rose from her seat and followed Dolly back inside her office with Mary following behind her. Much to her relief there was little evidence that the rat had ever been there beyond a faint lingering smell and a few tiny unsavoury looking smears on the topmost invoice.

She saw immediately what Mickey had meant. She was surprised she hadn't noticed it when she had first entered the room, but then, she had been somewhat distracted by the large, dead rodent in the centre of her desk.

A white rectangular card, edged with black in the style of a mourning card, was tucked slightly under the heavy brass base of her green shaded desk lamp.

'What's that, miss?' Dolly bent to peer at it.

'I rather suspect it may be a message from Esther Hammett.' Kitty voiced the thought that had been haunting her ever since she had first started to sense that she was being observed.

Kitty picked up her paperknife and teased the card from under the lamp, taking care not to handle it. She wasn't certain if it was contaminated in some way or if the inspector might be able to extract further clues from it. She had read some cases recently in the newspapers, and it seemed that more and more these days fingerprint evidence was being used to secure a conviction.

'What does it say?' Dolly, like Kitty, had noticed the black printed message.

'"Lest you forget. An eye for an eye... EH,"' Kitty read out loud.

A startled gasp from Mary reminded Kitty that the other girl had followed them inside the room.

'I don't want any word of this to reach my grandmother. Mary, make sure that Mickey knows that he too is not to say anything,' Kitty said. 'I don't want her upset.'

The girl nodded mutely, her eyes wide and dark in her pale face.

'Dolly, please can you place a telephone call to Inspector Greville at Torquay Police Station.' Kitty hoped the inspector would not be too busy with Natasha Bolsova's arrest to take her call.

She slipped the offending card into an empty envelope and set it aside. She would make certain that the police received it. Dolly was busy on the telephone, eventually handing the receiver across to Kitty when she had been connected with the police station.

Kitty found herself speaking to the desk sergeant who informed her that the inspector was out at present. Kitty gave the sergeant the details of what had happened, and the man promised to alert the inspector on his return.

After completing her call, Kitty turned her attention back to her receptionist. 'Mary, did you see anyone approach the office or enter or leave the hotel?'

The colour had returned to the girl's cheeks, and she shook her head, frowning as if attempting to recall anything out of the ordinary.

'There weren't nothing when I went to room nine. The gentleman there had been trying to open the window and had jammed the sash.' The frown lines on Mary's brow deepened. 'I weren't there very long. A bit of brute force soon shifted it and I asked Mickey to take a look when he had a minute in case as the runners needed a spot of grease. They probably dried out in the heat.'

'And you didn't notice anything out of the ordinary on your return? The door was still only slightly ajar? No one was leaving the lobby or loitering near the booklets on the stand at the far end?' Kitty asked.

'No, miss,' Mary said.

'What happened when the boy fell in the river?' Dolly asked.

'Well, I were at the desk, and I heard a shout go up. It were right outside the hotel so naturally I goes to the window to see what was happening.' The colour deepened in Mary's cheeks.

'Of course,' Kitty reassured the girl. 'And then what happened?'

Mary bit her lip. 'There was a commotion and a lady screaming as her little boy couldn't swim and some of the gentlemen was going into the water to fetch the child out so I grabs some of the old towels as we keep under the desk to take them outside. You know, miss, in case as they needed something to dry themselves off or to wrap the kiddy in.'

'That was very quick thinking, Mary, well done.' Kitty saw the girl's shoulders relax a little at her praise.

'They got the little boy out and give him back to his mother and then everybody sort of drifted away and I come back in here to the desk and the telephone was already ringing with the greengrocer wanting to check something with the kitchen,' Mary said.

'Did you notice anything then on your return?' Dolly asked, her eyes bright with enquiry.

Mary looked perplexed. 'Nothing definite. Somebody did brush past me as I were coming back into the lobby, and I did think at the time as I hoped he hadn't come from inside the hotel.'

'It was not one of our guests then?' Kitty asked.

Mary shook her head. 'No, miss. This was a tall thin bloke. I hadn't noticed him before. He wasn't from the town, I was sure. He were a bit scruffy-looking, not like one of the holiday people.'

Despite further questioning from Kitty and Dolly, Mary could remember little else about the man who had brushed past her near the entrance.

Mary turned in the doorway to return to her desk. 'There was one other thing though miss.'

'Yes, Mary?' Kitty asked as she took her seat.

'The little boy what fell in the river. His mother said as he must have over-balanced while he were giving the ducks some crusts but the child told one of the gentlemen who fetched him out as he had been pushed into the water.'

Dolly exchanged a meaningful glance with Kitty.

'That is odd. Thank you, Mary.' Kitty dismissed the girl back to her duties and picked up her pen ready to finish her day's work.

'If the boy were shoved in the water, then it would have given whoever wanted to put that thing in this tray the perfect opportunity,' Dolly observed as she gave the soiled topmost sheet of paper a disgusted look.

Kitty opened her ledger ready to enter the account and check the bill against her records. 'I agree.'

'You said as you thought that card were from Esther Hammett even before you clapped eyes on it properly. Is there something else going on, Miss Kitty?' Dolly asked in a low voice.

Kitty sighed. Dolly was even sharper than her sister, Alice. 'A couple of times just lately I have had the feeling that someone has been watching me,' Kitty confessed.

Dolly's eyes widened. 'Have you seen anyone, miss?' she asked.

'I thought I saw someone last night, but it was so quick I couldn't be certain.' It felt strange to finally be voicing her concern aloud. She hadn't even mentioned it to Matt for fear he would consider her fanciful or even worse insist on wrapping her up in cotton wool just to be on the safe side.

Dolly tapped the end of her pencil thoughtfully on the desk. 'It would fit in with that woman. Sneaky and devious, always up to no good.'

Dolly had worked at Elm House, a nursing home in Torquay, when she had first left school. It had been owned by Esther Hammett under another name. This had been when Kitty had first crossed swords with her.

The home had been a centre for smuggling and distributing cocaine and opium, and several residents and one of the nurses had subsequently died. Kitty herself had barely escaped with her own life after Esther had instructed one of her henchmen to cut the brakes on Kitty's car.

'The funeral for Esther's brother was only a few weeks ago in Exeter. Inspector Pinch informed us that it had taken place,' Kitty said.

'I suppose as she would have been back in town for that.' Dolly's gaze met Kitty's.

'We were led to believe that she had returned to London afterwards. I do wish that the police would arrest her and charge her with something. I can't believe the number of times she has wriggled her way out of jail,' Kitty said.

'She's as slippery as an eel that one. Have you told Captain Bryant any of this?' Dolly asked.

Kitty blushed guiltily. 'No, not yet. I thought I had been imagining things. Ever since Ezekiel drowned and Esther sent that awful bouquet of flowers to me, I've been a little on edge.'

After the fateful jail break when Ezekiel had kidnapped Kitty and had subsequently drowned in his attempt to escape, Esther had blamed Kitty for her brother's death. She had sent Kitty a bouquet of red roses tipped with black and a warning note when Ezekiel had been pulled lifeless from the river.

'T'would be best to let him know,' Dolly advised.

'I will. I don't expect he will be home yet. Let's get the last of these invoices and bookings dealt with and I'll telephone him,' Kitty promised.

TWENTY-ONE

They finished their work shortly before five o'clock with no word from the inspector. Kitty telephoned Matt while Dolly gathered up the letters, ready to take them to the post in time for the evening collection.

'There's no reply. Matt must be out, probably walking Bertie or seeing a client.' Kitty replaced the receiver on its stand.

'What are you going to do, miss?' Dolly asked.

'I think I shall drive into Torquay and drop this card into the police station.' Kitty looked at the envelope containing the warning message. She wanted to remove it from the hotel in case her grandmother should come across it.

If she was being honest with herself, she also wanted to try and find out what was happening with the Winspear case. Had Natasha had the murders added to her robbery charge?

Dolly frowned at her as she placed her straw hat on top of her auburn curls. 'I don't think as you should go alone, Miss Kitty. Not after that nasty thing was left on your desk. What if they's watching you?'

Kitty rose from her seat and collected her own hat from the small stand in the corner of the office. 'I'm sure it will be fine,

Dolly. That thing was probably just left to shock me. An unpleasant reminder that Esther hasn't gone away.'

The girl picked up the envelopes for the post. 'Well, I'm not so certain, miss. Let me come with you to the police station. We can takes these to the post on the way and at least you'll have a bit of company. I swear as I shan't rest easy otherwise.'

Kitty could see from the mutinous set of Dolly's lips that the girl was determined to accompany her.

'We may be there for a while,' she warned as she slipped the warning message inside her handbag.

'That don't matter. A nice bit of fresh air would do me good after being in here all afternoon.' Dolly grinned impishly at her employer.

Kitty resigned herself to the inevitable and the girls set off together towards the shed where Kitty garaged her car. She had to admit that it did feel reassuring to have Dolly with her as she kept a sharp lookout for anyone who might be lurking around as she unlocked the shed.

They drove to the ferry, stopping on the way for Dolly to post their letters. A few minutes later they were across the river and climbing the steep hill out of Kingswear. The heat from earlier had died down a little and a gentle breeze stirred the air as they drove along the lanes.

Kitty tried to see if Matt's motorcycle was parked on his driveway as they crossed the common near to his house. However, she was forced to keep her attention on the road as the fine weather and time of day meant that there was more traffic than usual. It seemed a little strange to think that after Christmas it would be her house too.

Dolly held on to her hat as they zipped along the coast road and on through Paignton towards the police station in Torquay.

'I'll wait here for you, miss. To keep an eye on the motor car,' Dolly said as Kitty pulled to a stop near the stone steps of the police station.

'Thank you, Dolly. I don't know how long I shall be, I'm afraid. It all depends on if the inspector is there,' Kitty warned as she climbed out of the driver's seat and collected her handbag from her friend.

'That's all right, miss. I shall be perfectly comfortable here, don't you fret. I've a book in my handbag,' Dolly assured her as she settled in her seat.

The desk sergeant she had spoken to earlier was at his post in the small reception area. Kitty was quite familiar now with the row of bentwood chairs lined up beneath the noticeboard covered in posters and the faint smell of disinfectant and stale bodies that tinged the air.

'Good evening, Miss Underhay. Inspector Greville has only just returned to the station. I'll put a call through to his office and tell him you're here.' The sergeant lifted the receiver suiting his actions to his words while Kitty waited patiently to see if he would let her through to the offices.

The sergeant replaced the receiver and lifted the hinged part of the desk before escorting her through the door behind the desk and along the corridor to Inspector Greville's office.

The inspector rose from his seat as she entered and dismissed his sergeant back to his post.

'Good evening, Miss Underhay. My sergeant told me that you received a rather unpleasant surprise this afternoon.'

Kitty took a seat opposite the inspector's untidy desk and opened her handbag to retrieve the message. 'This was left with the dead rat. It's signed EH, the same as the bouquet of flowers I received a few weeks ago. I can only assume it must be Esther Hammett letting me know that she is still out there.' Kitty handed the envelope across to the inspector.

He opened it carefully and peered inside to read the message. 'Most unpleasant. I shall have it tested but I doubt we shall find anything to link it to Esther. She is rather too sharp for that, I'm afraid.'

'Thank you, anyway.' Kitty didn't expect that Esther would have been so careless as to leave her fingerprints on the card.

'You don't know who may have been responsible for placing this and the rat on your desk?' inspector asked.

Kitty shook her head and told him about Mary's suspicions regarding the man who had brushed against her.

'Hmm, not much to go on. There have been no sightings reported of Esther Hammett locally. My last intelligence was that she had returned to London immediately after her brother's funeral. I shall of course try to verify that,' the inspector assured her.

'Thank you, I must admit it has unnerved me a little thinking that she might be back in the area.' Kitty shivered despite the warmth inside the office.

'I can imagine. Rest assured, Miss Underhay, if I hear anything I shall let you know,' Inspector Greville said.

'By the by, Matt told me that you had arrested Natasha Bolsova?' Kitty asked.

The inspector's moustache twitched. 'Yes, my constable caught her red-handed climbing out of the late Sir William's study window with Lady Lettice's jewellery.'

'I'm surprised she didn't leave via the front or back door?' Kitty remarked. She had been puzzling over why the Russian girl had needed to leave through a window.

The inspector's lips curved upwards. 'No doubt that would have been her plan but since the murders, Lady Lettice and Miss Elspeth Winspear have been quite nervy. The house-keeper had locked everything up good and tight and had charge of the keys. All the doors to the house were deadlocked.'

'Unfortunate for Natasha, but lucky for Lady Lettice,' Kitty observed.

'Indeed. Miss Bolsova had secreted a good deal of the fami-ly's small silver items and some of Mrs Padma Winfrey's jewellery in the grounds. She had packed her bags and they were stowed in the late Sir William's motor car. No doubt she intended to retrieve the goods and get away in his motor.' Inspector Greville leaned back in his chair, making the spring creak at the sudden shift in his position.

'It was a good thing that you had the foresight to leave a man on watch,' Kitty said. 'Do you think she is also guilty of the murder of Sir William and her brother?'

The inspector steepled his hands together and eyed her intently. 'I could make a case against most of the Winspears. My problem is that I have nothing definite to tie any of them directly to either Ivan Bolsova's murder or that of Sir William. I had thought Lady Winspear might be in the frame, but it seems an acquaintance saw her near the mansion at the time Sir William was killed. So Lady Lettice has an alibi once again. Natasha Bolsova, beyond denying that she is guilty of killing either of them, is refusing to say anything further at all.'

'I see. Matt said that Henry Winspear had telephoned him and said that since Natasha had been arrested, they had no further need of his services. I presumed from that that the Winspears thought the murder cases were solved.'

The inspector raised a brow. 'Interesting. I have just come from Palm Lodge. The Winspears have wasted little time in making their plans to leave Paignton for London.'

Kitty was surprised. 'Are they free to leave, Inspector? You do intend to charge Natasha, then?'

Inspector Greville shifted in his chair. 'I don't think I have much choice in the matter at the moment. She is certainly guilty of attempting to rob Lady Lettice and my superiors will have a view on the matter.'

Kitty frowned. 'I can see that she and Ivan would have been well placed to steal valuables as they travelled. I can also see that with Ivan's death she would have lost her dance partner and the means of securing a livelihood so she could have decided to risk all on one last heist. But I think that if Sir

William had thought that she and Ivan were dishonest then he would have had absolutely no compunction about throwing them out. He would also have gone to the police.'

'If he had proof,' Inspector Greville reminded her. 'This could have been the matter that he wished to discuss with Captain Bryant. That may have been what sealed his fate. Then if her brother had decided to propose to Lady Lettice, she may have decided it best to get rid of him too.'

Kitty could see that the inspector had a point. However, Elspeth, Lettice, Padma and Henry also had motives and opportunity.

'What are the Winspears' plans?' she asked.

'Henry and Padma Winspear are intending to travel to London. Henry has hopes of interesting some backers for his latest business venture. Lady Lettice and her friend Mr Fairweather also have meetings planned, something to do with an agent for the film industry. I believe they intend to fly to Paris for a couple of days. Miss Elspeth Winspear has arranged to stay with a friend locally. She said she doesn't wish to remain at Palm Lodge alone,' the inspector explained with a sigh.

'Gracious, they certainly haven't lost any time, have they?' Kitty blinked. Were the family all so convinced of Natasha's guilt or simply anxious to escape from the area? 'I wonder, Inspector, if I might see Natasha? Perhaps she may speak to me?' she suggested.

The inspector surveyed her for a moment, clearly turning her suggestion over in his mind.

'Very well. I can't see that it will do any harm. So far she has refused to say anything beyond denying any involvement in the murders. She has not even asked for any legal representation.' Inspector Greville rose, and Kitty followed his lead as he opened the door to his office.

They walked along the corridor and down the concrete steps that led to the cells at the rear of the police station. Kitty had visited them a couple of times before the previous year when Matt had been arrested on suspicion of murder. The memory chilled her as she waited for the inspector to unlock Natasha's cell door with a large black iron key.

The Russian girl was seated on the end of the narrow bunk, her knees drawn under her chin and a cigarette smouldering in the thin carved holder between her fingers.

'A visitor for you, Miss Bolsova.' The inspector stood aside to allow Kitty to enter.

Natasha frowned. 'Miss Underhay, I am surprised. What brings you here?'

Inspector Greville had withdrawn to stand just outside the cell. Kitty was in no doubt that he would be listening to every word.

'Henry Winspear told Matt that you had been arrested.'

Natasha gave a careless shrug and blew out a thin stream of pale blue smoke into the air. 'Bah, the Winspears.' Her tone was scathing.

'Inspector Greville's officers have recovered several of the Winspears' possessions from a hiding place amongst the trees near the edge of the drive. I saw you there the other day when I visited with Mrs Craven,' Kitty said.

Natasha unfurled herself, swinging her long, elegant legs down over the side of the bunk. 'So, why are you here, Miss Underhay? To get a frisson of glee from confronting a notorious criminal in her cell?' Natasha's voice dripped scorn. 'Something to run back and entertain your friends with over dinner?'

Kitty could feel heat creeping into her cheeks under the weight of Natasha's sharp gaze, but she stood her ground.

'No, nothing like that at all. I came to see if you really had murdered Sir William and your brother,' Kitty replied in a level tone.

The girl extinguished the remains of her cigarette in the

overflowing battered metal ashtray, which stood on a narrow shelf near the end of her bed.

Natasha rose from her seat to stand over Kitty. Her dark eyes flashed as she clicked her fingers in Kitty's face. 'You think I care that much about Sir William? No, I admit I do not like him, but kill him, no. I had no reason to harm the man. And I loved my brother, Miss Underhay. Ivan was all I had in the world. He was everything to me.' The girl took a few steps away and turned her back to Kitty.

A tremor ran through Natasha's body and Kitty could see she was trying to regain control over her emotions.

'You realise that the inspector has enough evidence to charge you with both murders?' Kitty waited for the girl to respond.

Natasha turned and sank down gracefully onto the edge of the bunk. 'I dare say that it would suit the Winspears very much if that were so. All of their problems disposed of so neatly with no inconvenience to them. To pin the deaths on a thieving foreigner. Pssh.' She pressed her lips together.

'If you didn't kill Sir William or Ivan, then who did?' Kitty asked. She had decided to take the bull by the horns. It seemed to her that Natasha might be the key to the whole puzzle. She had been privy to Ivan's relationship with Lettice and had the advantage of viewing the Winspears as an outsider.

'I do not know. If I knew for certain then don't you think I would have told the police? Do you think I like to sit here knowing I may have a noose around my neck because I took a few of Letty's baubles?' Natasha's eyes flashed once more.

'But you must have some suspicions? If you know or suspect anything about anyone in that house, then now is the time to speak up. They are getting ready to leave,' Kitty tried again.

Natasha's gaze met hers. 'The day Sir William was murdered I was with Ivan and we did as we said: We walked up onto the golf course. It was hot and we sat in the shade of a tree.

Then Ivan made some excuse about having to return for something. I thought it was an excuse to go and meet Letty. I had overheard them earlier talking about the grotto. For a while longer, I sat but then I was worried. I knew Sir William suspected something between them.' Natasha paused and looked past Kitty as if trying to recall the events of that fateful afternoon.

'What happened then?' Kitty asked.

'I decided to go and find Ivan. Time was getting on and we had to return to the terrace in time for tea. Elspeth and Sir William were very strict about timekeeping.' Natasha swallowed. 'I walked in the direction of the grotto looking out for my brother.'

'Did you see anyone else?' Kitty asked.

'I saw Elspeth, I think near the terrace, and then later I think maybe I saw Padma. Ivan met me on the path before I reached the grotto. He was out of breath and seemed, I do not know, how to explain...' She paused for a moment, clearly searching for the words to describe the scene to Kitty. 'He was excited somehow, but it was odd. He was trembling. I wondered if perhaps there had been a near miss and perhaps Sir William had almost caught them together.'

'And after you learned that Sir William was dead... what did you think?' Kitty asked.

A look of fear crossed Natasha's face. 'I did not know what to think. Had Ivan seen the murderer? Did he know who it was? I even wondered if it could have been him. Ivan could see that I was afraid. He said we must stick to our story that we were together.'

Kitty nodded her head slowly. 'Did you ask him about that afternoon?'

Natasha bit her lip. 'I tried but he would not talk. He was infatuated with Letty. If she asked him for the moon, he would have given it to her along with the stars. I do not know if he was protecting her from something or if there was something else. The day he was killed he was very happy about something. All morning I could tell he had this sense of excitement. He told me that everything was going to be wonderful. Our troubles were over.' Natasha shrugged. 'Perhaps he thought with Sir William dead, his dreams would come true.'

'How did you feel about his relationship with Lady Lettice?' Kitty was curious to know Natasha's feelings about her brother's affair with their patron.

The Russian girl's lips curved upwards in a mirthless smile. 'Ivan often made love with the wives of our patrons. Rich older ladies with time on their hands and ugly, old, boring husbands. At first this was no different except that Lettice was young and pretty.'

'But then something changed?' Kitty asked.

Natasha nodded. 'He became besotted by her. It was poor Letty, trapped in her marriage with that old, unpleasant man. I told him no good would come of it. Sir William had started to become suspicious. I think Elspeth and then Henry were telling him things. I asked him to stop the affair and he said that I should not worry.'

Kitty paced backwards and forward besides Natasha as she tried to process everything the dancer was telling her. 'And how did you feel about Lettice? Do you think she was in love with your brother?'

The girl gave a scornful laugh. 'The only person Letty loves is Letty. At first I think she did a good job pretending she was fond of Ivan but I don't know. Then when that other man came to the house within hours of Ivan being dead.' Natasha shook her head, her expression sombre. 'I knew then it had been a pretence. Ivan was just one of the toys she used to amuse herself with. I began to be afraid.'

'Do you think Lettice had a hand in her husband's death, your brother's?' Kitty asked. She could see how Lettice would have had a motive for murdering Sir William, but then what of the rest of the family? They too had motives and opportunity. Had Ivan seen something that day that he intended to use to his advantage?

'I do not know. If I had thought she had done it then I would not have stolen her diamonds. I would have killed her and stuffed them down her throat.' Natasha's voice cracked with anger. 'They have so many secrets, that family. Elspeth with her fancy man. I see her sneak out to take him gifts. She even knit socks for him; Sir William, he teases her about it. She could have killed him and then murdered poor Ivan if he had seen her. Then Henry and Padma. So busy claiming they are poor, always looking for money. Henry probably thinks he can manipulate Letty into giving him money to make him go away or to hand over Sir William's companies. I know that is what he wishes. I heard him say so to Padma when they thought no one was near them. Padma, she sneaks about the house, always so secretive.' Natasha came to a halt and took out another cigarette, her fingers fumbling as she inserted it into her holder.

'Thank you,' Kitty said as Natasha took a pull on her cigarette.

The Russian girl settled back more comfortably on her bed and fixed her dark stare on Kitty. 'You can believe what I have said or not, Miss Underhay. I may have stolen the jewels but I did not kill anyone.'

TWENTY-TWO

Kitty fell into step beside Inspector Greville as they made their way back along the corridor and up the steps towards the inspector's office.

'I take it that you heard all of that, Inspector?' Kitty asked.

The policeman nodded and waved his hand for her to retake her seat opposite his desk.

'Yes, I did. You certainly got more out of Miss Bolsova than I have been able to obtain.'

'She is adamant that she did not kill Sir William or her brother. If we are to believe her then that leaves Letty, Henry, Padma or Elspeth.' Kitty's mind raced as she considered all the possibilities.

'Well, she certainly cleaned out Lady Lettice's jewel box. The bag she had with her contained everything from diamond earrings to expensive costume jewellery.' The inspector indicated a black-and-white photograph, which lay on top of the paperwork on his desk.

Kitty picked it up and studied it with interest. The inspector was correct, there was quite a quantity of jewellery all neatly laid out and labelled for evidence. Her attention was caught by a small plain item. There was something Matt had said after he had spoken to Miss Loveday.

'This one is of Mrs Winspear's jewellery.' Inspector Greville passed her another photograph. 'We have returned the bank notes and silver to Lady Lettice.' He indicated another photograph.

Kitty recognised many of the fine gold bangles that Padma liked to wear, along with several elaborate rings in the picture.

'It's no wonder Natasha tried to get away with all of these.' Kitty passed the photographs back to the inspector. She could understand the temptation given the desperate state Natasha must be in following Ivan's death.

Kitty suddenly caught sight of the time on her wristwatch. 'Thank you for allowing me to see Natasha, Inspector. I really must get going back to Dartmouth. Dolly is waiting outside for me in my car.'

The inspector stood to see her out of the office. 'I'll see what I can discover about Esther Hammett's whereabouts. If there are any more concerns, please let me know.'

'Thank you, Inspector.'

The sergeant lifted the hinged portion of the counter to allow her through into the waiting area.

'I expect if no new information comes to light then I shall charge Miss Bolsova tomorrow.' Inspector Greville halted at the door to the corridor.

Kitty nodded. 'It's very difficult, sir, isn't it?' She could see that the inspector would have little choice in the matter despite Natasha's denials. No doubt his superiors would insist once they learned about the theft of the jewellery.

She hurried down the steps of the police station to where Dolly was patiently reading her book as she waited for her.

'I'm so sorry, Dolly. That took rather longer than I anticipated.' She jumped into her car and started the engine.

Dolly carefully stowed her book away and listened intently as Kitty told her of the conversation with Natasha.

'I don't know, miss. I agree it doesn't sound as if Miss Bolsova would murder her brother,' Dolly said.

'I know. There was something very definite about the way she spoke.' Kitty kept going back over everything they had learned so far. There was something about that comment Matt had made after interviewing Doris that kept niggling away at her.

She turned the wheel and took the road leading way from the coast.

'Where are we heading, Miss Kitty?' Dolly asked as she pressed her hand on top of her hat to prevent it from flying off into the road.

'I'm sorry, Dolly. Do you mind if we make a quick stop at Palm Lodge? We may already be too late as I don't know when the Winspears planned to vacate.' Kitty wasn't even sure about why she needed to go there, but there had to be something.

There were too many lies and half-truths that were bothering her and if Natasha were to be believed, then one of the family was about to get away with murder. Even worse, an innocent woman could be hanged.

Kitty swung the nose of her small red car in through the gates and along the drive to pull to a halt near the front door of the house. The lodge looked deserted in the early evening sunshine. However, Kitty noticed that the large wooden doors to the garage stood open and a large blue motor vehicle was still parked inside.

Dolly jumped out of the car and followed Kitty to the front door.

'I'm coming with you, miss.'

'Very well,' Kitty agreed, and rang the bell.

No one answered so Kitty tried the black cast iron pull once more. Dolly wandered over to the study window and cupped her hands around her eyes as she tried to peer inside.

'Why is no one answering? There must be someone here. There is a car in the garage. Surely they have not all left already?' Kitty stepped back from the door with a frown.

'Miss, come and take a look over here. I'm not sure but I think as there is someone collapsed on the desk.' Dolly's voice was sharp with anxiety and Kitty hurried to the girl's side to peer through the window.

A quick peek confirmed Dolly's words. A figure seemed to be seated in Sir William's chair, the upper part of their torso sprawled forward on the desk in an unnatural pose.

'I think you may be right. Come on, let's go around to the back of the house and try the doors there.' Kitty led the way around the side of the building and onto the wide stone terrace that ran along the rear of the lodge.

Dolly rattled the handles on the first set of French doors that led into the drawing room. 'These am locked up tight, miss.' Kitty was already trying the other set further along.

'These are locked too, and I can't see anyone else inside the house.' Kitty's heart pounded as she tried to think what to do next.

'Kitchen door, miss?' Dolly suggested.

Together they ran around to the side of the building to the glass small porch, which enclosed the tradesman's entrance to the scullery and kitchens.

'Locked,' Kitty said as she tried the handle.

Dolly was already pulling a pin from her hat. 'Here, miss, let me have a pop at it. It looks like the one they had at Elm House.'

Kitty stood aside as Dolly bent to apply her skill to the lock. Kitty had developed a certain amount of talent herself in this area, but Dolly was much nimbler and quicker. It was a skill she had acquired during her employment at Elm House.

'Got it!' Dolly straightened, a triumphant smile on her face.

'Come on, but be careful, we don't know if there is anyone else here apart from the poor soul we saw in Sir William's study.' Kitty again took the lead through the clean and deserted kitchens and through the baize door into the main hall of the house.

The hall was silent and deserted. All the doors leading into the other rooms were closed. The only one that stood partly ajar was the door to Sir William's study.

'Dolly, wait here just for a moment while I go in and see what has happened.' Kitty kept her voice low, uncertain if there was anyone else still lurking inside the apparently empty house.

Dolly nodded her agreement, her eyes wide in her pale face.

Kitty swallowed hard and pushed the door of the study open wider to allow her to enter. To her dismay, she saw that the sight they had seen from outside through the window was correct. Sitting in Sir William's seat behind the desk and sprawled across the blotter, Elspeth Winspear lay ominously still.

'Elspeth.' Kitty rushed to the woman's side looking for any sign of life or injury.

A cup of tea stood part drunk and cold to one side of the desk, a bloom forming on the surface. Kitty touched the side of the woman's face and discovered she was still warm. There was no sign of any wound that Kitty could determine so she searched for a pulse just below Elspeth's ear.

'Dolly!' Kitty called her companion to come into the room. 'I think she is alive, but only just. Her pulse is very weak.'

The younger girl snatched up the telephone receiver. 'I'll call for help, miss.' She placed it to her ear and tried the dial. ''Tis dead.' She looked at Kitty in alarm.

Before either of them could say anything more, there was a bang as the study door was slammed shut. The sound of a key being turned in the lock followed along with the slam of the front door.

Kitty rushed to the window. 'It's Lady Lettice and David Fairweather. They must have been in the house all this time.'

She watched as David reversed the car she had noticed in the garage out onto the drive. The rack at the rear was now piled high with luggage. Lettice jumped in alongside him without a backwards glance, and then the car roared out of the gate.

'They're getting away, and judging by the luggage they must be heading for the airfield. Whatever have they done to Elspeth?' Kitty turned back to Dolly. 'We have to get some help. She's fading fast.' She tried the heavy sash window that Natasha had used when she had tried to abscond with Lettice's jewellery. Unsurprisingly, she discovered it had been fastened shut and she couldn't lift it.

Kitty looked around the room before picking up one of the smaller bentwood chairs that stood in a corner.

'Stand well clear, Dolly. I'm going to smash the window.'

Dolly moved obediently to stand well clear as Kitty lifted the chair and smashed it with all her strength against the centre of the frame. Kitty flinched inwardly at the crashing of the glass and cracking of wood.

Shards of glass fell about her feet, and she realised she was covered in tiny cuts all along her arms.

'Miss, be careful.' Dolly had her hands pressed over her ears.

Kitty's shoes crunched on the broken glass that lay scattered across the polished parquet floor as she used the chair once more to clear the fragments of glass from the shattered pane.

'Thank heavens Sir William had a taste for old-fashioned heavy furniture.' She tried to make light of the situation in order to reassure Dolly. 'There, I've made a safe space so that I can get out.'

'You go ahead, miss, and try to stop those two. If you gives me a hand to climb out as well I'll run along to the other houses and fetch some help for Miss Winspear.' Dolly had seized a book from the bookcase and was using it to further remove any more of the small glass splinters left in the frame.

Kitty glanced at Elspeth. The woman was still unconscious, even the commotion of the smashing of the window had not roused her. She plucked some cushions from a nearby chair and used the heavy velvet drapes to pad the window frame in order to protect her as she scrambled over the sill. Once outside, Dolly passed a chair to her and Kitty assisted her companion to climb out.

'Get going, Miss Kitty. I'll go for help,' Dolly called over her shoulder as she set off at a sprint down the drive.

Kitty jumped in her car and started the engine. She could only assume that Lettice and David Fairweather must be heading for Haldon Aerodrome near Teignmouth – unless they had chartered a private flight to land at some local field and she thought that possibility unlikely.

They had a head start and were in a much faster car, but Kitty knew many of the shortcuts through the narrower lanes, which she was sure that Fairweather would not either know or risk. Plus, if Dolly could raise the alarm in time, then they might be prevented from boarding at the aerodrome.

The toll at the bridge to cross at Shaldon caused another small delay as Kitty fumbled in her purse for change. She overpaid the charge and drove away without waiting for change, an action that left the toll booth operator scratching his head.

Elspeth must have discovered something that tied Lettice and David to the murders, otherwise why would they have tried to kill her? Kitty gritted her teeth and pushed her little car as fast as she dared, earning herself several blasts of the horn from other motorists as she swerved around them.

She could only hope that Elspeth would pull through. With

no sign of any visible injury, she had to assume that there had probably been something in the cold half cup of tea left on the desk.

Her petrol gauge dropped as she drove up the hill out of Teignmouth towards Haldon. The aerodrome was sited just out of the town on the top of the hill. She had been past it a couple of times before but knew little of it beyond the air displays, which had taken place there during the summer in the last few years.

Kitty slowed her car when she saw the sign for the aerodrome and swung in from the road into a small flat area near a large building constructed from corrugated iron. The car David Fairweather had been driving was parked nearby. The luggage, which had been secured to the rack at the rear, had been removed.

Kitty stood up inside her car to try and see if there was any sign of Lady Lettice or David Fairweather. The airfield itself was fairly small with the runway consisting of grass and cleared patches of heather.

A de Haviland aircraft was at the end closest to her near the corrugated hangar and Kitty realised that the metal steps were just being removed, ready for the plane to start off along the runway.

Fairweather and Lady Lettice had to be aboard that plane. Kitty looked around in desperation. She had to try and prevent them from leaving, but how? She was too far away to alert the pilot or ground staff.

She looked around for some way she could prevent the flight. Remembering there was another track on the far side of the hangar that she had seen when she had pulled in, Kitty threw her car into reverse.

Gravel skidded from under the narrow tyres of her car as she roared forward across the car park and along the track leading around the building and onto the airfield. She had her fingers crossed that there wouldn't be any kind of gate or barrier in her way.

Luck seemed to be with her as the metal gate was open and she squeezed her car through the gap and onto the airfield coming out beside the airplane. She saw the startled face of the ground engineer who had removed the steps as she drove onto the runway sounding her horn.

The sound she made was swallowed up however by the noise from the airplane's propellers as the pilot finished his checks and prepared to start taxiing down the runway. Kitty pressed her foot to the floor, desperate to get ahead of the aircraft before it could start moving.

Her car bumped and jolted over the grass as she gave it her all to overtake the airplane, swinging in front of it at the earliest opportunity in order to block the take-off. The noise of the plane's engines was deafening, and she prayed the pilot would pull to a halt without hitting her as she tried to maintain a safe distance between herself and the plane.

Her blood hammered in her ears as she finally heard the aircraft splutter to a halt. She applied her own brakes to come to a stop, her heart pounding with the temerity of her actions. She drew a shaky breath of relief as in the distance she heard the faint wail of a police car drawing closer to the aerodrome.

'What the devil are you playing at? Don't you know how dangerous that idiotic stunt was? You could have been killed, along with the pilot and passengers.' Her car door was wrenched open, and she found herself face to face with a very angry middle-aged man dressed in navy-blue coveralls.

'I had to stop the flight. There are two wanted criminals on that airplane,' Kitty tried to explain as the man took hold of her arm clearly intent on removing her from her car. 'Ow! Please release my arm.'

'Not blooming likely, young lady, a right load of stuff and nonsense. You can save your explanations for the police.' The man tugged her out of her car onto the field just as the familiar black shape of a police car drove onto the runway towards the stationary aircraft.

Another police car turned in and followed the first onto the field. The sirens blared as one car halted at the airplane doors, and the other continued along and stopped where Kitty was still being held by her captor.

Two more men clad in navy overalls had emerged from the hangar near the windsock and were now hurrying down the field towards them.

'I've got a hold of her, here, officer. Arrest this woman now for endangering an aircraft and trespass,' Kitty's captor demanded as soon as the policeman driving the car opened the door.

'Miss Underhay, I presume?' The policeman ignored the man holding on to Kitty's arm.

'Yes sir. The people you want are on board that airplane.' Kitty's legs were trembling now, and she thought she probably would have fallen if not for the harsh grip of the aerodrome employee who seemed determined to hold her prisoner at all costs.

The other aerodrome employees halted and stood panting alongside the police car, clearly confused by the evening's turn of events.

The policeman turned his attention to the aerodrome workers. 'Right then, can you lads get some steps so we can have the people off that plane.' He looked at Kitty's captor. 'And, sir, you may release this young lady.'

TWENTY-THREE

The man holding Kitty's arm glared at the policeman. 'Now, just a minute, officer. This young woman almost caused a serious accident.'

The sergeant nodded. 'Yes sir, but she also prevented two dangerous criminals from escaping.' He turned away to walk towards his colleagues who were waiting for the steps to be brought to the aircraft door.

Kitty's captor muttered something under his breath and reluctantly let her go. The man strode away leaving her to rub the sore spot on her arm. No doubt she would have a nasty bruise to show for all this later. She watched as the steps were fetched and the airplane door opened.

Lady Lettice emerged first, her face a tight mask of fury. She was followed by David Fairweather who also looked less than pleased that their escape had been foiled. The police promptly led them both into the waiting car. Last to emerge was the pilot who seemed confused by the strange events that unfolded.

Kitty leaned against the side of her car and took a deep breath. Thank goodness she had made it in time. A few more minutes and the de Haviland would have been in the sky, bound for France. Lettice and David would have got away with the murders.

'Are you all right, Miss Underhay?' The sergeant who seemed to be in charge had walked back to join her.

'Yes, thank you, I'm just a little shaken,' Kitty reassured him. She probably looked a terrible mess. Her arms and legs were covered in scratches from where she had broken the study window and her hat and hair were windblown and untidy.

'If you feel all right to drive, miss, then can I ask you to follow me back to the police station in Teignmouth? It's near the railway station. Inspector Greville is on his way over to meet us from Torquay.' She was conscious of the sergeant assessing her as if to assure himself that she was safe to drive.

'Of course.' Kitty climbed back into the driver's seat of her car. She started her engine and followed the police car off the field and out of the aerodrome.

She wondered if the inspector would have any news about Elspeth. She could only hope that she and Dolly had been in time to save the woman. The police cars halted outside a brick building on a narrow street not far from the sea front. Kitty pulled to a stop behind them and followed the sergeant inside.

Lady Lettice and David Fairweather had already been escorted to the cells to await the arrival of Inspector Greville.

'May we offer you a cup of tea, Miss Underhay? That was quite a feat you pulled off back there,' the sergeant said as he showed her into a small, neat and tidy office with cream walls and utilitarian, brown wood furniture.

'Thank you, that would be most welcome.' Kitty could really have used something a little stronger after everything that had just happened. However, a cup of tea would be lovely and, even better, if the police might manage to rustle up a biscuit to accompany it.

Kitty had just received her drink when the door to the office opened again, and Inspector Greville entered.

'Good evening again, Miss Underhay, I gather from Sergeant Coombs that we have you to thank for preventing Lady Lettice and Mr Fairweather from making their escape to the continent.' He took the seat opposite Kitty.

'I think I was in the nick of time. May I ask how Miss Winspear is faring?' Kitty asked.

'She is at the hospital now, I believe. Thanks to you and Miss Miller, the doctor thinks that she may make a full recovery,' the inspector replied.

Kitty gave a sigh of relief. 'I'm so glad. I take it that there was something in the tea?'

The inspector nodded, his face grave. 'It would seem so. Fortunately, she hadn't drunk all the contents before she collapsed and then you and Miss Miller arrived in time to obtain help.'

Kitty shivered. 'Poor Elspeth, she must have discovered something about Lettice and David.'

'I daresay we shall learn more when we speak to them.' He eyed Kitty curiously. 'May I ask what prompted you and Miss Miller to call at Palm Lodge after you left the police station?'

Kitty blushed. 'I just had this niggling feeling that I needed to call and see if there was something I'd missed. I think it was brought on by the photograph that you had of the things Natasha had stolen.'

Inspector Greville's moustache twitched. 'Oh? Why was that, Miss Underhay?'

'This will sound a little odd, but Lettice loves her jewels. You saw what Natasha had taken: diamonds, pearls, rubies and then amongst all of that there was a small, cheap-looking gold band. Now, Lady Lettice doesn't seem to be a sentimental kind of person so why was that ring there? It didn't look like something Sir William would have given her and she has a very fine wedding band and engagement ring that she wears.' Kitty looked at the inspector and she could see his mind was considering the implications of that particular item of jewellery.

'Hmm, something else, perhaps, to ask Lady Winspear about?' the inspector asked.

Kitty nodded. 'I believe so. I think, if my guess is right then it holds the key to this whole case.' She finished her drink and set the thick white china cup back on its saucer.

'If you are feeling more recovered, Miss Underhay, shall we go and see what our prisoners have to say for themselves?' The inspector rose from his chair to escort Kitty to the cells at the rear of the small police station.

The sergeant unlocked the door to the cell containing Lady Lettice Winspear first. Lettice was dressed in a smart, pale rose-coloured summer two-piece of fine silk with a neat matching hat trimmed with silk roses. Diamond and pearl earrings glinted in her earlobes.

'Inspector Greville, I really must protest.' She rose from her seat on a plain pine chair as soon as the inspector entered the cell. She glared at Kitty as she followed the inspector inside.

'Please take a seat, Lady Winspear.' The policeman waved his hand towards the chair and Lettice subsided back onto it, a sullen expression on her pretty face.

'I should warn you, Lady Winspear, that I intend to charge you with the murder of your husband, Sir William Winspear, and also that of Mr Ivan Bolsova. I shall also be charging you with the attempted murder of Miss Elspeth Winspear. Have you anything you wish to say?' Inspector Greville asked as the sergeant took out his notebook, ready to record the conversation.

'I demand to see my solicitor. This is quite preposterous. What evidence do you have?' Lettice's eyes sparked and she glared at the occupants of the cell.

'You had been conducting a romantic liaison with Mr Bolsova. Something that your husband, Sir William, had discovered. He intended to sue for divorce and had already contacted his solicitor with a view to disinheriting you from his will. A matter that would have been financially ruinous for you,' Inspector Greville said in a mild tone.

'I could not have killed William. I was with Elspeth for most of the afternoon as you well know. There certainly would have been little time for me to have left the tennis courts and gone to the grotto in order to murder him. Plenty of other people could have killed him. There is nothing to tie me to his murder.' Lettice looked quite smug, and Kitty's hackles rose at the woman's complacency.

'I don't think that you did kill Sir William. You were seen at the mansion by someone at the time your husband was killed so you didn't commit that crime yourself,' Kitty said.

Her words caused everyone in the room to turn their attention towards her and Lettice's smile grew wider.

'Miss Underhay?' Inspector Greville looked at her.

'I think you persuaded Ivan Bolsova to kill your husband. Ivan was completely in love with you and would have done anything that you asked. You had told him all sorts of stories about your marriage and your treatment at Sir William's hands. No doubt you made him all kinds of promises about how you would be together once your husband was dead. You would of course be a wealthy woman and Ivan was a man who loved and needed money.' Kitty met Lettice's gaze squarely.

'Thank you, Miss Underhay. Lady Winspear?' Inspector Greville turned his attention back to Lettice.

'Rubbish. How dare you?' Lettice folded her arms defiantly.

'You made certain Elspeth overheard you telling Ivan that you would meet him at the grotto. You were confident that she would tell her brother and his jealousy would lead him to try and catch you with Ivan. Once you had left the tennis court, I think you watched your husband set off for the grotto and his death. The broken arrow must have been a bonus as a speedy and effective weapon.' Kitty looked at Lettice.

'I am inclined to think Miss Underhay is correct. You then decided to rid yourself of Ivan Bolsova. I think there were a few reasons for this. He was very close to his sister, and you were sure that Natasha Bolsova would take a keen interest in protecting her brother's interests. She and Ivan would always have a claim on the fortune you inherited from Sir William. Then, there was the small matter of your other lover, David Fairweather.' Inspector Greville placed a restraining hand on Lettice's shoulder, keeping her in her seat when she attempted to stand.

'David is an old friend from my theatre days. I hadn't seen him for years until we met again in London.'

Kitty noticed that Lettice's hands were shaking.

'That isn't entirely true, is it, Lady Winspear?' Kitty said. She looked to the inspector for the go-ahead to test her theory on Lettice.

The policeman gave a barely perceptible nod of approval for her to continue.

'I don't know what you mean,' Lettice muttered.

'David Fairweather was more than a mere friend or old theatrical acquaintance, wasn't he?' Kitty watched the colour leach from Lettice's cheeks and the girl licked her lips nervously.

'Nonsense.' The protest though sounded weak.

'You and David Fairweather had been more than friends when you were acting together. I believe you fell in love with him and were, in fact, married to him. The wedding ring that Natasha stole with your other jewellery was from that marriage and you could never bear to part with it. For some reason the two of you parted company and it was while you were apart that you met Sir William.' Kitty paused for a moment. Lettice's complexion was now paper-white.

'You married Sir Willam bigamously and probably thought that anything that had been between you and David was long over and would never resurface. But then you met him again and all the old feelings came back. What were you to do? Married to a rich old man who you had no doubt expected to die within a short time of your marriage. That would have left you free to return to David, your first love, with the money to keep him by your side. There was just one problem. Sir William despite his age was in rude health and showed no sign of curling up his toes for your convenience.'

A tear escaped from the corner of Lettice's eye.

'You needed to get rid of Sir William and fast if you were to regain your first husband. David was also in a position to black-mail you over your bigamous marriage and you knew there was only so much money you could give to him without Sir William becoming suspicious. Ivan Bolsova was the perfect tool to provide what you wanted. Freedom from Sir William *and* all his money. Then, get rid of Ivan and you and David could live the life you wanted. With you funding his dreams of stardom, he was hardly likely to say anything.' Kitty looked at Lettice.

'It was David's idea, not mine. He pressured me, saying that he would tell William that I was already married.' Lettice turned towards Inspector Greville. 'I had no choice. If I had not encountered him that day...' She broke off to find a small, lace-edged handkerchief from her pocket. 'You must believe me. After I left David, I thought he was dead. I would never have married William knowing that I was still a married woman.'

Inspector Greville's expression was impassive as he listened to Lettice's pleas.

'So, your marriage lines to Sir William will say that you were a widow?' the inspector asked.

Lettice faltered. 'Well, no, I don't recall. I mean. I didn't think it was that important. I was single, after all.'

Kitty smiled to herself. She was in no doubt that Lettice had declared herself a spinster and not a widow when she had married Sir William. It would be interesting when David Fairweather was interviewed, to discover how much he knew of Lettice's plans.

'And the attempted murder of Miss Elspeth Winspear?' Inspector Greville asked.

'I don't know what you mean,' Lettice blustered.

'When Dolly and I arrived at Palm Lodge a few hours ago we rang the doorbell, and no one answered. Your car was in the garage with the door open. Dolly and I saw Elspeth collapsed in the study. When we managed to enter the house to try to aid her, you locked us inside the study and drove away.' Kitty's voice was cold.

'We had to leave for the aerodrome, or we would have missed our flight. David insisted we go. I was unaware anyone was in the house.' Lettice looked at the inspector. 'I didn't know Elspeth was there or that Miss Underhay and her companion had broken in. I merely secured my property and we left for our flight.'

'Miss Winspear is expected to recover from the sedative overdose that had been added to her tea, thanks to Miss Underhay and Miss Miller's intervention. No doubt you thought that the fake suicide note you had left under Miss Winspear's head would lead us to assume that she had been responsible for Sir William and Mr Bolsova's deaths. An insurance policy if Natasha Bolsova were not charged with the murders.' Inspector Greville frowned at Lettice who visibly wilted under the sternness of his gaze.

'I don't know anything about any sedative. That must have all been David's doing.' Lettice tried one more plea, but she must have realised it was falling on deaf ears.

'I presume poor Elspeth had discovered something to connect you to the murders? Or was it a good opportunity to make sure that someone took the blame if Natasha wasn't charged. After all, if Elspeth was dead, she couldn't deny her guilt. To be extra certain that she would die you even cut the telephone line to the house so help could not be summoned.' Kitty saw that her words had hit home.

'I think, Miss Underhay, we are done here. Sergeant, if you would please.' Inspector Greville took Kitty's arm to lead her from the cell as he motioned to the sergeant to relock the door.

'A nasty, calculating woman. She'll say anything to save her own neck,' the inspector observed in a low tone once they were back in the corridor and Lady Lettice's cell door had been resecured.

'I must admit, that was quite unnerving.' Kitty shivered despite the air in the narrow corridor still being warm.

'I take it that you would like to see Mr Fairweather?' the inspector asked, a half-smile tweaking the corners of his mouth.

'Oh yes, I would very much like to hear what he has to say, especially after hearing Letty's version of events.' Kitty had to admit she was very curious to discover if the murder plot had been Lettice's brainchild or if David had been the instigator – or even a willing accomplice.

He had certainly been keen to get away from Palm Lodge and he must have realised that Elspeth was either dying or dead. Kitty's car had been parked outside too so he would have known that someone had called at the house, even if Lettice alone had been responsible for administering the sedative to Elspeth and disconnecting the telephone.

Inspector Greville gestured to the sergeant who promptly unlocked the door to David Fairweather's cell. Once again, he led the way inside with Kitty following as the sergeant took up his station beside the door, his notebook in hand.

David Fairweather was seated on the edge of his bunk. His

jacket lay discarded in a heap on the thin pallet mattress. He was crouched forward, his head in his hands.

'Good evening, Mr Fairweather. No doubt you are aware of the circumstances that have led to you being apprehended and brought here,' Inspector Greville said.

The man straightened to look the policeman in the eye. 'Is Letty all right?'

'Lady Winspear is perfectly well, although I should tell you that she is facing very serious charges.' Kitty sensed the inspector was choosing his words carefully. 'Perhaps you would care to tell me what you know of this story,' Inspector Greville invited.

The inspector drew his cigarette case from the pocket of his jacket and proffered it to David Fairweather. Once the man had taken a cigarette, he selected one for himself and lit them both.

'Letty and I knew each other some time ago. We were members of the same theatre company. Touring around, performing at various small venues throughout the country. We grew very close, Lettice is a beautiful woman.' David took a pull on his cigarette and blew out a cloud of smoke.

'Yes, you and Lady Lettice mentioned this before. However, we now know that there was more than a mere friendship between you back then,' the inspector said.

Kitty could see the sergeant busy making notes in his book.

'We fell in love and got married. Letty had thought she was going to have a child. You know how it is? I wanted to do the right thing by her. Then it seems she was mistaken. I don't know, after that we started to argue. Lack of money, Letty's career was going down. That's the thing with the girls, as they get older, there's always another younger, prettier face to take their place. Letty was jealous and the company broke up. She went away and I found another touring company.' He took another pull on his cigarette, seemingly unaware of his surroundings as he revisited his past.

'Time passed by, and I lost touch with her. Then I was in an accident and couldn't work for a while. I broke my leg in two places, it was quite bad. Well, Letty heard something on the grapevine, I suppose, and by the time the rumour reached her I had gone from being injured to being dead.'

It seemed then that Lettice had been telling the truth about believing herself to be a widow if that were the case, Kitty thought. It was probably the only wholly true thing Lettice had told them.

'The next time I ran into Letty in London, she looked at me as if she had seen a ghost. And, in a way, I suppose she had. She was married to Sir William by then. I think he acquired her like a kind of ornament to show off to his peers. There she was all rich and glamorous, covered in jewels and furs.' David shook his head at the memory.

'What happened then?' the inspector asked, his tone full of mild curiosity.

David sighed and flicked some ash from the end of his cigarette into a small metal ashtray. 'Obviously I didn't want to rock the boat. Letty was set for life and Sir William was so much older than her. It was only a matter of waiting. At least that's what I thought. Letty gave me some money and we met for lunch a few times and I, well... I realised that I still loved her. She said, "Well, I don't know how we can be together". Her husband was very suspicious of her friendships. We got to talking about the future and what life could be like if...'

'If Sir William were dead?' Inspector Greville said.

Ruddy colour tinged David Fairweather's cheeks. 'Well, yes.'

'Lady Winspear says that it was your idea to kill Sir William and that you coerced her by threatening to go to her husband to reveal the truth about your marriage, knowing she would lose everything,' Inspector Greville remarked casually.

Kitty's eyes widened while she waited to see what reaction

this statement got. Did David Fairweather love his wife enough to try to save her from the gallows by placing his own neck on the line?

David looked up and Kitty saw alarm flash through his eyes as he realised the implications of what the inspector had said.

'No, that's not true. That's not how it was at all. Letty said she knew someone who would do anything for her. She only had to suggest something, and he would see that she was free. No one would be any the wiser. She couldn't even be blamed.' David stubbed out the remains of his cigarette. His posture had changed to one of tension, as if he were about to spring from his seat.

'And that person was Ivan Bolsova?' kitty said.

David nodded, a lock of hair falling forward onto his handsome forehead. 'Yes. Letty had become quite a patron of the arts. It was a good cover for us to remain in contact without arousing suspicion. She had discovered something about Bolsova and his sister. Something she used to persuade him to help her. I don't know exactly what, she didn't say. Plus, well, Ivan was besotted by Letty. It happened quite often, men falling for her. It was one of the things we used to row about.'

'Ivan killed Sir William at Lettice's instigation,' the inspector confirmed, and glanced towards his sergeant as if to be certain he had noted this down.

'Yes. I asked Letty what would happen about Bolsova. She assured me that she could deal with him. Pay him off and use the leverage she had against him and his sister to keep his mouth shut. It would be expensive but worth it.' David looked miserable as he admitted this part of the story.

'What went wrong?' Kitty asked. 'Did Ivan expect more as he was in love with Lettice? Or did she suddenly decide the price was too high and it would be cheaper and safer just to remove him from the equation altogether?'

David licked his lips nervously as he glanced first at Kitty and then at the inspector. 'Letty said she would sort everything out then she telephoned me and asked me to come. Something had gone wrong. Ivan was dead and she was frightened. I arrived shortly afterwards as you know. She said Ivan had threatened her, saying he wanted to marry her, and she had been frightened and lashed out in self-defence.'

Kitty's brows rose. 'Self-defence? And what of Elspeth Winspear?'

'Elspeth already disliked Lettice. All the Winspears disliked Letty. They would have jumped on anything to get rid of her so they could have the old man's money for themselves. Elspeth was behaving very oddly. Henry and Padma left for London after lunch earlier today and Elspeth said she just had a few things to do in Sir William's study. Letty was worried. I went to collect our bags ready for the flight. I had booked a private charter to take us to France. I thought the sooner we could leave the country the better it would be. Natasha was in jail, and I thought that she would take the fall for the murders.' He blew out a sigh.

'You must have seen my car outside the lodge and heard Dolly and me inside. You knew Elspeth was in the study and something had happened.' Kitty said.

David pressed his hands to either side of his head as if trying to shut out what she was saying.

'Letty said that she had given Elspeth something. A sedative. She'd overheard her on the telephone placing a call to Somerset House, presumably to check the wedding records. Letty had kept her wedding ring – the one from our marriage – and when it was returned with the things Natasha took, Elspeth saw it. It must had sparked an idea in her head. She was desperate to find something to challenge the will.'

Kitty looked at the inspector. It seemed she wasn't the only person that had seen the significance of that cheap wedding band. 'Lettice thought that Elspeth had found out about your marriage?'

'Like I said, she would have challenged the will. Gone to the police and then everything would have been for nothing. Letty said that if we got away quickly then we would be all right. She had taken all the money from the safe.' David gave Kitty a despairing look.

TWENTY-FOUR

Kitty was glad to finally exit David Fairweather's cell and return to the comforting safety of the police station corridor with its faint smell of disinfectant and old cabbage.

'Are you feeling all right, Miss Underhay? I realise that must have felt quite wearing after the events of the evening.' Inspector Greville led her back to the office she had occupied earlier and requested a fresh pot of tea from his sergeant.

'Yes, thank you. It was quite eye-opening. David clearly loves Lettice and was prepared to risk everything for her. Much as Ivan Bolsova was,' Kitty said as she sank down gratefully onto her chair.

'He was certainly just doing his best to tread a fine line between blaming her for everything in order to save his own neck and trying to protect her at the same time,' the inspector agreed as the sergeant reappeared bearing a wooden tray with a fresh pot of tea and a plate of biscuits.

Kitty smiled as she saw the inspector's eyes brighten at the sight of the biscuits and made sure to take two for herself when he offered her the plate first. She knew if she didn't, they would be gone by the time she had consumed the first one.

'I suppose it will be interesting to hear what Elspeth has to say when she recovers.' Kitty felt better once she'd taken a drink of her tea. The afternoon's adventures had left her rather more shaken than she cared to admit.

'It was fortunate that you and Miss Miller arrived when you did. I arranged for Miss Miller to return to Dartmouth in a taxi by the way. No doubt she will be anxiously awaiting your return. Are you feeling recovered enough to make the drive home, Miss Underhay?' the inspector asked as she set her empty cup down.

'Perfectly, thank you. I need to go home and reassure Dolly and Alice, and also to let Matt know that the case is solved.' Kitty hoped Matt wouldn't be too annoyed when he discovered that she had stopped the de Haviland from leaving by physically driving onto the airfield.

Inspector Greville rose and opened the door for her. 'I'll telephone the hotel and tell them you are on your way home. Thank you for your assistance, Miss Underhay, and do take care driving back to Dartmouth.'

Kitty said farewell to the inspector and his sergeant and set off towards the Dolphin. The light had faded considerably now, and the sun had almost slipped completely from the sky painting the sea with gold, orange and pink streaks. She turned on her headlamps and forced herself to concentrate on the road. At least on the return journey she could travel at a more sensible pace.

It was completely dark by the time she boarded the ferry to cross the Dart from Kingswear. Once she and Matt were married at least she would not have this part of the journey to contend with so often. Her arms and legs were aching now, and she longed for a nice warm bath and a cocktail followed by a good supper.

The lights were on in the Dolphin as she drove around and parked her car back in its shed, taking care to lock the door. The fine night meant there were still plenty of people around as she walked back towards the hotel. Something she found reassuring after the discovery of the dead rat earlier in the afternoon.

Mary, the receptionist, had left for the day when she entered the lobby and Bill, the night porter, greeted her from behind the desk.

'Miss Dolly and Miss Alice are with Captain Bryant upstairs with your grandmother, Miss Kitty. They've been waiting for you to come home. The inspector telephoned and said as you were on your way,' Bill said, discreetly not mentioning her somewhat dishevelled appearance.

'Thank you, Bill.' Kitty headed for the staircase and hoped that the story of her adventures wouldn't alarm her grandmother too much.

So much for trying to keep the discovery of the threat from Esther Hammett from her beloved Grams. No doubt she would have winkled the full story out of Dolly while they had all been waiting for her return. She hoped Matt would not be too cross that once again she had placed herself at risk.

When she reached the landing, she took off her hat and tried to tidy her hair in the reflection of the windowpane before entering the salon. Then, bracing herself, she tapped on the salon door.

'Thank heavens you're home.' Matt met her in the doorway engulfing her in a heartfelt embrace. 'Dolly has told me everything she knows. I've been so worried,' he murmured in her ear as she relaxed into the clean, male smell of his jacket.

'Grams?' Kitty murmured back.

'It's all quite all right,' her fiancé assured her as he placed a tender kiss on her forehead. 'Now, come and let Alice and Dolly see that you're in one piece while you tell us what happened after you went off after Lady Winspear and David Fairweather.'

Kitty gave in and allowed him to guide her into the lamp-lit salon under the watchful and anxious eyes of her grandmother and her friends. Once settled in a comfortable chair with a gin in her hands Kitty gave them a slightly edited version of the day's events.

'Oh, Kitty darling,' her grandmother remonstrated as she finished her tale.

'Well, miss, I think you was very brave, and Miss Winspear owes her life to you and our Dolly.' Alice looked with pride at her younger sister.

'Lady Lettice and David Fairweather are both behind bars and at least Natasha will only face theft charges and not murder ones.' Matt gave Kitty's hand a tender squeeze. 'Well done, darling.'

'All I can say is thank goodness it's over. Now, do you think that we can focus our attention back on the wedding and on recruiting a manager for the Dolphin? We do still have a business to run,' her grandmother asked, looking at Kitty and Matt.

'I think we can all drink to that,' Matt said, raising his glass to meet that of the others. 'To our wedding and a smooth course for the Dolphin Hotel.'

A LETTER FROM HELENA

Thank you so much for choosing to read *Murder at the Country Club*. If you enjoyed it and want to keep up to date with all my latest releases, just sign up at the following link. Your email address will never be shared and of course you can unsubscribe at any time.

www.bookouture.com/helena-dixon

If you read the first book in the series, *Murder at the Dolphin Hotel*, you can find out how Kitty and Matt first met and began their sleuthing adventures. I've always enjoyed meeting characters again as a series reader, which is why I love writing this series so much. I hope you enjoy their exploits as much as I love creating them. All of the Miss Underhay series feature fictional characters in real-life settings. The setting for this story, Oldway Mansion in Paignton, is especially lovely and if you ever find yourself in the UK in Devon, you can tread in Kitty's and Matt's footsteps.

I hope you loved reading *Murder at the Country Club* and if you did, I would be very grateful if you could write a review. I'd love to hear what you think, and it makes such a difference helping new readers to discover one of my books for the first time.

I love hearing from all my readers – you can get in touch or follow me on my Facebook page, through Twitter, Goodreads or my website.

Thanks,

Helena Dixon

 facebook.com/nelldixonauthor
twitter.com/NellDixon

ACKNOWLEDGEMENTS

My thanks go to Teignmouth Museum for all the information on Haldon Aerodrome and helping me to track down the site of the police station.

Special thanks go to Kathy Hughes and all the volunteers at Oldway Charitable Trust. I had a wonderful tour of the mansion and took some fantastic photographs, which helped enormously in bringing the world that Kitty and Matt inhabit to life. Of course, there are many fictional events within the book and I took a few liberties with geography within the grounds and the house. I am indebted to everyone who gave me valuable information and pictures of the period when Oldway was a country club and the earlier period when it served as a hospital for wounded US servicemen in the Great War.

The volunteer gardeners do such an incredible job of maintaining the grounds and helped me to see where the Parterre and Italianate gardens were and are situated. The grotto is beautiful and I would recommend anyone visiting Paignton to call at Oldway for a cream tea and a walk around the grounds.

My thanks as always also go to the fabulous team at Bookouture, including my wonderful editor, Emily Gowers, and also my agent, Kate Nash. I am so lucky to work with such brilliant people.